Dedication:

This story is dedicated to anyone who has lost a loved one and to all the mothers around the world who have lost a child. The pain of losing someone you love is unimaginable, but it is a thousand times worse when it is your child.

I want to thank my both of my sons; Alex and Hunter for always believing I was a Wonder Woman and giving me the courage to take chances.

I want to thank my husband Tim and my son Hunter for helping through the rough times after Alex was killed by a drunk driver in June 2014.

I want to thank my Fall 2016 Law and Justice students for believing in me and giving me the courage to try and publish this story. I also want to thank my 2016-2017 fourth period Geography students for helping me brainstorm and for being so wonderful to have in class.

Alex's Room

Footsteps echo down the hall.

Gentle sounds softened by walls.

Muffled snores travel through the door.

Your quirky laughter fills the air.

Six months later you are no longer there.

Quiet whispers and hush tones now dominate this once happy home.

Table of Contents

Capricorn: I

Aquarius: II

Pisces: III

Aries: IV

Taurus: V

Gemini: VI

Cancer: VII

Leo: VIII

Virgo: VIIII

Libra: X

Scorpio: XI

Sagittarius: XII

Ophiuchus: XIII

Appendix

Capricorn: I

Every story has a beginning, middle, and end; however, in my case, the end is the beginning of my story. My name is Alexander Xavier; I prefer Alex, but for some reason, my family refuses to consider my preference. Mom tells me all the time in her teacher voice that if she wanted me to be called Alex, she would have named me Alex. So, for now, I pretend I understand her logic. I have learned over the last 17 years that it is better to pick and choose my battles, and this is one battle I know I will not win.

I will not pretend that I am a straight-A student or that I have been the perfect older brother. I will admit to being a typical teenage boy consumed by the thoughts of girls, video games, and sleep, but not necessarily in that order. If asked, I would say that I am a laid-back person, but I can be serious when the need arises.

I am incredibly psyched about this upcoming school year. I cannot wait until the end of the year when I will be a freshman at Western Kentucky University. It feels great finally getting on with my life, and now I can focus on the things I want to learn instead of being told what to learn and how to think. It has been two weeks since I graduated from Greenwood High School in Bowling Green, Kentucky, home of the Gators. I like my school, and to be honest, being a teacher's kid has its rewards, such as raiding your mother's classroom for snacks, getting money when you want to stop at Culver's after school, or just seeing your mom when your teacher has a sub you do not care for in the least.

I know I will miss seeing some of my other friends and my kid brother at school, but I am sure we can do stuff outside of school. My little brother at one time was picked on in middle school, but I made sure the other kids at Greenwood knew not to mess with him. He used to eat lunch with my friends and me every day at the senior table, and I would never tell him this, but he is not that bad of a baby brother. Sorry, I tend to get a little sidetracked; my mom claims I have attention deficit disorder, ADD, anyway, as I was saying back to my story.

The day started out like any summer day since school let out; I slept in until around 10 am and gradually started the process of stretching and waking up. Once awake, I left my room and noticed the house was eerily quiet and seemed deserted. I peeked into my brother's room and saw he was still sleeping with a YouTube video playing in the background. Gently I eased the door shut and headed toward Mom's room. It looked like both of my parents were also gone. "Oh well, that just meant I could take as long as I wanted in the shower without having to hear everyone complain about how much hot water I used." We really do need to replace the water heater, I thought.

After taking my shower, I started to dry off when it suddenly occurred to me that if I called Mom and Dad, I could convince them to feed me. I picked up my cell phone with one hand and attempted to dial Mom's number while holding the towel in a knot at my waist with my other hand. At first, it sounded like the call would go to voice mail when suddenly, Mom's voice blasted into my ear. Pulling the phone away from my ear, I yelled towards the phone. "Hey, Mom, lower the volume," I said.

"Bubba, what do you need?" asked Mom. "Since I am a broke college student, what do you think about buying me lunch?" Mom laughed, and I could hear her telling Dad I was a big mooch." I waited a few more seconds for Mom to finish talking to Dad. "Ok, we are at Kyoto Gardens on Campbell Lane. Be careful, and I do not want you speeding on that bike," she said.

A week after graduation from Greenwood High School, my mom surprised me with a vintage 2007 Suzuki Savage motorcycle to help me get to and from WKU. My mom, her sister, and my uncle graduated from WKU, so they knew just how lousy parking on campus could be. A motorcycle seemed the perfect solution. Plus, fifty miles per gallon would make my pocketbook euphoric.

I named my bike Shelia, and she had a gorgeous royal blue gas tank with chrome rims and exhaust. On the bottom of the black leather seat, she has an embroidered imprint of the German Iron Cross from World War One. I loved my bike. I quickly put on a pair of light blue jeans, added a black Fruit a Loom V-neck t-shirt, grabbed my silver-gray helmet, and walked out the door admiring the mid-morning sun as it reflected off Shelia's chrome rims.

I must admit the day was perfect for riding, I thought as I swung my leg over my bike and eased her up the gravel driveway. The day was beautiful and cloud-free; the temperature was around 78 degrees, and the wind blew from the northeast at about six miles per hour. I love riding my bike; it makes me feel free like a bird; I imagine being on my bike is like flying but better.

As a kid, I used to love to sit on the swings during recess and pump my legs back and forth until it seemed like I was flying. I still like to swing on the swings at the local playground near my old elementary school, especially when I am worried about something. It is slightly ironic that my elementary school's mascot is the Alvaton Blue Jays; my eyes are blue, and I love feeling like I can fly. I am so glad Mom got me this bike, and this has been the best summer of my life. Slowly I eased out of the driveway and turned left to head towards town and to my favorite place to eat, Kyoto's. Mom always liked to tease me about my obsession with everything Japanese, but as I told her when I registered for my Japanese class at WKU, all my time spent watching anime will finally pay off.

I knew what I wanted to do with my life; I had it all planned; I would attend WKU and study computers, learn Japanese, join the United States Navy, and get stationed in Japan. One day retire and buy a beachfront property and creates fusion cuisine for tourists based on Japanese/American recipes. Then on my days off, I would polish up the fantasy stories I started writing when I turned fourteen.

My mother was also a writer. She encouraged me to draw and write and gave me my first writing journal for my fourteenth birthday; before that time, I wrote down ideas on every scrap paper or napkin I could find. During the past four years, I have filled my journal with portraits of the characters, maps of kingdoms, and brainstorming ideas that Mom and I created during our weekly conversation.

The smell of good food pulled me from my introspection as I pulled into the parking spot next to the outdoor patio in front of Kyoto just in time to see Mom and Dad heading out the door with two Styrofoam glasses of sweet tea. "Mom, I thought you were going to feed me?"

Mom laughed and shook her head, "You took too long; Dad and I have errands to run; you should have gotten here sooner."

I turned my soulful baby blues in her direction and, in a pleading voice, said, "Mom, please.... I will get lonely, and I want to sit out here and look at Shelia; plus, don't you want to visit with me and talk a little bit?"

With a long-drawn-out sigh, my mother looked at Dad and motioned towards the black wrought iron table set just under the eaves of the porch area in front of Kyoto. "Oh, ok, go in and get what you want, but you will have to eat it out on the terrace, and your dad and I are leaving the minute you are done."

I headed in with Mom's credit card firmly grasped in my hand. Whenever I ate at Kyoto's with Mom, I ordered the medium rare hibachi steak with extra mushrooms, a California roll, and a coke. I loved this place with the excellent food and authentic Coke products; I was in Nirvana. After ordering my food and sitting at the patio table, Mom reached over and tried to snag a bite of my steak, "Hey, I thought you already ate," I said.

Laughing, she popped the stolen goods into her mouth, "I did, but I just couldn't resist another bite." I angled my Styrofoam container away from her, blocking access with my upper torso. Dad chuckled as he told us to behave ourselves. Mom exited her seat, the wind blowing her blonde hair into her blue eyes; they were the same shade as mine.

"When you finish eating, we must stop at AutoZone and pick up a filter and oil. "Your dad and I will teach you how to take care of your bike and change your oil," said Mom.

I stood up, shoveling the last of my food into my mouth. "I am ready; I mumbled as I threw the remaining food into the trash can. At AutoZone, I looked at the colorful display of different types of oil with little to no clue about what I was looking for as Mom nudged me toward the counter where a frazzled middle-aged, balding man talked to a customer on the phone. About five minutes later, after a lot of fidgeting on my part, the man hung up the phone and looked at me expectantly. I turned towards Mom and Dad; thankfully, Mom took the lead.

"We need an oil filter and synthetic oil for a Suzuki Savage 2007', she said. The guy chuckled, turning towards me. "First time doing your oil"?

I turned bright red as my parents laughed along with the man. Moving toward the end of the desk, the clerk said, "Follow me."

We went down a couple of aisles and gathered the necessary supplies; by the time we returned to the counter, Mom had already pulled out her credit card.

With a hasty scribble on the signature pad, Mom turned towards me with a grave expression, "Add that to what you owe me, and remember I am not US Bank of Mom"! I sighed a long-drawn-out sigh. "Yes, Mom, I know, and I plan to pay back every penny."

Walking toward my bike, A.K.A Shelia, I could not help but feel a thrill go through me as I thought about riding her to work and showing her off to some of my friends. A friend of mine Dee was returning to town from Chicago for a visit; I could convince her to go for a ride with me. A light slap on the back of my head dispelled all thoughts of tonight. "Hey, what was that for"? I asked Mom.

"You know I love you, but I want you to be careful, no speeding, and seriously no riding your bike without your helmet," said Mom.

"I know; I promise to be careful. I plan to go home and take a nap before going to work, and then after I get off, stop at Southern Lanes bowling alley, and say hi to some of my friends, ok?"

Mom gave me a warm embrace and said just be careful. I slowly swung my leg over the bike, and gradually opened the throttle, Shelia responded with a mellow purr and a silent promise to fly like a bird in the wind. Mom and Dad climbed into the SUV and headed home.

Later that evening Alex started to get ready for work, grabbing his red polo shirt off the floor and giving it a quick cursory sniff. He thought it would work for one more night as he shrugged his arms into the short sleeve shirt. He grabbed his khaki pants and black shoes and turned towards the door.

Suddenly Mom came into the room. "You are up; I was worried you would sleep through your alarm."

Alex groaned, "Mom, I only did that once." Without any warning, Allen, Alex's best friend since elementary school, jumped off the top bunk and grabbed Alex from behind, and started to give him a bear hug.

"So, who is the girl you plan on seeing tonight?" asked Allen with undisguised glee. Struggling to get free, Alex whined, "I'm going to be late for work."

Mom laughed and told Allen to let him go with the parting comment, "Make sure she does not have a boyfriend because I did not raise you to be a home wrecker. Also, it is time I let you ride your bike home from work without driving behind you."

Looking at Mom and Allen, a smile spread across my face, and my voice jumped an octave in surprise, wonder, "Are you sure?"

Mom nodded with a solemn look on her face. "In two months, you and Allen will be going off to college, and I think it's time I start letting go of the apron strings a little bit."

Alex smiled and rushed to give his mother a hug and a kiss. "Thank you, I promise I will wear my helmet, I will not speed, and I will wear that ugly safety vest you made me," said Alex as he rushed out the bedroom door. The noise of the motorcycle leaving the driveway echoed through the night, fading with each passing second, becoming a distant memory with every rotation of the wheel. Alex waited at the light at the intersection of Scottsville Road and Cave Mill Road; he knew he had ten minutes to get home before he was late for his curfew.

He knew he could make it with at least two minutes to spare, but he was still worried because this was the first time his mom had let him ride his bike home at night by himself. Usually, Mom would meet him at work and follow him back in her car. However, she was just starting to trust him to do the right thing, and he did not intend to give her a reason to second guess her decision and not trust him in the future. He looked forward to going home and getting some sleep; Allen was out on his date with Jamie. And his brother rode down with his aunt to visit his cousins in Nashville so he would have the game console all to himself for the rest of the night.

He had a great day at work; he helped a soon-to-be mom pick out decorations and toys for her first child's nursery at Babies-Tots-N-More and gave some of his friends at the bowling alley a ride on the bike before having to head home. Dee, one of the girls he attended school with during his sophomore year, was visiting from Chicago. He had a wonderful time talking to her and catching up on the last two years; she planned to move back down to Bowling Green in the next month.

Later in the night, he was able to convince her to take a spin around the parking lot. He really liked her, and if luck were with him, he could persuade her to go out with him on a date once she settled into her new apartment. The night was beautiful; the stars shined like diamonds in the sky, the wind had died down, and the temperature was perfect for a bike ride.

"This is the best summer of my life," he thought.

The left turn signal turned green, and he started to ease the bike forward, not even noticing the fast-moving headlights speeding toward him; suddenly, he felt a moment of intense pain followed by nothing. The last thoughts that drifted through my mind were of his mom and how he had done everything right....

Huntington: Indiana

Xavier rolled over and groaned as the chipper voice of his mother crashed around his ears. He was temporarily blinded as his eyes tried to adjust to the intense sunlight streaming into his room as his mother shoved his curtains to the right side of the window. Turning to look at the sleep-tousled teenager Deanna Hanson tried to keep the smile off her face, "time to get up, sleepy head. Your father and I plan to go to Fort Wayne," said his mom as she bent to retrieve dirty clothes from under the bed. "I want your room cleaned up, and I mean my version of clean, not yours, where you shove everything into the closet."

Swinging his legs over the side of the bed, Xavier put his head into his hands and mumbled incoherently. Lifting the laundry basket into her arms, Deanna leaned over and kissed Xavier on the head, "Hey, I love you," she said.

The door closed with barely a sound as the teenager on the bed struggled to untangle himself from his sweat-soaked sheets and blanket. Looking at the clock, Xavier realized it was 10 am. He had overslept, but it was no big deal, what with school being out for the upcoming Christmas holiday. Plus, he had not been sleeping too well lately; the nightmares from his childhood were getting worse, the feeling of intense pain followed by absolute blackness. Waking up soaked in sweat and feeling like your heart would burst out of your chest did not make for a restful night's sleep.

Looking across the room, he noticed he was not the only one who had overslept. Newsprint with eyebrows, the cocker spaniel he got when he turned ten, was sleeping next to his dresser on a memory foam doggy bed that cost as much as his recently acquired Biophone chip. The boys had named him Newsprint with eyebrows because he was black and white like a newspaper but with shocking brown eyebrows.

Newsprint, as he was affectionately called, was getting older, and he needed more loving care now that he was eight. Mom and Dad promised to keep him while attending the University of Indiana at Bloomington. However, the thought of getting a phone call from Mom and Dad telling him he had passed away filled him with dread.

Xavier sauntered towards the closet and mentally reviewed his options for the day (HNHS). Huntington North High School was out for Christmas break, and his parents were going to Fort Wayne to some festival; grabbing his phone, he dialed his best friend as he looked in his closet for something to wear.

A voice yelled in his ear, "This better be an emergency." Matt was Xavier's best friend and an all-around genius, but he hated getting up before 2 pm during breaks. "Hey, stop being a baby; maybe if you went to bed like a normal person, you wouldn't be so tired," said Xavier.

Matt's voice cracked as he swore at Xavier in German. "Does your mother know you talk like that laughed Xavier? "No," said Matt. "What do you want? In about two seconds, I will hang up on you."

Quickly Xavier explained his idea of hanging out at Matt's house since his parents would not be back until later in the evening. Meanwhile, downstairs, Deanna paced back and forth in front of the fireplace mantle with little thought given to how beautiful the holiday garland and red bows looked on the mantle. A fire crackled in the fireplace as she struggled to keep from crying, her voice cracking from the strain; she looked towards her husband, Blaine.

Upon meeting the Hansen family, most people thought Xavier looked like his mom and Will, his brother, looked like his dad. It was true; however, both boys' temperaments mirrored the opposite parents. Xavier's dad Blaine was a quiet, laid-back person with jet-black hair streaked with silver. Most people would assume it would be coarse and thin, but it was ultra-soft and thick. During movie night, Deanna loved to run her fingers through his hair as they watched television in the great room. Blaine's steel-rimmed glasses and lean and lanky build reinforced his studious appearance. They made it easy for him to pass as a college professor instead of the owner and operator of a mechanic shop.

On the other hand, Deanna was a college professor who was more anxiety-prone and tended to worry about everything from mundane to catastrophic. Her compulsion to obsess was passed on to Will. Her beautiful ash-brown hair had natural blond highlights that were the envy of women half her age. Her blue eyes were a mirror image of Xavier's, and her facial features were a feminine version of her youngest son. While she only stood five feet tall, many of her college students could attest that she was scary when she was riled up. Even though she was outnumbered by the men in the family, they also knew better than to make her angry.

Deanna turned toward the mantel picking up the picture of Xavier and Will when they were young and carefree; both boys reclined next to each other on a snow-white carpet, dressed in matching black shirts and slacks with the light glinting off their dishwater blonde hair. Now that they had grown up, their hair had darkened to ash brown like their mother's. While it was confirmed that the boys sometimes had minor disagreements, most of the pictures of them together showcased their infectious smiles. They captured their playful spirit and love for one another.

Rosie, the family dog, half beagle, and half Australian Sheppard sat on the couch close to the fireplace in Deanna's favorite spot. Rosie had the build and coloring of a beagle, her caramel-colored fur was dotted by soft snow-white spots, and her beautiful soft brown eyes were rimmed in dark chocolate brown as if she were wearing eyeliner. Her soft whimpers and body language mirrored Deanna's.

While Newsprint was Xavier's dog Rosie was 100 percent Deanna's. Blaine slowly crossed the room, enveloping his wife in his arms and comforting her as she started to cry her heart out. Her muffled sobs and tears barely left the room as the sounds were absorbed by his comforting arms and plaid shirt. Once dressed, Xavier headed down the stairs; upon hearing his mother's crying, he stopped midway down the stairs cocking his head to the side; he held his breath, hoping the silence would magnify what his parents were saying. Xavier knew that eavesdropping was a bad habit, and he was aware that, eventually, it would get him in trouble, yet he had never been caught.

Mom's voice drifted up the stairs. "I'm scared, Blaine; Xavier is starting to have nightmares again. The doctor promised they would go away once he finished puberty. What if he gets worse or finds out what we have done and hates us for the rest of our lives? I lost him once. I can't go through it again."

"I never thought that a simple question. What would you be willing to sacrifice to have a loved one back? Little did I know it would lead to all of these lies and having to give up everything we knew and loved," she said. A hiccup interrupted her comments, followed by a sniffle and a loud trumpet sound as she blew her nose.

Blaine's voice was calm and gentle but firm, "Deanna, you are worrying too much; everything will be fine. We all agreed at that time that no matter the price, it would be worth it if we could guarantee Xavier would live a long, healthy, and happy life. We delivered on that promise to the best of our ability, and we have additional time with him. He will graduate in about six months, and then it's on to the University of Indiana to study Psychology and Creative writing and then on to Law school."

Xavier moved down one step, trying to hear his mother's mumbled response to Dad's comment. What was she talking about, he wondered when suddenly the stairs squeaked in protest; turning quickly, he raced toward his bedroom. Gently closing the door, he moved towards the end table next to the bed, acting like he was searching for something.

When the bedroom door opened, his dad poked his head in the room, "son, brunch is ready when you are," said Blaine.

Xavier turned his head and prayed his father did not know he had been eavesdropping. I am getting my phone, and then I will be down in a minute," he said. Walking down the stairs, Xavier thought about what he had overheard. He wondered if his nightmares and the weird bits and pieces of conversations he had heard were somehow connected.

Why would his mother worry about him having nightmares, and why did the doctor say they would go away once he had finished puberty. He felt like he was on the verge of remembering something important, but what was it, and would it help stop the nightmares?

The kitchen was a bright, airy room with an oversized island in the middle of the kitchen and a comfortable breakfast nook off to the left in front of a set of big bay windows. Even this place was not safe from Mom's Christmas decorating spree. A festive six-foot tall artificial evergreen tree decorated with colorful lights and handmade ornaments stood off the side of the breakfast nook, with the lights blinking in sync with jingle bell rock.

Deanna turned from the stove, sliding scrambled eggs from the skillet onto a plate next to crispy bacon and golden-brown toast with butter and apple jelly. Her eyes were red-rimmed but not so much as to give away the fact that she had been crying a short time before.

Biting into the bacon, Xavier acknowledged that his parents truly complemented each other; his mom made the best-scrambled eggs, and his dad made perfectly crisp, flat bacon; together they were an awesome team. Mom was book-smart, adventurous, and extroverted, and his dad was introverted, handy, and liked to observe everything around him. Taking another bite, he had to admit the quality of the food served by his parents was the type you could only get with years of practice, and it was better than anything you could ever get at a restaurant, or at least he thought so.

Deanna put the pan back on the stove. She pointed her index finger at Xavier as he shoveled food into his mouth, "Your dad and I are going to Fort Wayne to meet some friends and enjoy Aunt Millie's Northern Lights festival. We will listen to the carolers, drink cider, and sample Apple Swirl bread. We will only be about forty-five minutes away, so if you need us just give us a call, but it better be important, not something trivial or juvenile. You can have Mathew or Packer over, but that is it! No parties, no girls, and no alcohol!"

With a gulp and a quick drink of orange juice, Xavier said, "Mom, you know I do not drink; only losers feel the need to drink to have fun. Plus, I refuse to spend money on alcohol or drugs when all you will do is pee it out and have nothing to show for it. Now video games are a different story. Can I have some money? There is a new RPG game I want to play, SKYRIM: Lost History XVI?"

With an exasperated sigh, Mom said, "Yes, just get my purse out of my office upstairs."

Bounding up the stairs two at a time, he pushed open the room door and grabbed the pink and rose gold bag off the mahogany desk that dominated the small space. Black filing cabinets lined the wall with pictures of Xavier and his brother Will during different stages of their life scattered throughout the room. Suddenly a picture frame started to fall off the filing cabinet; lunging forward, Xavier caught it before it could hit the floor. Turning the picture over in his hands, he inspected it for damage when he noticed a piece of paper sticking out of the back corner.

Mom's voice carried the stairs, "Hurry up, your dad and I want to get started; we still have to meet Angie and Mark Bear at the Antiqology."

Putting the picture back on the edge of the filing cabinet, he headed towards the door, meeting his parents in the foyer as they put on their coats, "Why are you meeting Angie and Mark?" asked Xavier.

Deanna flipped her dark brown hair over her collar. She explained, "The Antiqology has this new eggnog ice cream your father and I want to try, and we plan on carpooling with Angie and Mark Bear to Fort Wayne."

Turning towards the door, Dad winked at me and said, "Don't stay up too late and no messes."

Finally, they were gone; racing up the stairs, he paused outside his mother's office; what was that paper sticking out of the picture frame? With Mom and Dad gone, this may be the only time he would have to look at it without them knowing. Shutting the door behind him, he approached the filing cabinet and removed the picture, turning it over; he tried to take the back off without damaging it further.

He soon realized the little pegs holding the back of the picture frame were stuck; looking around, he spotted a monogrammed letter opener with the initials EDH. When he was little, he had asked his mom who EDH was, and she replied that she did not know because she picked it up at a garage sale before he was born. She claimed she purchased it because the last two initials were the same as hers.

She would then take it away from him, and it would be hidden somewhere out of sight and out of mind, only to turn up a month or two later. Using the pointed end of the letter opener, he pried the clasps up and removed the black cardboard from the frame; the paper was crumpled and had a yellow tint hinting at its age. The word "Xerox" was written in cursive; the penmanship was graceful and delicate, leading him to think it had been written by a woman, even possibly his mother.

As he put the picture back, it fell between the wall and the filing cabinet; great, not only was he pushing his luck by snooping now he had to move office furniture. Xavier hated moving furniture, especially when mom got it in her head to clean before the holidays. The house was always spotless, no matter what time of the year. With a sigh, he pushed the filing cabinet to the side when he noticed the outline of a key under black duct tape on the back.

Why was a key taped to the back of the filing cabinet? Taking the key off, he started trying to open the filing cabinet lock with no luck. He then tried to open the locked desk drawers again, with no such luck, when suddenly he realized that the key looked like one of the keys you would use for a Sentry fire safe. He knew his mother had one hidden in the back of the closet in her bedroom.

He had found it when he was around five years old and liked to find hiding places to take naps. One time when he was just three years old, his mom told him she almost called the police to report him missing after his dad lost track of him when he was babysitting him. When she came home and asked where he was, his dad had to admit he could not find him. The entire time everyone was looking for him. He was sleeping in a partially closed guitar case he had seen on the enclosed front porch. Since then, Mom consistently enforced the rule that he takes naps in his bedroom and nowhere else.

Leaving the office area, he headed towards his parents' bedroom. His parents' room was spotless and tastefully decorated like the rest of the house. The room differed from the rest of the house primarily because instead of hunter green and burgundy dominating the color scheme, it was a chocolate brown and a light mint green. He wondered if it was a compromise for his dad's sake. Blaine often stated that he did not care for green and only indulged his wife because he loved her. It was a standing joke in the family that if Mom and Dad ever had a daughter, she would have wanted to name her burgundy; it made him wonder why Will was never named Hunter after the shade of green his mother preferred.

With that thought in mind, he moved the pile of clothing and boxes stacked in front of the safe. Now that he thought about it, the only place that needed to be cleaned and organized was this part of Mom's closet. If he did not know better, he would think his mother was trying to hide the fire safe. The key slid into the lock without any trouble; it was a perfect fit for the Sentry safe; luck must have been on his side because it fit and opened.

Once inside, he found a file labeled Gemini September 8th, ironically his birthday, except the year was different. He was born years later. Removing the folder, he noticed that both the safe and file folder were empty; why would anyone keep an empty folder in a fireproof safe?

Looking at his watch, he realized time was getting away from him. Pushing off the floor, Xavier put everything back in its proper place. He shut the safe and the mystery temporarily into the lockbox in his mind. He would have plenty of time to solve the puzzle later after visiting with his best friend Mathew down the street. Matt should have a few ideas on where to look for more information and whatnot.

Aquarius: II

A knock sounded on the door, temporarily distracting the young man hunched over the dissected parts of a computer tower, the gaping hole giving evidence of its traumatic demise. A muffled shout of "come in" was drowned out by Xavier barging in, yelling, "Lucy, I'm home."

Mathew looked up. "Ha, very funny; you've been watching I Love Lucy on ReTV?"

"Please, I own all the episodes on Holocene," said Xavier. The creation of the Holocene in 2029 allowed anyone who owned the software system produced by the NIMAGE Corporation to become the character of their choice and relieve the movie via virtual reality. Limits were put on the type of shows and movies produced due to the unforeseen death of a teenager and an older woman from stress cardiomyopathy during an intense simulation of a historical documentary.

Mathew asked, "So who were you this time, Ricky or Lucy?"

Throwing himself down on the bed and speaking in a fake Cuban accent, Xavier answered, "Ricky, of course! I could never do justice to Lucy; she is the Queen of Comedy."

Mathew shook his head sporadically, causing his out-of-control curls to bounce around as his vivid green eyes showed intelligence. Most people were intimidated by Mathew's 145 IQ and his membership in Mensa. Then add his above-average height of six feet six inches tall. You had the perfect recipe for social isolation and limited social interaction with kids his age. At Abraham Lincoln elementary school, Xavier, Mathew, and Packer first became friends. In this kindness-certified school, students were encouraged to do random acts of kindness daily and pass them on. The school's philosophy matched his parents in that you help others because it is the right thing to do and not because of a desire for recognition, money, influence, or power.

For Xavier, his random act of kindness in second grade consisted of helping Mathew pick up his books after he tripped over his own two feet and spilled his stuff in the hallway at the end of the school day. After Xavier helped him, they talked about computers, cartoons, and random facts. The two became inseparable for the rest of the school year until the arrival of a new kid during third grade. All three boys were placed in the same 3rd-grade class under the supervision of the new teacher named Ms. Saehan. She was the best third-grade teacher any active young boy could ever have; she knew how to keep them engaged and cultivate a love of learning without suppressing their spirit of adventure.

Parker moved to the area from Green Bay, Wisconsin. He gravitated towards Xavier and Mathew after the three boys ran headfirst into each other in the bathroom and gave themselves mild concussions. While Packer was not considered a genius like Matt, he was extremely loyal to those he called friends. His hobbies included binge-watching dystopias, documentaries, and historical research from the early 1950s to the modern day. His childlike innocence and gullibility made him highly likable among his peers and the subject of numerous jokes and pranks.

The wait in the school nurse's office gave the boys plenty of time to get to know each other as they waited for their mothers to pick them up and take them to their respective pediatricians. Over the next ten years, the three boys became known as the three musketeers by friends and family members; where one was, the others soon followed, as did creativity, confusion, and chaos.

"Mom and Dad are in Fort Wayne, and I thought since we did not have school, why don't you and me and Packer have a SKYRIM marathon. We could play all sixteen versions of SKYRIM."

"Wait, said Mathew you don't have number XVI?"

Xavier laughed as he pushed the clothes off the bed onto the floor and plumped up a pillow with the cartoon character of the Greek god Dionysus riding a spotted jaguar. "I do now. Mom gave me money to buy the game when she and Dad left."

The door swung open as Packer staggered into the room with a half-gallon of milk in one hand and a plate loaded with red and green frosted holiday sugar cookies in the other hand. The crumbs from the cookies littered Packer's vintage Aaron Rogers Green Bay Packer jersey. Once he finished the mouthful of milk and cookies, he said, "Hey, what's buzzin, cuzzin?

Xavier rolled to his right side to look at Packer, "What does that even mean, and who even talks like that anymore"?

Packer smiled, taking a sip of milk from the gallon, "I am officially up to 1960s slang and can tell you the history of Mr. Potato Head and what cereal was popular right before you were born."

The other two boys laughed and yelled nerd.

"See, that is a prime example of 1950s slang that has survived through the years", replied to Packer as he sat on the floor, leaning against the bed and watching Mathew tinker with the computer. "So, what is the game plan? Are we staying here to watch Mathew play Dr. Frankenstein, eat junk food, and chill out or what"?

Xavier looked at Packer and said, "Mom and Dad are in Fort Wayne, and I thought we could have a SKYRIM marathon. What do you think?"

"Wicked" said, Packer. "But whose house will host the marathon, yours, mine, or Mathew's? My mom has her church group discussing the upcoming Christmas pageant. Mathew's room does not have enough room with all these spare computer parts lying around; we barely have room to sit."

Matt's exclamation drowned out Packer's additional observation; "I can't help it; I am a prolific inventor, fixer-upper, and genius extraordinaire," he said.

Xavier smiled. "Then that means the marathon will be at my house. How about 3 pm? Everyone brings two liters of Coke; no Pepsi products are allowed. Also, bring a bag of chips or dessert, and I will make the pizzas."

Sitting on the bed, Xavier paused momentarily, gathering his thoughts; "Guys, since we are going to have the marathon at my house, I want to talk to you about something unrelated to video games or food. In Mom's office, I discovered a piece of paper hidden behind a picture of Will and me; the paper had one word "XEROX." Then I found a key taped behind a filing cabinet, and it unlocked a sentry fire safe in my mom's closet. The paper in the safe had September 8th, and the birth year was nineteen years before I was born."

Packer interrupted Xavier's monologue momentarily, "Dude, you know how private your mom is and how territorial she is about her personal office. Remember when we inadvertently spilled her coffee on a story written by a former student who had died while we were playing hide and seek. I remember the look on her face and how she yelled at us and then burst into tears. I have never seen your mom so upset, angry, and sad all at the same time. Your dad had to come to get us, and we stayed out all afternoon until he thought it was safe for us to go back and tell her we were sorry."

"I know but let me finish what I was trying to tell you guys," Said Xavier. Walking down the stairs, I heard Mom in the living room crying and talking to Dad about the nightmares I had been having lately. She worried about something, but I could not exactly hear what she said. She was just as upset as she was that day, we ruined that story. I feel like my parents are hiding something from me, but I do not know what it is, and I am starting to get worried; what does it mean, and why are my nightmares coming back?" Xavier leaned over the side, resting his head in his hands.

Mathew was the first to break the silence, "Man, when did the nightmares start returning? I thought that quack in Fort Wayne told your parents they would stop once you finished growing. What was his name?" Mused Mathew, "Crock, Cracker, Potter?"

"No, his name is Jameson Proctor, and he specializes in Neurological Cancer treatments," said Xavier. "However, now that I am almost eighteen, I do not plan to see that psychopathic quack again. I do not care if I never stop having nightmares. It is better than dealing with his stupid sense of humor and his love of needles. I can see it in his eyes. He takes great pleasure in hurting me when I go to see him. I have even told Mom and Dad this, but Mom says I am imagining things."

Packer quietly piped in, "How about I research it for you, what with my mad research skills into historical periods? It should be easy. I need to correlate the information with the term XEROX, the date, and any other information you could give me, and we can take it from there."

"Sounds like a plan to me," said Mathew. The boys stood up and headed towards the door.

"OK, then everyone meets at my house at 3 pm, the last one there gets cleaning detail," said Xavier.

Packer shouted, "Hey, that's not fair. You live there." Everyone laughed light-heartedly and went their separate ways to collect goodies for the upcoming marathon.

The morning before Christmas, the house was quiet as Will and his wife slept in the den on the pull-out couch; Xavier's nephew Carter slept in Will's old room. Mom and Dad were sleeping in their bedroom down the hall. On the other hand, I was wide awake, busy trying to beat Skyrim before the house exploded with chaos and confusion typical during the holidays when the entire family came to stay. My brother Will was born May 4th, and with a sixteen-year age gap between us, you would expect us to be more like strangers than brothers.

I know I was a surprise baby because I had never seen a picture of my mom pregnant with me, only pictures of her pregnant with Will. However, despite that big age gap, Will always made time for me. He even told me once that he decided to attend the local technical college to ensure he was there for Mom and me.

He looks more like Dad; they have the same slender build, wear the same glasses, and have similar mannerisms. His coloring is like mine and mom's, with ash brown hair and blue eyes the same color as a dad's. Will has always seemed closer to Mom and me than to Dad, but he says it is because Dad is just more introverted than Mom, me, or Will. Sometimes Mom and Will look so sad, but when I ask them why they are unhappy, they say it is nothing and change the subject. It makes me feel excluded, and sometimes I wonder if I am adopted, and they just do not want to tell me.

The smell of pumpkin pie and oatmeal cookies with cranberries permeated the house as the muffled sounds of *Jingle Bell Rock* echoed through the downstairs living area. During the holiday, Mom always made pies, cookies, and her special Egg Nogg the day before Christmas to have something to eat when we binged watched Christmas movies. Mom's famous crock pot lasagna with six different types of cheese simmered in the kitchen in preparation for dinner tonight. It is a standing joke within the circle of family and friends that the amount of cheese in Mom's lasagna would bind a person up for a month. Will, Lynda, and Carter planned to head back to Fort Wayne later tomorrow night or early tomorrow morning, depending on the mood of Carter, or the little emperor, as I like to call him.

The riot of noise and confusion moved like a wave throughout the day as Mom, Dad, Lynda, Will, and I attempted to corral two-year-old Carter Alexander. I passionately believe that the terrible twos were god's way of paying parents back for their misbehavior as children. Dinner was loud and chaotic as everyone sat around the dining room table and traded stories back and forth about their favorite holiday memories. Will turned towards Mom when suddenly a dollop of lasagna smacked him in the chest as Carter scooped another spoonful, looking towards his grandma with a playful sparkle in his eyes.

"Hey, you little ankle-biter," said Xavier. "Packer and Mathew would have a stroke if they found out you were throwing grandma's famous crock pot lasagna around like that."

Blaine looked up, wiping his mouth, then leaning towards Carter. He said, "Don't waste food."

Everyone at the table laughed because they knew how serious Dad was about his food. When Xavier was a child, he remembered his dad telling him not to waste food. It seemed as if Blaine had the metabolism to eat whatever he wanted when he wanted. On the other hand, Mom always joked about how she could gain ten pounds by looking at a Hershey's bar. She ate salads and watched her sugar intake religiously, stating that diabetes ran in the family. He often wondered how she knew it ran in the family when her parents had died when she was young.

Xavier sometimes wished they had not died when he was little because it would have been great to have grandparents to play with and eat the junk food not usually allowed at home. He could imagine the fun and games he would have had learning to throw a ball and going to swim meets with them cheering him on. He had always wished his family were bigger than what it is currently. Now that he thought about it, he realized he did not even know his grandparents' first names and could never recall what they looked like. Were there even any pictures of his maternal and paternal grandparents in the family albums in his mother's office?

"Mom," said Lynda as she used a washcloth to clean up Carter, "don't you and Xavier have an appointment on December 27th at Dr. Proctor's office in Fort Wayne? I wondered if you and Xavier wanted to have lunch with Carter and me after the appointment."

My head whipped around, my eyes narrowed, and I put my fork down carefully, all humor and holiday cheer wiped from existence by the mere mention of the psychopathic quack.

In a slightly monotone voice I said, "since I am almost eighteen, I no longer needed to see Doctor Proctor."

The silence at the table was stifling; even baby Carter was holding his breath in anticipation; Xavier was usually a laid-back person, but when he got angry, he was known for having an explosive temper equivalent to a volcanic eruption. Only mom had a temper to match, and she could be just as stubborn.

Mom shook her head, "Yes, but you need a physical, a booster shot, and a meningitis shot before you go to college. I have no intention of shopping around for a new doctor at the last minute only to find out they are not accepting new patients or our insurance, especially when the one you have gone to for years is only a short trip away. The subject is now closed for discussion."

Savagely I pushed away from the table, "I'm not hungry anymore, and I don't want to see that idiot, Proctor."

I stormed up the stairs, hating that I would have to see the psychopathic quack. No matter how much I complained about him to my parents, they did not want to listen to what I had to say in the matter. One good thing, after tomorrow, I will be able to tell him precisely what I think of his stupid sense of humor and his horrible bedside manner.

Xavier waited in the cold, brightly lit examination room, his right hand gripping the back of the tissue-thin dressing gown to maintain his modesty and prevent his butt from being exposed to the elements. He wondered who the person was who thought it would be cute to put little rubber duckies wearing red galoshes and carrying a red umbrella on the examination gowns, so not cool.

He hated going to the doctor's office, what with the cold temperatures, the indignity of the attire, and the smell of antiseptic mixed with the scent of illnesses; not one of which was on his to-do list. Impatiently he waited, reminding himself repeatedly that he only had to make it through one more visit with Dr. Quacko (Quack plus wacko); after this, he could choose who he wanted to see rather than deal with him and his decrepit nurse.

The door opened, and in walked the devil and his evil sidekick, Susan Davison, also known as Nurse Cruella da Ville. Dr. Quacko stopped reviewing a medical file with Xavier's name on it. He was a white-haired gentleman about six feet tall, two inches, give or take, weighing about 180 pounds. The two most prominent things you noticed about him were his dad's gut and his hawk-like nose that constantly turned up in the air as if he smelled something foul and unpleasant.

While Nurse Davison was one of those people who always had what was referred to as an angry resting face; she was about five feet eight inches tall with cold, steely gray eyes, a harsh profile, and black plastic framed old lady glasses rimmed in fake rhinestones with silver chain attach to the earpieces to keep them from falling off or being misplaced. A blanket of silence engulfed the room as Dr. Quacko stared at Xavier; putting the file folder down, he adjusted his glasses and reached for his pen light, a slight curve to his mouth indicating his personal enjoyment as he took in Xavier's discomfort and anxious attitude.

"So, there were two peanuts that walked into a bar; one was salted," Dr. Quacko chuckled and looked at Xavier expectantly when no laughter emerged; he moved on to his next joke. "OK, I got another one, which is even funnier than the last one. "A dyslexic man walks into a bra." He waited for a reaction, "get it? Instead of B-A-R, he switched the letters to spell bra." After no response from Cruella or Xavier, Dr. Quacko replied, "Well, we seem to have captain grouchy pants in the house today."

No matter how often people told Xavier that he was lucky to have such a great doctor, he could not shake the feeling that the doctor was not who he said he was, and it was all a façade. His skin crawled whenever he had to be around the doctor and his nurse, but no one wanted to listen to his suspicions. Clicking the button on his pen light, the doctor stood in front of Xavier and the examination table as Cruella took her position to the left side of the exam table as if trying to block any escape attempts.

"Let's see how your optic and Oculomotor nerves are doing today," said Dr. Quacko. Xavier shook his head, "English, please." Doctor Quacko laughed and said, "Just checking to see if you were brain-dead again. He started chuckling.

Xavier thought this man's sense of humor was stupid and twisted, who would think joking about being brain-dead would be funny.

He tilted his head, "is that another lame joke? I don't get it, and it's not really funny."

The chuckling abruptly stopped as he lowered the penlight and asked Xavier, "Is there anything out of the ordinary I should know about or any questions you want to ask me?" Instead of answering, Xavier pushed off the end of the exam table, forcing both the doctor and the nurse to step back to avoid being knocked down.

"Are we done? I just want to get my clothes on, go home, play some video games, and enjoy what is left of my Christmas break before school starts back up again."

Putting the pen light away and moving towards the door, Doctor Quacko said, "The only thing left to do is have Nurse Davidson give you the last immunization shots, and we will finish the paperwork for the University of Indiana; then you can go home." Both Cruella and Dr. Quacko left the room.

Xavier hurriedly dressed while muttering, "I hate this place."

He never really was a fan of hospitals or doctors' offices. He could not pinpoint why, but he felt extreme fear and anxiety every time he went to either. It physically became hard for him to breathe; it felt like he was suffocating and dying. He never told his parents of his concern because they already worried about him as it was due to cancer he had as a child and his constant being sick or having to be admitted to the hospital.

He looked towards the door and noticed a military green file folder with his name on it. He grabbed the folder and opened it, scanning through each section, vital signs, allergies, the reason for the visit, and diagnosis. He noticed off to the side of the last heading a note stating that the patient's development was accelerating faster than anticipated; atlas protocol was to be enacted with a recommendation to contain and confine the subject with removal from the current environment, effective immediately.

Startled, Xavier stopped to think before dropping the folder on the counter and silently easing open the door; leaning his head out slightly past the door frame, he tried to ascertain whether anyone would see him sneak out. He did not know what was happening, but he would be darned if he was contained or confined by anyone, much less the doctor and Nurse Cruella da Ville.

Sliding out into the deserted hallway, he made his way toward the sound of multiple voices, hoping to find out more information before telling his mother what was happening. Looking around the edge of the corner wall, he noticed two men talking to Dr. Quacko. Both men looked like pro wrestler wannabes; the one on the right was at least six feet tall and weighed 260 pounds, with the muscular build of a famous actor from the early 2000s named Dwayne the Rock Johnson. The second man, who was just as big, leaned against the wall cleaning his fingernails with a small case pocketknife; his blonde hair, cut close to the scalp, made him seem almost bald. Xavier was getting ready to turn around and head toward the direction of the stairs when he heard the Hulk Hogan look-alike speak up.

"So, doc, how are we going to get the boy out of the building; if you want, I can hit him upside his head or use a choke hold on him and put him to sleep for a while?"

The doctor shook his head no and gestured towards the receptionist desk/nurses' station.

"Susan will give him the last of his immunization shots; one of the shots will be a sedative called Rohypnol that was banned in the United States, it will take about 15 minutes to take effect, and it will knock him out for a few hours. We will then wheel him out the back door and load him into the SUV, and you two will head to the safe house. Once he comes to, he will not remember his being drugged."

Both men nodded in understanding and started to head towards the door leading to the parking garage when the Hulk suddenly stopped and looked over his shoulder toward the doctor.

"How will you keep the mother from raising all kinds of grief? You know she will get slightly suspicious; we do not need the police on our back-door step. The boss will not be happy if we must deal with the fuzz."

Dwayne looked at the doctor. "Do you want me to take care of her?"

With a quick look around, Dr. Quacko lowered his voice and said, "No, I told the mother that I suspected that cancer he had as a child is starting to come back. I suggested she go home and get some stuff, and I would send him to the hospital for an MRI and some blood tests."

Smirking, the doctor outlined his plan, "The boss already took care of everything. Once she gets halfway home, the bomb in her car will take care of her. Goodbye, dear old mom; Merry Christmas, and Happy New Year. When the police investigate the explosion, it will look like a gas leak. The mother's remains combined with the body of that runaway kid you put in the trunk, and poof, no one will ever suspect that Xavier is alive. Now get the car ready and bring it to the back-physician's entrance, it will take a little bit before the drug takes effect, and I do not want to raise suspicions. Now do not mess anything up."

Xavier took off, heading towards the rear of the building and the emergency stairwell leading down to the ground level of the parking garage. He knew he had to escape before Cruella Da Ville and Dr. Quacko discovered he was gone; Mom would never believe him, and if he let her take her car, she would never live to see him again. Stopping suddenly in his tracks, he quickly looked around the area next to the stairs; he did not see any signs indicating the potential for sounding an alarm when using the exit. Well, no time to waste, it was just a chance he would have to take if he wanted to save his mother and get away.

No alarm sounded; charging down the stairs two at a time, he planned out what he needed to do to get away and keep his mom safe. First, he needed to convince Mom to let him take her car; thankfully, they brought two cars because he had planned to go to the mall. Mom had some work she said she needed to do at St. Francis University, where she taught incoming first-year students English Composition and Early American Literature.

Second, he needed to get money out of the bank; he had three thousand dollars in savings he had planned to use to purchase an Alienware computer before going off to college. That would be enough to tide him over until he could figure out what was happening and who was pulling the strings of this operation. Thirdly he needed to contact Matt and Packer without being seen by his friends, family, and enemies.

It was apparent even to him that the complexity required to murder someone and make it look like an accident required a level of organization and skill beyond that of a common criminal. Finally, he needed to get rid of the car, his phone, and anything they could use to track him down. Packer's obsession with dystopian movies and doomsday scenarios made it easier to think of what must be done to live off the grid. Exiting the building, he headed deeper into the parking structure. He looked for his mother's vehicle, a Ruby red Mazda CX72 with Wonder Woman decals.

Mom always picked cars that stood out among the drab gray, black, and white cars; she said it made it easier to find. Putting his fingerprint on the handle, he waited for the fingerprint identification system to recognize him and unlock the door. With an audible click, he opened the door and tapped his hand to initiate his Biophone. The technology was still relatively new and expensive and typically only made available to middle or upper-class families due to it being in beta phase.

Biophone technology was initially based on radio frequency identification devices created by the former Soviet Union. In the early stage of development, Microchip implants consisted of a silicone glass plate the size of a grain of rice implanted in a person's hand. The South Korean company Samsung originally purchased the RFID patent. It was later adapted and revised to allow individuals to text, make calls, and listen to audio recordings of emails by tapping the top of the hand and listening via an implanted microphone chip placed behind the right ear just under the skin.

The Biophone was kinetically powered through body movement and was exceptionally durable, with a built-in tracking system for children under sixteen. The tracking system was designed to track lost children and kidnapped victims and prevent juveniles from fleeing home. However, once a child reached the age of sixteen, federal laws required the deactivation of the tracking system unless the child was mentally or physically disabled or had a mental illness or terminal disease.

He knew he had to text his mom before Dr. Quacko talked to her and convinced her his cancer had returned; time was of the essence. Xavier tapped the top of his hand three times to activate the Biophone; he quickly dictated the following message. I am done and now leaving the doctor's office, getting ready to go to the mall; I hope you do not mind I am taking your car because Dad's belated Christmas present is too big for my trunk. Doctor Proctor had to leave suddenly, and I have a copy of my medical records for the

University of Indiana. See you at home and Mom, I love you...

The top of his hand, where the quarter-sized biochip was located, turned red, then rapidly flashed green three times, indicating his mom had received and read his message. His mom's response to his previous message was almost immediately relayed to the audio microphone embedded under the skin behind his right ear. The statement was concise and to the point, KK, heading to St. Francis University to get some work done, see you at home, love you too. Tapping his hand to disconnect from his Biophone, he pressed his right index finger to the fingerprint identification sensor below the ignition starter. Xavier felt relieved; he must have gotten to his mom before Dr. Quacko, and his goons did. He also felt guilty because he knew his mother loved his brother Will and him with all her heart.

His mother never hid how much she loved them. Sometimes she could be overly protective and clingy, like when she would not let Xavier spend the night at other friends' houses. He was lucky that his mother even let Matt and Packer stay over at their home. With her having no extended family due to the death of her parents in a car accident and having no siblings, aunts, or uncles, he understood her need for family, affection, comfort, and the insane fear she had that something terrible would happen to her boys.

He knew in his heart that the pain and grief she would feel upon his demise would be horrific, and he dreaded causing her so much pain. Still, it was better to suffer a little now than to suffer forever because he did die or because he was imprisoned for the rest of his life as a test subject for

Dr. Quacko. As the old saying goes, the best-laid plans of mice and men often go awry. It was time to make a new plan and hopefully get his life back on track as soon as possible.

He knew he had to get out of there before they discovered him, and Hulk Hogan decided to make good on his suggestion to knock him out. In the rear-view mirror, he thought he saw one of the goons heading into the garage briskly; just for a moment, he thought he saw the man aim his gun in his direction, and it looked like the barrel of the gun was fitted with a silencer, but he could not be sure.

Gradually, he pushed down on the accelerator, picking up speed in a steady manner. His head started to hurt from trying to pay attention to his surroundings and every minor detail. Mentally he repeated his goals to maintain his composure. "Do not draw undue attention; find the nearest TX3 bank branch office and get back to Huntington."

Five minutes later, he pulled the car over to the side of the curb and went into the lobby of the bank, he knew taking out that much money would require presenting his personal identification, but it could not be helped. Standing in line seemed to take forever, and his fidgeting and anxiety levels increased in direct proportion to his wait time.

The holiday music and Christmas decorations did little to soothe him as the soft crooning sounds of Bing Crosby's "I Am Dreaming of a White Christmas," pushed him further into a depressive state. His mother loved listening to Christmas music from November 4th until January 1st of the New Year. Mom always said that her great-grandfather's last name was Christmas, so celebrating the holiday season was a tribute to her ancestors. Everyone in the family enjoyed teasing her about her Christmas obsession. Dad even put a limit on the number of Christmas trees in the house.

Finally, the silvered-haired, mild-aged woman behind the counter said, "May I help you?"

Xavier took a deep breath and nervously reached for his wallet in his back pocket. He prayed that the woman would not give him a hard time or insist on calling his mother to verify the removal of the funds since his account was linked to her account. It was easier for his mother to give him money if they were connected. It would also save on transfer fees if he ever needed a large sum of money once he was in college. Going to college seemed like a pipe dream from a far-off time and place.

"Yes, I am getting ready for college and plan to buy a new computer. Can I please withdraw three thousand out of my savings account?"

The bank teller typed the information into the computer and asked, "Do you need it in a cashier's check?" Xavier shook his head no. The teller looked at his driver's license, comparing the picture to his features. Finally, after what seemed like a thousand years or more, she put down the identification card and asked, "Would you like it in large denominations such as the fifties, one hundred, or small bills?"

Xavier thought about it for a moment; large denominations would attract too much attention, but the twenties, on the other hand, would be just one of many thousands of twenty-dollar bills. "I want all twenties, please."

The woman looked startled, "OK, but I will have to get more bills from my manager because I do not have enough in my till to pay out that large amount. Would you like a security guard to walk you to your car?"

With a slight negative shake, Xavier declined the offer. He acknowledged that he would wait for her to obtain additional monies. In a matter of minutes, the bank teller returned with the bundles of twenties; slowly, she counted out the cash, her voice barely above a whisper so no one would overhear and know how much he was leaving the bank with. Once he signed the receipt, she happily wished him a Happy New Year. The sound of holiday music slowly faded away, as did his dream of a bright and happy New Year's Eve with family and friends.

Pulling the car over to the side of the road under a deserted underpass, Xavier prayed that the bomb Dr. Proctor had mentioned had not reached the point of detonation. Still, if it had, he would not care one way or the other. Moving around to the back of the SUV, he hesitantly reached for the release button, praying he had overreacted or imagined the entire conversation between Dr. Quacko and his goons. The hatch moved in slow motion, inch by inch, upward until finally, the body of a young man was revealed, similar in height, build, and coloring to Xavier; he looked more like Xavier than his own brother Will did.

A part of him wondered if the boy's family would miss and grieve him to the same degree as his own family. His mom always told him that life was unfair, but he never realized just how unfair it was until faced with the image of that young boy who could have been his own brother lying dead in his trunk. He now understood why the death of a child violated the natural order of life. No parent should have to bury their child and spend the holidays relieving the past and thinking about what would happen if I had done this or done that.

Xavier promised himself that after everything was resolved, he would visit the parents of this missing young man; he was not sure what he was going to say or if he was even going to introduce himself. Still, he did know that the kid in the trunk deserved some form of acknowledgment for helping Xavier escape with his life. He gently removed the body from the trunk and positioned him in the driver's seat, and used an old, discarded T-shirt he found in the trunk.

Once he tore off numerous strips of cloth from the T-shirt, he used them to tie the body to the seat so he would appear to be running the heater to keep the car warm as he waited for someone. He knew that the fire would eliminate any trace of the wrappings before the fire department, or the police arrived.

The only thing he kept from the trunk of the car was a bandana with a small amount of blood on it; he suspected the blood belonged to the young man and hoped it would help him later find out his identity so he could notify the family. Grabbing some miscellaneous items from the back-cargo area, Xavier placed a ball cap on his head, shut the trunk, and threw a wad of clothing into the back seat with a lit match. He knew that the combination of the fire within the car, the heating up of the engine, and the material in the upholstery would ensure the fire spread rapidly and possibly ignite the makeshift bomb. He stood and watched the fire burn until he was sure it would not inadvertently go out.

Pisces: III

The sound of sirens approaching motivated him to hitch his backpack on his left shoulder, as he turned towards the road leading away from the scene of his demise. He pulled out a hoverboard decorated with scratches, scuff marks, and numerous dings. By the time the fire department and police responded to the scene, the evidence of the accelerant would be history, the body would be burned beyond all recognition, and he would be long gone.

The only safe thing he could think of right now was to head back home and hide in the treehouse until he could get word to his friends. He knew he could count on Mathew and Packer's help to figure out what was happening; However, it would take a while to get back to Huntington based on his current mode of transportation. Traveling via hoverboard was barely faster than walking but much less tiring. An electric bike would be better, but they were banned due to the lithium batteries exploding due to extreme weather conditions.

Hopefully, by the time he got home, he would have some idea of what to do because right now, he felt slightly detached from the world, like he was watching a movie, and everything was happening to someone else. Would he always be this detached, or was it just temporary? He hoped it was just a way for his mind to make sense of everything and protect him from emotional overload. Funny how you never fully appreciate what you have in life until it is ripped away from you. Mom always said life was unfair and looked so sad and beaten down whenever she said it. At that moment, he would have given anything to know what made her so sad and why she had such a cynical outlook toward life in general.

Xavier calmly sat in the tree house named the "The Doghouse" he, Mathew, and Packer had built in middle school with the help of his dad as a place to escape from parents and talk about everything from Pokémon to girls. His dad, being mechanically inclined and handy with electricity, had wired the tree house with electrical outlets and lights. The clubhouse roof had solar panels angled to take advantage of the sun's rays from sunrise to midday. The generator was housed in a wooden bench and a small heater for unexpected cold nights. All the outlets in the tree house were connected to the solar generator.

His dad even figured out how to run water to the hideout by anchoring PVC pipes to the side of the tree and painting them brown so they would blend in with the tree trunk. The water hose from the house connected to the PVC pipe and provided clean, cold water which could be heated via a solar-powered heating wand. The water was drawn up the tree trunk via a USB-powered faucet in the makeshift sink/cabinet created using a standard Lowe's cabinet and a silver extra-large doggy bowl with a hole cut out for connecting to a drainpipe. The grey water was removed from the tree house by another PVC pipe, and it was directed towards the back of the yard and was used to irrigate his dad's garden.

Xavier was exhausted, and a part of him was worried; heck, the fire could have sputtered out for all he knew. They could have already found the body and were hunting him down, intending to put him on trial for murder. How could he prove he had not killed that young man and that he was dead before he was taken out of the trunk. He made sure to check but he also knew that it was illegal to conceal or alter the remains of a deceased individual. Taking a deep breath, he stopped and focused on one of the streetlamps just before his house; he knew he needed to distract himself because if he kept thinking about what was done to that young man, the injustice of it all, he would go crazy, and that would undo everything he had achieved so far.

It had been a while since the three boys had spent time together in the tree house; they had built it with his father the summer before his fifth-grade year. Looking back, he wished he had spent more time with Matt, Packer, and his loved ones. Life had gotten a little hectic since the start of his freshman year of high school, and it got worse as he got closer to graduating.

Waiting for Mathew and Packer to show up was nerve-racking. He was counting on the fact that they would eventually need to escape the noise, confusion, and chaos surrounding his disappearance and death. The shutters covering the windows rattled a little as the wind blew against them, trying to force them open. The tree house provided some protection from the elements, and he knew it was better to be here than having to hide under an underpass or a bridge in the freezing cold.

Looking around the dirty, cluttered one-room clubhouse, he spotted a pair of scissors under a pile of comic books. He figured he would do the messy stuff before the guys showed up; Packer did not handle the sight of blood very well. The more blood involved, the more likely he would pass out. He had no doubt that removing the Biophone implant would be bloody and extremely painful, but it had to be done. Grabbing an old shirt one of the boys left behind, he made some makeshift bandages. He heated the scissor blades with a lighter to disinfect them.

Slowly he lowered his right arm, bracing it on his thigh and turning his hand over, pressing the point of the scissors into the skin until a bubble of blood welled up and dribbled down his hand and soaked into his jeans. Pressing down with more force, he took a deep break. He gritted his teeth, dragging the blade along the edge of the Biophone implant until it caught the outer edge of a thin piece of glass half the width of a microscope slide and one-third of its length.

The pain became unbearable, but he pushed through; stopping was not an option; there was only one direction to go; the glass slide popped out with surprising ease; releasing the breath he was holding, he pressed the sweatshirt to his hand, wishing he had a belladonna patch for the instant migraine he had acquired. The cut was not too deep, but it required consistent pressure to be applied to get the bleeding to stop.

The clubhouse floor started to vibrate as footsteps ascended the ladder, each step causing the tree to shudder in displeasure. The crunch of leaves and debris echoed through the night; some unknown person or persons were climbing up the ladder towards the only entrance to the clubhouse and Xavier's temporary sanctuary. Scooting back behind the makeshift couch, which was more of a wooden frame with discarded couch cushions, he minimized his profile to hide his presence until he knew if the intruders were friends or foes. The door flew open with a loud bang; snow, wind, and cold frigid air poured into the room as Xavier huddled further behind the couch, attempting to conserve body heat.

The faces of the two young men were hidden from view, but that did not stop Xavier from recognizing the sound of Mathew's voice as he started talking to Packer, only for his voice to trail off in mid-sentence. Mathew shuffled into the room; his shoulders hunched over as if he were Atlas carrying the world's weight on his shoulders. Packer quickly followed and shut the door, turning around, he set the bundle in his hands on the floor next to the coffee table; it appeared to be Xavier's favorite Green Bay Packer blanket, given to him by Packer on his 10th birthday. It was his favorite, not because he liked the team but because it reminded him of his friendship with Packer and his obsession with the team.

Secretly Xavier also liked how soft and warm it was. Mom enjoyed teasing him about his inability to pass up touching anything that looked soft. It was one of the reasons he made sure his hair was so soft and luxurious, and she teased him about that as well, often commenting on how it was a crime for a guy to have such smooth and silky hair. He wondered how his mother was taking the news of his death; she always told him how much she loved him; he knew his death would break her heart, and he hated to cause her pain. Keeping his breathing quiet, he watched as Mathew and Parker settled down on the white, oval shag carpet, not bothering to keep their wet and dirty shoes on the wooden planks of the clubhouse floor.

Packer was the first to speak, his voice cracking with emotion, "I cannot believe Xavier is gone; I do not understand it. He was heading home; he always did everything right. He did not drink and drive, did not do drugs, and had a heart of gold. Why did it have to be him and not someone who deserved it? Why would he even go to that side of town? No matter what they say, I do not believe it was an accident."

Mathew stared off into space. His voice sounded hollow as if coming from a great distance. "I don't know, it doesn't make sense, it doesn't seem real; I expect him to come through that door any minute and make a joke about some stupid show he liked."

Both boys sat in silence, each immersed in the past, relieving the good old days, refusing to think about the potential changes to come with the death of their best friend.

It made Xavier feel good inside, knowing that his friends were indeed on his side and not on Dr. Quacko's payroll. However, he did feel bad for the pain he was causing them by hiding his existence. He knew this was an excellent time to make his presence known.

"Hey guys, said Xavier as he crawled out from behind the couch, cradling his bloodied, injured hand to his chest. Standing up, Xavier started to move into the center of the room.

Mathew swung his way, his jaw-dropping open in shock; Packer started to choke on the soda he was drinking as it started to go down the wrong tube and back out his nose.

"Oh my god, it burns like hades," yelled Packer as he jumped up and down in shock over Xavier's surprised entrance.

As both boys rushed Xavier, the force of the charge pushed him back onto his heels, "hold up, guys, give a dead man a chance to take a breath," Xavier joked.

Mathew looked at him. "Man, so not funny."

Packer tried to silence his laugh, then his face started to turn multiple shades of green after he noticed the blood dripping from Xavier's fingertips. Before either one could react, Packer's eyes rolled into the back of his head, and he started to fall towards the floor in a dead faint. Matt and Xavier caught him and dragged him to the makeshift couch. Xavier got up, cleaned the blood from his hand, and grabbed a glass of water for Packer as Matt patted his cheeks until his eyes started to open.

"I am so sorry," said Xavier. "I planned on cleaning everything up before you arrived, but it took a little longer than I thought. If I could have warned you that it was not me that died in the car, I would have." Holding up the piece of glass he had removed from his hand, he asked, "Is there a way for you to short-circuit this thing so no one can use it to find me?"

Mathew took the piece of glass from him and held it up to the light to get a better look at the inside circuitry. "All it would take is a little bit of juice from the outlet, and it will be another piece of useless glass," said Mathew.

Moving towards the wall, he inserted the corner edge into the outlet; Both Packer and Xavier watched with fascination as smoke curled up from the sliver of material he held between his forefingers. The acidic smell of burnt plastic, glass, and circuitry lingered in the air making the boys' eyes water.

Packer turned towards Xavier, "OK, what is going on, and why does everyone think you are dead? Why are you hiding in the doghouse when Momma D is heartbroken over your death?"

Xavier sank onto the shag carpet that had seen better days and shook his head, "to be honest, I am not sure what is going on? I went to my last doctor's appointment thinking I would get the last immunization shots and the paper I needed to complete the admission process for the University of Indiana. Then when I was looking at my file, I noticed his handwritten notes, so I started to leave the examination room to find my mom so we could get out of there."

He then explained how once he got halfway down the corridor; he overheard Dr. Proctor and two of his thugs discussing killing his mom and kidnapping him. Then just when he was getting ready to make a break for it, the doctor and his goons started talking about a dead body in the trunk, a bomb, and a safe house.

"After hearing all that, I realized I needed to get out of there as soon as possible and somehow draw them away from my mom and family. He was so casual when discussing blowing my mom's car up and making it look like we both had died in a car crash. All I could think about was how I would protect my family. Since they wanted only me, I figured it was better to fake my own death and try to get back here and figure things out. I thought about everything as I was trying to get back to Huntington. The only thing I can figure is that he must be very well-connected or well-financed and that this entire whacked-out situation cannot be put into place on the spur of the moment."

Lost in thought, each boy coped in his own way, Matt sitting silently on the couch, Xavier picking at his newly applied bandage, and Packer pacing back and forth, tossing the football into the air, and catching it rhythmically. The only sound in the room came from the wind whipping through the tree branches and limbs slapping against the wooden structure.

Suddenly Packer stopped, and the ball fell to the floor unnoticed as he looked at the other two, "Hey, do you think the stuff you discovered in your mother's office is connected to what you overheard?"

Mathew grabbed a piece of paper and a pen, "let us review what we know so far, and maybe we can connect the dots. First, we have a piece of paper with your birthday but the wrong year, then the word Xerox, the conversation between your mom and your dad, the attempted murder and kidnapping of Momma D and you."

Xavier interrupted, "Also, write down that they are well financed and have access to illegal weapons such as explosives and high-tech gadgets. All the goons had a handgun in a holster on each side of their waist, and one even had what looked like a silencer on the end of his gun barrel. Not to mention Dr. Quacko has been my doctor for as long as I can remember, that would be about thirteen or fourteen years, give or take a few months. So, what does it all mean?"

Mathew shook his head and looked towards the shuttered window, listening to the whistling of the wind,

"Xavier, I hate to say it, but right now, we do not have enough information to figure out the puzzle; all we can do is gather more intelligence. We need to get into your mother's office, get my computer, and figure out how to get into those medical files."

Packer piped up, his face lit up with excitement, "How about we use the memorial service as a cover for getting into your mom's office? It is scheduled for Saturday, and we can leave the service a few minutes early and look in the office before everyone meets back here."

"That is not a bad idea," said Xavier. "However, I want to attend the memorial service. Before you get your knickers in a wad, I plan to go incognito. I do not know yet what disguise I will use, maybe a baseball hat and sunglasses."

Mathew casually flipped the fried circuit chip across his knuckles, mimicking the moves of Criss Angel, the magician they had seen in Las Vegas when Xavier's mom had recently attended a convention for the National Teacher Leadership Conference, "Do you think attending the service is a good idea?"

Slowly letting out his breath Xavier leaned forward and put his hands on the back of his head, "Look, this may be the last time I get to see my family until we figure out what is going on. I need to see them," he pleaded.

Mathew moved towards Xavier, patting him on his left shoulder; he said, "I understand; I am just worried that you will be spotted because you know there is a good chance that Dr. Quacko and his thugs will be in attendance."

With a triumphant shout, Packer started jumping up and down like a crazy man. The random outbursts and jumping from topic to topic were not new to either Matt or Xavier.

Both boys understood and accepted that it was a part of Packer's personality, so they patiently waited for him to explain.

"I got it," said Packer. "I know how we can sneak in, and you can watch from the back of the church. "Hey Xavier, does your mom still have the baby cam she keeps for when Carter visits? The camera is small enough; we could use it to bug the flowers at the service, and Mathew can hook up to the Church's WIFI and set up a remote recording station. We can review the audio after the service for additional clues."

Xavier was the first to point out that it would look suspicious if two teenage boys started sniffing flowers or paying too close attention to the decorations. Placing listening devices would require someone who could blend in and not look suspicious if seen smelling or rearranging the flowers as they planted the devices."

"Of course," Mathew said, laughter tingeing his voice. Xavier, remember when you got the lead in the play at school?"

Confusion lined Xavier's face, "Which play? I have had the lead part in every play since eighth grade?"

Packer nodded enthusiastically, "The one where you played George Cohan in Yankee Doodle Dandy. Not the young version but the old one. Old people tend to become invisible in large gatherings, so if an old man casually starts sniffing the flowers and looking at the pictures of Xavier and his family, no one will think twice about it."

Once everyone understood the basic premise of the plan, the boys all started jumping wildly around the room, fist-pumping the air, and trying to keep their yells to a dull roar.

When they finally collapsed on the couch in exhaustion; Xavier said, "We need to change the costume a little maybe update the clothes. We can keep the white wig and the beard and add some makeup to age me. The clothes will be easy to modernize, I will just grab one of my dad's blue and black flannel shirts, an old pair of my Wrangler jeans, and hiking boots, and it will be the perfect disguise."

St. Mary's Catholic Church was eerily quiet, with the occasional sob breaking the silence and echoing around the room as Deanna Hanson attempted to muffle her heartfelt cries as she greeted visitors. The Hansen family stood to the left of the table decorated with lush red roses mixed with white and pink carnations; a silver, Spartan urn stood in the center of the table. The name Xavier Alexander Hanson was etched on it, and underneath his name were two intertwined roses bearing the date of his birth and death.

Behind the grief-stricken family, a white projector screen played a video of Xavier as a small child chasing his dogs around the backyard as Will leaned on the edge of the swimming pool laughing at his brother's antics and the dogs. Both dogs were full-blooded cocker spaniels; Ravenclaw was red, black, and white, like a calico cat with curly brown hair on both ears. The other dog was about a year younger than Ravenclaw, and her name was Hufflepuff, with jet-black fur and a white star on her chest. Both dogs barked happily and chased the little towhead boys around the yard as laughter rang out from all directions.

The images changed to a more modern picture of Xavier dressed in a royal blue and white ski suit holding a set of skis, laughing, and beaming into the camera. He looked to be around fifteen, standing on the snowpack slopes next to his family on a Christmas ski trip in Swiss Valley in Jones, Michigan. The tune of "Carry on My Wayward Son," by the band Kansas, played in the background; it was one of Xavier's favorite songs; he had a thing for music from the 1970s and the 1980s.

The music volume gradually faded as Father Andrew waited for the remaining visitors and family to have a seat.

"Normally, I would start the service with a spiritual blessing, but in this case, Deanna and the family would like me to start with an excerpt from a poem written by Robert Frost, "Two roads diverged in a yellow wood, and sorry I could not travel both. Xavier was a wonderful, happy, laid-back young man with his whole life ahead of him. He thought the road he would take would lead him to a bright future, like most young men his age, but for some unknown reason, he was destined to follow the road laid out by our heavenly father rather than the one he chose for himself."

Xavier stood in the back of the church, leaning against the back wall close to the front doors of the church. A hand-carved cane in his right hand, the bent carriage, and white hair and beard combined with a well-used blue and black flannel shirt and wrangler jeans gave him the appearance of a man in his mid-seventies. Closing his eyes, he let the warm, smooth, and peaceful baritone voice of Father Andrew wash over him. He knew in his heart that the only way to keep his family safe was to play dead, but how long would it be before he could tell his mother he loved her, hug his brother Will, goof around with his dad, chase Carter and give Lynda a kiss on the cheek.

He silently watched as his mother's shoulders shook with grief, occasional uncontrolled sobs escaping from her as his father stared off into space as still as a stone statue, his brother Will mimicking his father's actions. At the same time, his sister-in-law sang the snuggle bunny song his mother had written for him and his brother as children to his sleeping nephew Carter.

Mathew and Packer's family sat directly behind the first pew reserved for the family; both boys looked straight ahead, showing little to no emotions. It seemed surreal, seeing Mathew and Packer sitting in the pews without being with them, nudging each other, whispering, or trying to play games on their vintage game consoles as the adults around them scolded them for their inattentiveness. A movement to the left in the Sanctuary near the altar diverted his attention from his family and friends.

Dr. Quacko and a tall, thin woman moved toward the fifth pew directly behind his parents. The woman wore a red pants suit that complemented her dark mahogany shoulder-length hair. Her expensive handbag swung in cadence with her powerful strides. The woman was about five feet eight inches tall but looked taller because of her black pumps. Her build was average, weighing about 132 pounds, and she looked to be in her late 40s with the elegant, coffered look of someone with great wealth and power.

The doctor and the woman in blue whispered to each other as they reveled in the anguish and misery they had inflicted on his family and friends.

Person after person stood up and talked about how wonderful, loving, and kind he was and how much his passing would alter their lives. Xavier never realized that his life had touched so many people, and some things that impacted others the most he considered trivial or mundane. He never thought twice about picking up another student's books in the hallway, stopping a bully from picking on a new kid, or how he liked randomly sitting with the new kids and helping them adjust to a new school. How could these small acts of kindness impact someone's life so radically?

It was difficult to keep everything together and not run up to his mom and family and plead for their forgiveness. He felt like his mind was fractured into small pieces; his thoughts were scrambled, moving from one random thought to another. His thoughts shifted to the woman, then jumped to the fact that he needed to find a new favorite color because he had no doubt that any person associated with Dr. Quacko was up to no good. She looked familiar, but he could not find a place where he knew her.

Most people believed you could not judge a book based on its cover, but for some reason, Xavier always had a sixth sense about who to trust and who to avoid. His instincts told him that Dr. Quacko's companion was a nasty word that would have his mother making him brush his teeth with dish soap if she ever heard him say it aloud.

Mathew and Packer looked towards the doctor and his companion and whispered to each other; after a quick conversation with their parents, they got up and headed towards the boys' bathroom. That was Xavier's cue to meet them in the parking lot by their car; they only had twenty minutes to make it to his house to search his mother's office for clues before the service ended and the place was overrun with family and well-intentioned friends. Turning away, he headed out the doors slowly but steadily as he wondered if he could ever come home again.

Xavier walked into his house and immediately noticed the bare, spartan appearance of the home. He was surprised his mom had removed all evidence of holiday cheer; she usually put up the Christmas decorations on November 4 and took them down the first weekend in January after New Year's Day. The house was morbidly silent; the footsteps of the three teenage boys, muffled by accent rugs, littered the foyer.

Packer and Mathew stopped behind Xavier at the base of the stairs. "You, OK?" whispered Mathew.

Xavier turned his head to look towards the dining room; the farmhouse chic-style table groaned under the weight of the casseroles and potluck dishes set out to feed family and friends after the service.

"This seems so weird," said Xavier. "I do not think I have ever seen this house this devoid of holiday cheer. Even the first Christmas we were here after I went into remission, Mom still tried to decorate and maintain a prominent holiday spirit."

Packer moved into the dining room and started swiping food off plates shoveling it into his mouth. "Look at all this food," he said around a mouthful of ham and deviled eggs.

Mathew grabbed him by his suitcoat and pulled him towards the stairs. "Let's go, Chef Ramsey; we have a small amount of time to search before the service lets out, and we are bombarded by everyone," he said.

Creeping up the stairs, the boys noticed that the door to Momma's office was slightly ajar; pushing the door open, Xavier walked into the room and saw three white moving-style boxes sitting in the middle of the floor in front of the desk. One of the box lids was leaning against the desk with pictures of him and Will on top. Reaching to pick up a picture, he noticed a white envelope peeking out from under the desk close to the open box. He wondered if it fell out when his mother looked in the box and if it could explain what was happening.

"Hey guys come here; look what I found; it was lying under the desk; I am not sure if it came from this box," Xavier said as he pointed to his mom's desk. Both boys put down the items they were looking at and moved around the desk to look at the envelope. The plain white envelope had the word **CITRUM** written in an elegant feminine script like Chinese calligraphy. Xavier turned over the envelope looking for other writing but failed to find any.

Mathew was the first to speak, "Is that the only word written on it? Is there anything in the envelope?"

Hesitantly Xavier opened the envelope only to find it was empty, he knew that finding a letter would be too easy and nothing was ever that easy. "Nope, it's empty; I wonder what CITRUM means;" the sound of a key being inserted into the front door, accompanied by the muffled sound of voices, interrupted Xavier's question.

"Quick," Xavier said, "hid in my room, and if anyone asks, say you were looking for something, maybe the picture of all three of us from that summer up by Lake Roush. Play up the fact that you want a memento to remember the good times we had before I passed away. Mom will not be suspicious if you tell her that. Then once the house is filled with more people, we can sneak out the back door and go to the doghouse. We must leave one at a time to avoid drawing attention to ourselves."

Xavier mingled around the house, listening in on conversations and playing the part of an old family friend while avoiding his mother, father, brother, and sister-in-law, fearful they might recognize him regardless of his disguise. Leaning by the banister, he took out his silver, engraved pocket watch; in about 5 minutes, he would head out, and no one would be the wiser.

A gentle tug on his leg had him looking down to see that Carter, his nephew, had escaped the clutches of the adults and was trying to get his attention. Hands raised in the air; Carter demanded to be picked up by his favorite uncle.

Quickly looking around, he squatted down, tweaking Carter's nose as the toddler tried to grab hold of his clothing.
Xavier hugged Carter quickly, whispering into the toddler's hair, "I love you, Car-car. Now find G-ma," he said as he attempted to disengage himself.

Planting a wet sloppy kiss on Xavier's cheek, Carter happily turned around and strolled toward his grandmother's voice.

His sing-song voice singing "the snuggle bunny" song Xavier used to sing to him when he put him to bed on the nights he stayed with Grandma and Grandpa.

Straightening up, Xavier thought, "Whew, that was close," when voices off to his left caught his attention, Dr. Quacko and his companion were talking, the rapid rise and fall in volume and tone signaling a potential disagreement.

Xavier stopped suddenly; wait, it sounded as if the woman was giving him a dressing down. His assessment of the character of the woman was correct.

The woman looked around; venom dripped from her words as she spoke harshly to the doctor.

"You were told to initiate the Atlas Protocol and bring Xavier in for observation," she said. "Instead, you screwed up your assigned task, and because of your incompetence, he escaped, and then to make matters worse, you actually blew him up. If you mess up one more time, you will be on the receiving end of a memorial service. I will not have this entire operation jeopardized by your gross incompetence. Do I make myself clear? Now you need to retrieve the next child on the list, and this time do not make any mistakes and do not draw attention to yourself. Because you decided to get creative and blow up our test subject, I now must clean up this mess with the Indianapolis PD."

Running his hand through his hair, the doctor nodded in affirmation.

"Look, Xavier was smarter than he looked, the hippy beach bum image he projected fooled me, and I will not underestimate the next candidate. I promise the next grab and bag will go off without a hitch."

The woman looked at the doctor with a frown that marred her mature features, "Don't make promises you can't keep; because I guarantee I do keep my promises."

Xavier turned left, heading towards the back-kitchen door; it was time to regroup and figure out the next step in this game of cat and mouse. Hopefully, he would continue to be the cat and not the mouse. The boys discussed their clues at the doghouse as Mathew searched the internet for additional hints.

Turning away from the computer screen, Mathew's hands poised above the keyboard, he looked at Xavier and Packer and said, "OK, so what clues do we have so far?"

Xavier grabbed the paper he and Packer had written everything down. Reading everything aloud made him realize they did not have much to go on, just vague unconnected reference points. Mathew and Packer must have thought the same thing, as their faces mirrored the same sense of hopelessness.

Mathew shook his head and said, "Let us focus on one thing. According to my research, CITRUM is either an elixir made of heterochronic parabiosis in which there is an exchange of blood between older and younger people designed to rejuvenate the livers and muscles of the older ones, or it is a company based in Chicago founded by the great-grandchildren of former presidential candidates Henry

Simon Trudel and Dewitt Mason Cyder, both who lost closely contested presidential races."

Xavier's face brightened as he said, "Maybe this is the break we need, and if we go there, we might find something that may lead to the next clue. What is the address?"

Mathew turned towards the computer, his fingers flying across the keyboard rapidly; suddenly, he stopped and turned the monitor towards them.

"Does this lady look familiar?" On the screen was a picture of a young woman who looked like the older female companion of the doctor.

"Wait," said Xavier. "That looks like the woman I saw talking to him at the house, an older version like they might be related rather than the same person. The one at the house seemed regale and more authoritative like she was giving him orders or a harsh scolding. She even threatened him if he screwed up getting the next kid."

Mathew nodded, his eyes shining glee; "we are one step closer to discovering where the money, thugs, and research facilities come from," he said.

Packer finally spoke up, "So what do we do now? We cannot always stay here, and eventually, Xavier's parents will come out and start asking questions. Plus, hiding Xavier out here will not get us any closer to finding answers to our questions. We need to find out what is going on. Based on the numerous dystopian movies and the comic books I have read; this has a mastermind plot and conspiracy written all over it."

"Packer is right," said Xavier. "We need to figure out what the next step is, and we need to divide and conquer.

"Mathew, you stay here and work on the computer angle and see what you can find but be careful. We do not know how deep this goes or who we can trust. Packer, I need you to watch my parents and see if you can pick up any more tidbits of information. Mom knows you love her cooking, and she will think nothing of you being there since you are always at the house. I want you both to help her deal with losing me, but we cannot let her know I am alive. They will be watching her, and her grief must appear genuine, and mom is a horrible actress and liar."

Both boys stood silently patiently waiting for Xavier to continue.

"I plan to go to Chicago and see what I can learn about the CITRUM corporation; I withdrew three thousand dollars from my bank account before the accident. I can use that to fund my trip. I will go dressed as a drifter/homeless person, try to scout the area, and see what I can find out about the company. Most people do not censure what they say about the homeless because they are invisible. Being homeless will allow me to wander around and gather information without being discovered. I will stay in the homeless shelters and use the public library to contact you via email. We can arrange a meeting if needed."

Shaking his head, no, Mathew asked, "you do realize that pretending to be homeless will not work; for one, it is the middle of winter in Chicago; two, you have never been homeless a day in your life, and you will stick out like a sore thumb and three there is no way a company like CITRUM will allow a homeless person within 100 feet of their doors."

Throwing a stress ball into the air and catching it, Packer spoke up in agreement with Mathew's assessment of the situation.

"Think of it this way who in their right mind wants to sleep out in the cold in a box in a urine-soaked alleyway with rats, cats, and dogs crawling all over them?"

"OK, maybe you are right, but then that means we need to come up with a new plan that has a chance of success," said Xavier.

Mathew laughed. Oh, I am already five steps ahead of you, which is why I always beat you in chess. Before you leave, there are a few things we need to pick up for you, the first thing being a disposable burner phone for all three of us. That way, we can stay in contact without fear of being traced. Once we have the phones, I will place a device on the outside of it to jam listening devices from being used to access our conversations.

I have been working on a prototype, and I think it might be ready, or at least I hope it is ready. You can use your hoverboard to get around from place to place while in the city.

Second, we need to get you a bus ticket to Chicago, and I have a friend who is a computer whiz in Chicago who might be able to help. I met him at that gifted and talented Mensa-sponsored computer summer camp mom made me attend before our first year of high school. He was a former attendee turned camp counselor. Not that I would ever tell Mom this, but I made some rather good contacts at that camp."

"Now, I have to warn you that the guy is different, and he is constantly talking about conspiracy theories," said Matt.

Do not get him started on the JFK assassination, the Trump-Russian election theory, or how Socialism is the stepping-stone to communism. Otherwise, he is a good guy, and whether you decide to share details with him is up to you, but if it were me, I would tell him what is happening. He comes from a wealthy family and is not your typical rich kid. Castor has his own tale of woe; if he trusts and believes you, he will move heaven and earth to help you. However, it is his secret to tell, and you just need to know that I would not suggest you confide in him unless I was 100 percent sure we could trust him.

The third thing we need to do before you leave," said Mathew. "Is to alter your appearance so that if someone does see you, they will not make the connection between you and the kid killed in Indianapolis. I have been thinking maybe you need to add a tribal tattoo along the left side of your face and pull your hair into a man bun."

"Wow, stop there," said Xavier in a rush, his face becoming flushed with agitation. "I am not getting a tattoo on my face; I don't mind one on my arm, leg, chest, or back but not on my face,"

Mathew shook his head. "No, listen, I have this special effect skin film I developed to help cover up damaged skin in burn victims. When you place the film in the microwave and heat it for 15 seconds, you can place it on your body, and once it cools, it cannot be removed without soaking it with a hot washcloth, like how kids use it to apply temporary tattoos. Parker can design and print a tribal tattoo onto the skin, mold it to your face. Next, we change your hair color to dark brown, almost black, and then no one will ever think that you are Xavier. We can use the 3D printer to make extra sheets of film with the tattoo on it, and you can then remove the fake tattoo and later reapply it when necessary. The tattoo will make it easier to claim mistaken identity if you are spotted by someone who knows you from before your untimely demise."

With a dramatic flourish, Mathew pulled a card from the 3D printer and presented it to Xavier.
"Say hello to Mr. Joseph Christmas Jackson, his friends call him Crip, and his enemies don't call him at all," said Mathew with a laugh.

Xavier shook his head, "your sense of humor is almost as bad as that quack doctor."

When he looked down at his new driver's license, he saw a stranger with black hair, blue eyes, and a tribal tattoo on his face. The bone structure and eye color matched his own, but that was where the similarities ended. He was supposedly twenty-one years old, and he did not look like the type of guy who was the class valedictorian, a letterman in swimming, or a future thespian.

Xavier paused to think about what Mathew had said. His face slowly morphed into a smile as his brain processed the implications of being able to transform himself into someone else without any permanent damage being done or having to sit in a tattoo parlor and endure the agony of having needles inject ink into the sub-layers of skin to make the tattoo a reality. He hated needles of all types. Add that to the list of things not to do; it ranked up there with death, doctors, hospitals, and pop quizzes.

"What about a place to stay since you think my passing as a homeless person is unbelievable," asked Xavier?

Mathew swiveled back and forth in the chair. "That is an easy solution, Mr. Jackson, to a not-so-difficult problem. A hostel close to Wrigley Field costs about fifty-four dollars a night, provided you do not mind sharing a room with three complete strangers. You get to sleep on a bunk bed, and if you are anxious about it, just pretend you are spending the night at Packer's house."

Unexpectedly Packer started laughing. His voice echoed around the suddenly quiet room. "This is going to be so epic," both boys looked at him with disbelief. "You must admit that this will be a remarkable story for when we have kids one day."

Grabbing the pillows off the couch, Xavier and Mathew proceeded to pummel Packer to the ground. Laughter mingled with grunts and groans as the three temporarily forgot about the upcoming separation, danger, and heartache they would be forced to deal with in the coming days. The battle royale continued until each participant collapsed in an exhausted heap, locking the door the boys settled down to sleep waiting for the darkness to descend and provide the boys with much needed camouflage.

Chicago

Xavier shivered in the old, frayed jacket he had borrowed from Packer; its dark blue color faded from too many days spent in the sun and from the constant washes Packer's mom, Mrs. Barrington, insisted it needed to maintain its hygienic quality. Walking past the shop windows. Xavier was startled by the tribal tattoo that ran along the side of his face from the top edge of his hairline along his neck, only to disappear underneath the collar of his jacket.

The sudden change in temperature from the frigid wind jerked him back to awareness of his surroundings. He now understood how Chicago got its nickname, the windy city. The wind chill made the temperature feel more like -10 degrees than -2 it was. What a great way to start the New Year, thought Xavier as he shuffled along the street, tucking his head into the jacket collar to keep the wind out and his body heat in. Morosely he thought I might as well be dead; No friends, my parents think I am dead, and my college plans are in the toilet.

A blare from an ugly green and cream checkered taxicab startled Xavier as he realized he had inadvertently entered the street in front of a car. Shaking his head and yelling sorry as the wind snatched the words out of his mouth, he hurried to the other side of the crosswalk.

He took the paper from his pocket and looked at the name and address Matt had written on it. Castor Lee, Mitchell Towers, 198 W Randolph apartment #252, (773) 508-2934. He stopped in front of the building and looked up, telling himself it was time to stop feeling sorry for himself. It was evident from the outer appearance and the location of the building that whoever lived here had a lot more money than he was used to and even more money than his parents were used to.

The red brick building resembled the Lego towers he made as a kid, and the windowpanes shined at the top of the building. The glass doors leading into the apartment foyer had etched designs on the glass giving the inhabitants within the lobby a sense of privacy. An elderly man stood outside the door and wore a long black woolen jacket that resembled a navy pea coat ending just above the knees. He shivered as the wind whipped past him.

With one black-gloved hand on the door handle, he looked at Xavier. "Are you coming in," he asked politely and respectfully, "or are you waiting for someone to come out?"

Glancing down at the paper and then back up towards the gold lettering above the door, he asked, "is this Mitchell Towers?"

The elderly gentleman looked down at the paper. He said, "Oh, you are looking for Mr. Walker, his apartment is on the second floor, but you will need to see the young lady at the front desk if you are parked in the parking structure so your car will not be towed."

Xavier smiled, "That is OK, I just moved here, and so I live a couple of blocks over. It is easier to walk than try and find a parking space."

The elderly man responded with a deep throaty chuckle, "I wish others thought like you. It would make the traffic downtown so much easier."

With a short nod of agreement, Xavier walked into the lobby of Mitchell Towers. He felt as if he had been transported to another world. On the left side of the bottom floor was a Scottish pub called the Duke of Atholl in the middle, with a concierge help desk on the left and a coffee shop called *"I Do Not Give a Sip"* on the right. The cup logo over the coffee shop door showed a cup of coffee with a drop of dark liquid suspended over the center of the doorway. A random thought crossed his mind; if a person tilted their head a certain way, the drop of coffee above the door resembled a poop emoji. He silently chuckled and wished he could tell Mathew and Packer about it.

The flow of customers was constant; most were too busy talking on their Biophone or scanning the news on their virtual glasses. The information feeds reflected off the tinted glasses as audio was delivered via the Biophone linkage in their earpieces. Xavier tapped his right hand before he realized he no longer had access to his Biophone. He never realized how much he came to depend on the device until after he no longer had it. Pulling out the disposable phone, he looked at the paper in his hand and started to dial the phone number listed.

Xavier silently prayed that Mr. Lee would answer the phone; he did not like the idea of going back out into the cold. So far, pretending to be homeless was a terrible idea; staying warm and finding a dry place to sleep in a strange city invoked a feeling of dread and despair.

The phone ringing magnified his dread; just when he thought it would be transferred to email, an abrupt, impatient voice demanded, "Who is this?"

Startled by the abruptness of the disembodied voice, it took Xavier a moment to respond. "My name is Xavier; I am a friend of Mathew Murray. He told me to come to see you."

The phone went silent for a second, and Castor asked, "Where are you? If you are downstairs in the coffee shop, go up the escalator, and I will come to get you. What are you wearing?"

Xavier responded, "I am wearing an old dark blue frayed jacket with a Green Bay Packers baseball cap and a pair of ratty blue jeans with holes in the knees." The shrill sound of an automated dial tone signaled the abrupt end of the call.

He took the escalator steps two at a time, too impatient to wait for the snail-like steps to carry him to the second floor. At the top of the steps, he looked around and did not see Mr. Lee; he assumed with an Asian name like Lee, he would be looking for a short little man with dark hair. Surprisingly enough, the man who stepped up to him was anything but Asian in appearance; his 6-foot-four frame towered over Xavier, his blonde hair, green eyes, and pale skin attesting to Scandinavian heritage.

The only feature hinting at Asian ancestry was his slightly almond-shaped eyes surrounded by lush honey-gold lashes. Mr. Lee laughed, "I take it you were expecting a short little Asian man? I am Asian on my father's side, but my mother is Bavarian, and that is where I get the height and the coloring. Now my father looks like what you would expect a Mr. Lee to look like."

With a rueful smile and a shrug of his shoulders, Xavier said, "I am sorry; I was not trying to stereotype you. If my mother had been here, she would have slapped me upside my head and read me the riot act simultaneously."

Turning back the way he came, he said, "No problem, I have had to deal with the questions and looks all my life. Most people are convinced I am adopted. How about we return to my apartment, and I will make some hot tea, and you can tell me how you know Mathew."

He stopped before a mahogany wood door; an oval-shaped glass panel dominated the door with an etching of a wooded forest. The artistic details were breathtaking, and the leaves on the trees seemed to move to the rhythm of the wind.

The glass etching was functional and decorative, giving the inhabitants inside very little privacy. But then again, thought Xavier, who needed a solid wood door when you had a doorman, a concierge, and your own security force.

Xavier was amazed by the beauty of the apartment. Still, he should not have been too surprised, considering the front door was a piece of artwork in and of itself. The marble floor was a glistening white with veins of onyx running here and there in no discernable pattern. The side table matched the door with its glossy mahogany finish reflecting the light from the chandelier hanging down.

The apartment had an open floor plan with the living room directly in front of the foyer; the first thing a person noticed was the matching marble fireplace with onyx running through it. The mantel was solid black granite with a painting hanging above it. The artwork consisted of a long winding winter road with gold trees glistening against the white backdrop of newly fallen snow. Off to the left of the living room was a kitchen designed to complement the white and black decor of the living room. While the apartment was beautiful, it lacked a homey feel; it was obvious that Castor was a bachelor who spent extraordinarily little time in the residence.

Moving to put a silver kettle on the stove, Castor started to boil water for tea as he removed two black teacups and saucers from the all-white cabinets. Xavier knew that the amount of money used to decorate the apartment was more than what his parents made in a year, the place screamed money, but to be honest, it was a little too much white, black, and gold for his taste. The whistle from the tea kettle startled Xavier from his HGTV decor assessment.

"So," Castor said as he removed the kettle from the stove and poured hot water into the waiting teacups. "What brings you here, and how do you know Mathew?"

Xavier took a moment to respond, "Mathew is like a brother to me. I have known him since elementary school, but we did not like each other. There are too many differences. The first time I spoke to him was in second grade when I helped pick up his books after he tripped and spilled his stuff in the hallway at the end of the school day. We still did not like each other, but we started to thaw a little toward each other. Then one day, we got caught throwing rocks at each other. Mathew told the principal that we were practicing football throws, and then one thing led to another, and we have been friends ever since. It is amazing how giving each other a concussion helps cement a friendship. Mathew is one of my two best friends, and I would do anything for him," said Xavier.

"So why are you here?" Asked Castor, his intense green eyes pinning Xavier to his seat, the layers of silence building upon itself to the point of being painful and awkward.

Clearing his throat, Xavier spoke hesitantly, at first afraid that Castor would think he was crazy. "Well, it may sound crazy, but you are talking to a dead man."

Castor laughed, "The last time I checked, dead men did not drink tea, socialize with strangers and tell jokes."

"No, seriously, I am not joking, " said Xavier, pointing at the laptop on the kitchen island. "Just look up Xavier Alexander Hansen Obituary, Huntington, Indiana; the information should be online by now."

A quick internet search resulted in Castor looking back and forth, comparing the photograph from the obituary with the live specimen sitting across from him. His stunned expression testified to his willingness to believe Xavier's story. A half-hour later, after much stopping and starting, Xavier was able to answer all of Castor's initial questions. He had finally reached the part of the story leading up to their meeting in the lobby. Leaning back in the chair, he waited for Castor's response.

After an eternity of silence and discomfort, Castor walked around the end of the island and slapped him on the back of his right shoulder. "Mathew was right to send you to me; I know you do not know me or trust me, but I promise to help you in any way I can. So do you have a place to crash, or would you like to go to the hostel like you originally planned?"

Shaking his head in disbelief, Xavier said, "You would let a complete stranger stay with you?"

A somber expression replaced the jovial vestige previously worn by Castor, his green eyes darkening with his mood, a prelude to what was to come. "I take it by your reaction to my appearance and to my humble abode that Mathew told you very little about what I do. Not only am I a computer whiz but I am also the chief executive officer and President of my father's company CaLa International. He named the company after me and my sister right after we were born and before my mother passed away."

Walking towards the hall closet, he removed a black Burberry Kirkham Pea coat that easily could have cost 2,000 dollars. "Here, I have an extra coat you can wear. Before I tell you my story, there is someplace; I need to take you first. Because no matter how crazy your story seems, I know you will not believe mine unless you see it yourself."

Struggling to remove his ratty jacket, Xavier slipped his arm into the sleeve of the Pea coat. The immediate sense of warmth enveloped him, the same feeling you got after putting a shirt on that had just come out of the dryer. The heat was heavenly; strangely, Xavier lost everything that made him who he was, only to find contentment and joy in a warm jacket. Turning towards the foyer, Xavier started buttoning the coat as he watched Castor put on an identical black trench coat. Xavier laughed, "Hey, we are twining, man."

Suddenly, Castor scowled at him as if he had said something so hateful that it did not dignify a response.

"Sorry, I was just joking," said Xavier. "Mathew and Packer and I liked to wear the same clothes and make jokes about being long-lost twins or triplets."

Castor adjusted the collar of his coat and looked off into space as he stated in a monotone voice, "Well, I definitely know Mathew didn't tell you much about me other than my name based on your surprise at my appearance, and your twinning comment."

Stopping just short of the door, Castor took a deep breath. "Let me start at the beginning; I am a fraternal twin, and my sister's name was Lauren Elizabeth Lee. When we were six years old, we were on our way to school, my driver was a new hire, and he was not vetted to the extent he should have been. I wonder why I looked up when I did because I usually did not bother paying attention to the route taken to school. I was typically engrossed in playing a video game on my dad's prototype gaming system, a precursor to the Holocene created by my dad's company NIMAGE. When I looked up, I noticed we had pulled up outside an unfamiliar building, and I nudged Lauren to wake her up. When the driver opened the side of the door and jerked her out of the car, I grabbed her arm and tried to hold on. She started to struggle, and I lost my grip on her. When my side of the door opened, I bolted under the arm of a strange man and took off down the street. Running away probably saved me from the kidnappers. Still, I have always wondered if my running helped Lauren escape."

Xavier looked at Castor, "Oh man, I am sorry; I have a brother named Will, while there are quite a few years between us, about 14 years. I would be devastated if anything happened to him."

The look on Castor's face conveyed the pain he had lived with every day since he lost his sister. "I am," he said. "I have never forgiven myself for being a coward and not being there for Lauren. I have spent all my time, efforts, and talents to track down the men who took her." Walking towards the escalator, Castor said, "Let us get something to eat, and once we get where we need to be, I will explain in more detail why Mathew's sending you to me was a blessing in disguise."

The trip down the escalator went by quick as Xavier looked around at the opulent lobby; while outside the double doors, the snow and wind swirled together in an intricate dance that only mother nature could control; with a shudder and the bunching of his shoulders, Xavier gritted his teeth in anticipation of the cold. The weather in Chicago seemed colder than he had ever experienced in Huntington, Indiana.

Castor's voice was grabbed by the wind as he struggled to ask Xavier if he had a particular food preference. After the third attempt to converse Castor said, "never mind, I know just the place to go. Giordano's off West Jackson Boulevard makes the best deep-dish pizza in Chicago. It's not much further, and I promise you will smell it way before we get to it."

Six minutes later and chilled to the bone, the warm, glowing red Giordano's sign on the corner of the red brick building provided a beacon of hope for weary travelers seeking to escape the harsh and unforgiving demands of a Chicago winter. Castor was right, he thought. The aroma of warm fresh bread drifted on the wind. The tinkle of the bell above the door greeted Xavier as a wall of heat and heavenly smells enveloped him in a cocoon pushing back the biting cold that had permeated his bones.

Castor held up two fingers in response to the young hostess's unspoken question of how many, turning to lead the way towards a booth in the back of the restaurant close to the kitchen door. The heat from the kitchens drifted toward the men; the table was perfect as it provided warmth and privacy.

While Xavier was used to the cold weather and freezing temperatures associated with Indiana, he had to admit it was nothing compared to the biting wind that accompanied the sub-artic temperatures that moved in from Lake Michigan. Looking around, Xavier noticed that most of the restaurant's occupants seemed unaffected by the harsh temperatures and chilly winds that swept through the city; instead, the room was filled with laughter and noise, and he could see why this was an excellent place to sit and regroup.

Sliding into the black leather booth, Xavier noticed that the red and white checkered tablecloth and white and red candles placed in discarded wine bottles gave the restaurant a quaint Italian café feel. The food on nearby tables produced mouthwatering aromas. The visual appeal of the variety of dishes being carried out from the kitchen and the aromas made it challenging to choose what to order.

The waitress, a young woman around the age of eighteen with ash blonde hair upswept into a messy bun, approached the table with a half-smile on her face; the red polo shirt hugged her generous curves, the black slacks molded to her body mirrored the attire worn by the hostess, but that is where the similarities ended. The appraising look she directed toward both men made Xavier slightly uncomfortable. However, Castor barely noticed the flirtatious attitude of the young lady, instead focusing on the menu, only looking up after he and Xavier had decided what they wanted to eat.

After the waitress left to get their drinks and place their order, Xavier turned to face Castor. "So, is this where you planned on taking me?"

Shaking with silent mirth, Castor placed a red cloth napkin across his lap; picking up the saltshaker, he sprinkled some on the napkin on the tabletop to prepare for the placement of his drink. "No, that will come after dinner, but I want to ask you a few questions to understand what you know and what blanks I may need to fill in for you. So, what do you know about a group named "ANONYMOUS?"

Xavier stopped to wait for the server to place their drinks on the table and leave before answering the question. Well, I know that Anonymous was a loosely associated international network of activist and hacktivist entities active from early 2003 until the 2030s. The branch acted as an independent cell, so removing one cell did not endanger other cells. I remember someone mentioned that the only individuals who had access to the complete membership information of the individual cell leaders were the eight members of the committee that governed them.

Each committee member was chosen from within the seven regions of the North American continent, and the head or chairman of the committee was held by the founder of the group or his/hers designated heir. The Federal Bureau of Investigation, formerly the FBI, used an inside man to act as a Trojan horse to bring the organization to its knees.

He stopped talking as another waiter helped the flirtatious waitress place a deep-dish pizza on a silver stand in the center of the table; the aroma of the mushroom, sausage, and cheese made his mouth water and stomach rumble with hunger. The young lady placed the bill on the table and told them there was no hurry and to stay and enjoy the meal before winking at them and writing her phone number down at the bottom of the ticket.

Castro nodded as he wiped off the excess salt from the tabletop, "Yes, that is true, but most people do not know that my father was the one who started Anonymous and then later helped the FBI bring some more radical members to justice. The terrorist attacks on the Arch in St. Louis and the San Francisco Bay Bridge in 2024 helped him realize that the movement he originally started to help people was now just as bad, if not worse, than the ones he was fighting to bring down.

In exchange for my dad's cooperation then, President Thomas Fitzgerald granted him a blanket pardon for all crimes he may have committed as a member of Anonymous before 2025. According to my dad's journals that I found after he died, he claims he never committed any crimes. However, he still wanted the pardon to guarantee the government would not fabricate anything later.

Xavier knew from history class and living with a college professor that ignorance is anything but bliss.

Castor finished his last bite of pizza. "My father died soon after Lauren was kidnapped, and I grew up under the care of my mother's brother, who taught me how to hack into computers and efficiently cover my tracks due to his experience as a former Navy seal and security advisor for the Pentagon. When he first became Lauren and my guardian, I hated him. I blamed him for my father's death and, later, anything related to Lauren's kidnapping and continued disappearance.

However, over time I realized he was not the one to blame. Instead, I needed to blame the ones who took Lauren. I decided instead to channel my anger, hatred, and guilt into building an organization that could help me find my sister and punish those responsible for her disappearance."

Both men were silent for the remaining time it took to eat most of the pizza in front of them and drink at least two glasses of coke. Xavier had just realized that he was hungry when he entered the restaurant and placed his order. The noise and laughter flowed surrounding the two men as they focused on meeting their basic needs: food, warmth, and companionship. Neither man knew each other well, nor did they really trust each other, but all that was forgotten for a moment as they enjoyed the best pizza they had ever eaten.

Xavier stared at the last remaining piece of pizza sitting on the metal stand between them; the rest had long since been eaten as Castor told his story. He slowly chewed the pizza, frantically thinking about what Castor had just told him. He knew the next couple of questions could determine whether he could count on his help and possibly infiltrate CITRUM's facilities. Xavier gestured towards the last remaining slice of pizza; "so you going to eat that?"

Castor laughed, "That is the question you want to know. Not was my dad really a criminal, or if I am a criminal as well. Instead, you want to know if you can eat the rest. Matt told me you were a funny guy when we first met at camp, but I had no idea how funny."

With a telltale blush painting his cheeks a dusty red, Xavier looked down at the plate and mumbled, "Hey, I'm a growing boy, and I need a substance." Shifting uncomfortably, he looked across the table and asked, "So you going to help me?"

Castor wiped the tears of mirth from his eyes with the clean side of his napkin and placed it across his lap. His face became serious, his eyes darkening to emerald, green, intense with some hidden emotion. "There are still a few things I need to tell you, and to be honest, if it were not for Matt vouching for you, I would not be sitting here right now talking to you about the past. However, before I agree to help you, there is one more thing I want you to do. I have a friend I want you to talk to before we go any further."

Castor silently watched him, his visual assessment making him moderately uncomfortable. Still, Xavier knew he needed assistance, an ally in this strange city and against those working with Dr. Crocker. With his fingers beating a steady rhythm on the table, Castor broke the prolonged silence that engulfed the table.

"She works at an upscale private clinic as an LPN, but I trust her, and she has excellent instincts about people. I know you do not like medical personnel or hospitals, but she is cool, and I promise she will not hurt you; she will only ask some of the same questions I have asked you. If afterwards you still want my help, then you will have it."

Xavier frowned, pushing his plate away, and said, "Let's just get it over with."

Waving his left hand, Castor motioned to the waitress to collect the payment.

The wind and snow swirled in the background as the two men prepared to leave the warmth and comfort of the restaurant. While Castor paid the bill, Xavier's thoughts temporarily turned dark. He dreaded going out into the cold, but he reminded himself that it could always be worse; however, at this moment, he could not conjure up anything worse than what had already happened to him.

Xavier reluctantly stepped out of the black Mercedes, walking up the street from the parking space parallel to the multi-level homes and businesses historic district of Jackson Park Highlands. He hunched forward, trying to keep the wind and snow from migrating south under the multiple layers of clothing protected by the peacoat. However, he wished instead he was sitting back in the passenger seat with the heater on full blast.

Taurus: V

Castor walked upright with confidence garnered from years of experience battling the wind, snow, and rain common to Chicago. Stopping in front of a 1927, five-story building with a beautiful terra cotta exterior and antique lead glass window. A beautiful cheery slip-glazed terra cotta panel complemented the exterior design with the words "The Clinic" stenciled on the front in an elegant calligraphy style reminiscent of the late 1920s. "We are here," said Castor. "Let's go in before we freeze to death."

Opening the door, Xavier noticed a desk inside the foyer; a twenty-something young lady with straight shoulder-length brown hair and non-distinguishing features worked quietly. The sounds of a crackling fireplace located to the left of the entrance, the foyer with hardwood floors, casement windows, and 9-foot ceilings. The sound of typing, punctuated by soft classical music in the background, combined to create a warm and soothing symphony of sound that could easily lull a person to sleep.

The inside of the facility was protected from view by elegant hunter-green floral Jacquard brocade satin fabric curtains that afforded clients an illusion of privacy. Early 20th-century French Louis XV-style walnut Bergere armchair with gilt trim and burgundy upholstery created an elegant seating area for clients to wait and enjoy tea or coffee in front of the warm fire on a cold, blustery winter day. Notably absent from the waiting room was the presence of television and modern electronics other than the laptop the young lady was working on and an old-style rotary telephone silently sitting on her desk.

Xavier looked to his right towards Castor, "when you said a clinic, I was thinking more like a sterile, antiseptic-smelling place with long wait lines, screaming, crying children, and harassed parents. Instead, this place looks like a country club, and it smells like old mahogany and Old English wood polish."

Castor laughed, "I told you it was an upscale private clinic."

A frown punctuated Xavier's face replacing his typical, good-natured grin. "I don't know if my parents or I can afford the cost of this visit, plus I don't want to give out my insurance information to make it easy for others to find me," said Xavier.

Castor shook his head, "this is all off the record he whispered, and Angie will not even mention that we were here." Xavier still looked unconvinced.

"Look, you want my help, then you are going to have to suck it up, buttercup, and get past your aversion to medical personnel and procedures," said Castor as he walked towards the executive desk that blocked the door leading into the inner chambers.

Angie looked up with a smile; Xavier noticed she did not look as plain and nondescript as he thought when she smiled; her soft melodious voice also played havoc with his first impression that she was an average girl next door type.

"Castor, what trouble have you gotten into now?" She teased, her honey-brown eyes lighting up with undisguised mirth.

Castor laughed as he sat on the corner of the desk and attempted to brush a lock of hair from her face, only for her to wag her forefinger in his direction. He sighed heavily, "I am a reformed man, and Pollux would box my ears if she had to bail me out again. But if you must know, my friend Xavier needs to see Deralyn."

Slightly angling his body to include Xavier in the conversation, he motioned him closer to the desk. Angie looked at him with interest, sweeping him from head to toe as if looking for something. With a slight nod, she pushed a button under the desk. A muffled click and a soft puff of air were the only sign she had disengaged the lock for the wooden mahogany door behind her.

Castor, with the tilt of his head, motioned Xavier to follow him; the shotgun-style hallway was lined with beautiful pastel oil paintings, and one image, in general, caught his eye, halting his progress.

Castor casually strode back towards where he stood, "That painting was titled Christ Episcopal Church of Bowling Green, Kentucky, signed by William Herman Lowe in 1960. My dad purchased the painting from Western Kentucky University special collections."

Xavier continued to stare at the painting, "I do not know why, but I have this unsettling feeling that I have seen this place before in real time; it is like Deja Vue. However, I know that is impossible because until now, I have never been out of Huntington, Indiana."

Castor shrugged his shoulders, "Come on, we need to focus on the here and now, and Deralyn is waiting." Together the two men continued down towards the end of the hall; Castor punched in a ten-digit code next to the door, turned the antique pitted brass doorknob, and ushered Xavier into the room.

The new room no more resembled a clinic exam room than the outer waiting area. The décor mirrored what was found in the lobby apart from the sideboard buffet with English dovetailed drawers and cabinets that dominated the back wall.

Closing the door behind them, Castor gestured to Xavier to sit in one of the burgundy chairs as he took the opposite chair beside the door.

"Let me give you a heads up; Deralyn will ask you a few questions; some may seem unrelated, but please answer them anyway. So far, my instincts tell me that I can trust you, but it is not just my neck on the line if I am wrong about you."

Xavier's response was cut short as the door opened.

Deralyn could only be described as breathtaking her raven black hair flowed freely around her shoulders, her blue eyes were a rival for his own, and even her above-average height did not detract from her overall beauty; instead, it accented her athletic build and grace.

Castor smiled and looked at Xavier. "I think he is smitten with you." She laughed as she stretched out her hand;

Xavier stared at it awkwardly before accepting it and ducking his head in embarrassment.

Castor laughed, "Don't worry, Deralyn's nickname around here is Xenia Warrior Princess, a popular television show from 1995 to 2001." Smiling, she said, "Hush, you embarrassed him."

Clearing his throat, Xavier mumbled, "Nice to meet you, Deralyn." Moving towards the sideboard, Deralyn opened a drawer and pulled out a stethoscope and blood pressure cuff as she turned towards Xavier. "Has Casanova mentioned that I will monitor your vitals and ask you a few questions?" Looking towards Xavier, she motioned for Castor to leave.

"No," said Xavier. "It is okay if he stays provided, I do not have to undress."

Deralyn shook her head. "No, I just want to listen to your heart and lungs and ask you a few questions. Take a deep breath," she said as she placed the stethoscope on the inside of his shirt, the cold metal making him jump in surprise. "Sorry, I forget how cold it gets sitting in a drawer all day." Moving silently to the back, she leaned in and listened to his lungs before standing up and draping the stethoscope around her neck. "So, tell me, "She said mesmerizingly, "what time is it?"

He looked at the clock on the wall and mumbled 3:30 pm.

Then she asked him, "What day is it?"

Xavier struggled to answer and shook his head without looking away from Deralyn's blue eyes; her voice sounded like it was coming from far away. His lids started drifting shut, and he realized it was getting harder and harder to concentrate on the words coming out of her mouth. He knew that something was wrong, something he should be worried about, but he could not seem to rouse himself to the point that he cared.

After about five minutes, Castor's muffled voice broke the silence in his mind. "Deralyn, do you think he is ready to answer our questions?"

She responded with a slight nod and never breaking eye contact with Xavier, "Yes." At that point, Xavier lost himself to the smokey gray fog clouding his mind.

Gradually his thinking started to clarify, the hushed whispers of Deralyn and Castor seized his wandering thoughts in a vice grip and propelled him toward wakefulness. Strangely both of the room's occupants were no longer standing where they were when they started asking him questions about what time and day it was; with a crack in his voice, Xavier stated, "Talking about people as if they are not in the room is rude. I thought you were going to ask me some more questions?"

They turned towards him, Deralyn smiling, while Castor had a slight frown marring his smooth features. Deralyn moved towards him, "We did ask you questions, and you answered them completely and honestly."

Castor nodded as he moved closer and took a seat across from him. "Okay, so tell me what time it was when we started asking you the first question?"

"What? You only asked what time it was and what day it was, said Xavier?" He looked at his watch, stunned to realize that over an hour and fifteen minutes had passed since the first question had been asked. How could that be? They only asked him what time it was, and he remembered answering with 3:30 pm, not 4:45 pm? What was happening, and why couldn't he remember beyond the time and date? Was he losing his mind because of everything that had happened, or was it a byproduct of something Dr. Quacko and his nurse had given him? Xavier started rocking back and forth to calm his nerves and make sense of all the craziness around him.

"Listen, Xavier," said Castor as he pulled up a burgundy leather chair, leaning forward with his elbow resting on his knees, "now, I do not want you to get angry, and I want you to promise to listen to what I have to say before you decide whether accept my offer of assistance. Matt sent you to me for a reason, and I believe we can find out what is going on if you give me a chance. I use this building as an unofficial headquarters slash residence when I do not want people to know what I am doing, or for those I deem worthy of offering my protection should they ever need it."

With a bewildered nod, Xavier attempted to stop fidgeting and sit quietly, but it was easier said than done. He had a strange premonition that his life would get even more chaotic and complicated than it already was.

"Before leaving Giordano's, I started talking about the Anonymous group, and we got sidetracked. I let you believe I created a non-profit organization to help others but what I did not tell you was that I actually followed more in my father's footsteps and founded a group similar to Anonymous. We, however, call ourselves "Subreption," said Castor.

Xavier quickly interrupted him. "Wait, wasn't Anonymous completely disbanded? Also, what does it have to do with you, and doesn't Subreption mean concealing pertinent facts?"

"Yes, it does mean to conceal facts, but that is not why I did not tell you everything immediately. Even though Matt sent you, I could not risk everything I have achieved to an unknown individual who may or may not be telling the truth. Remember the story I told you about my sister Lauren and her kidnapping? What I did not tell you was that over the years, through my research and investigations, I have reason to believe someone connected to those in power within the United States government is somehow connected to Lauren's kidnapping. I just do not know how or why," sighed Castor. "I just know I must do something; I must find my sister and make sure those responsible pay for what they have done to me, my family, and Lauren. I must either bring her home to reunite with her family or bury her with my parents."

Deralyn stepped forward lightly, placing her hand on Castor's shoulder, "Xavier, Castor has built an organization dedicated to righting the wrongs and advocating for those who cannot like what his father tried to do just without the bombings and misguided terror tactics. Now it is my turn to come clean; you do not recall my questioning you because before listening to your heart, I coated the stethoscope with a hybrid chemical created by Dr. Robert House in early 1922's. The serum is absorbed through the skin, inducing a hypnotic effect in which the individual will answer any all questions put to them; a type of truth serum."

Angrily, Xavier jumped up, sprinting towards the closed door, "screw you, I don't need your help."

"Wait, I can get you into CITRUM," shouted Castor. "Xavier, I promise not to trick or lie to you again. I just needed to know if you genuinely needed help or were a spy planted in our mist."

Xavier looked over his shoulder at him; his hand hovered over the doorknob, indecisiveness freezing him in place. The awkward silence seemed to stretch on and on. Only the thought of putting his family in danger stopped him from opening the door and walking away from the only help he would get. He knew in his heart and mind that the chances of seeing his family again would decrease with every step he took out this door. He was being hunted by soulless killers who had no problem silencing anyone they deemed a threat to their plans, including family and friends.

"Okay, but I want you to be straight with me and stop lying to me; I may not have the knowledge and experience you have, but it is my life, and I deserve to make informed choices," said Xavier.

"Listen, Xavier, based on what you said while you were under the influence of the serum, I want to run a few additional tests, such as a Nanoparticle MRI, which will use

Nanos in combination with Magnetic resonance imaging (MRI) to produce an accurate image of your the anatomy and the physiological processes of your body and if we can obtain a copy of Dr. Procker's medical files on you then maybe we can reverse engineer what has been done and identify why he seems so interested in your development," said Deralyn.

"I agree with Deralyn's assessment," said Castor. "The only way we will get answers or figure out where to go next is if we do the tests. I promise we can do the tests without alerting anyone to what we are doing. I have connections with a company that tests the NMRI machines before delivering them to the hospital. We can put you down as a test subject, and the records will never make it into a hospital database."

With a smile and a nod of his head Xavier agreed.

"In the meantime, you are welcomed to stay in the condo on the fifth floor; it is 2,500 plus square feet with three bedrooms, a spacious kitchen and living area, and a warm and cozy grand wood-burning fireplace."

Just as Xavier opened his mouth to state he could not afford that generosity, Castor interrupted him. "Don't worry; the clinic and the entire building are owned by a dummy corporation which in turn is owned by me."

Xavier was flabbergasted, he knew that Castor was wealthy, but until now, he had no idea how rich. However, it was a relief to know that he had someplace warm to stay and people willing to believe him and provide him with sanctuary during his time of need. He had no desire to stay at the hostel with strangers and worry about potential assaults, thefts, and drug usage.

Three days later, sitting in the oversized conference room on the ground floor of Castor's unofficial headquarters, Xavier reflected on the changes over the past seven days. This time last year, he was busy making New Year's resolutions centered on graduating from high school, getting accepted to college, and finding a girl to ask to prom.

Since his subsequent death, his life goals had changed dramatically; protecting family, uncover the reason for the threat against his family, and finding a way to get his life back without sacrificing himself or those he loved.

The rising noise level pulled him out of his internal reflection; three stereotypical medical personnel followed Deralyn and Castor into the room. The chatter between the two men and the female abruptly died when they noticed Xavier sitting at the conference table. The sudden silence was unnerving as Xavier became the center of attention. The three individuals sat down, each opening a file folder placed in front of them by Deralyn as she organized materials and turned on the table projector.

"Okay, would everyone have a seat, please," said Castor as he sat at the head of the table opposite the projector. Xavier was grateful for Castor placing himself between him and the three unknown individuals who represented everything he hated about the medical community.

Deralyn activated the projector and pulled up a complicated-looking report that gave Xavier a migraine as he tried deciphering the information.

Freezing the image in place, Deralyn turned towards the room's occupants and instructed them to open the folder in front of them.

"Xavier and Castor, if you would rather look at the screen, you will notice the same report; the NMRI was completed two days ago. I want Dorian, Adam, and Katherine to break down the information for you because this is more their expertise than mine."

The three doctors looked at each other, silently communicating who would go first. Surprisingly, Katherine was the first to push back her chair, clearing her throat; her soft, cultured voice with a hint of a southern twang was a pleasant surprise, breaking the oppressive silence that blanketed the conference room. Katherine looked at the individuals within the room.

"The first thing I want to mention is that my specialty focuses on neurology, orthopedics, and spinal cord injuries. While completing RMRI, we noticed that your exoskeleton differed from the average individual."

As if on cue, a 3D hologram revolved and hovered above the center of the table. "If you look at the 3D image displayed, you will notice that the skeleton has a slight shimmer to it; at first, we thought it was a glitch in the imaging software, but then we noticed that even your teeth had a slight shimmer as well." She turned to address Castor as she said this. "After we noted this anomaly, we asked

Xavier if we could look at his teeth and possibly remove one of his back wisdom teeth."

With a wave of her hand, Katherine directed everyone's attention to the rotating 3D hologram model of Xavier's teeth that had replaced the model of his exoskeleton.

"After the extraction, we shaved a small amount from outside his left back molar. The analysis of the tooth showed that the bone structure consisted of calcium and diamond flakes which look like remnants of nanobots. Typically, nanobots are made of organic materials that dissolve over time. However, that is not so in this case, and we were able to determine that this new form of nanobots fused with Xavier's bone structure and dramatically increased the tinsel strength of his skeleton. Because of the fusing with the bones, we could not separate and access the primary program function of the nanobots without causing Xavier considerable pain and injury. Right now, we believe that the primary purpose of the nanobots is re-enforcing your skeleton and preventing potential catastrophic injuries."

With a click of the remote, the image on the screen was replaced with what looked like a tattoo of an interlocking lowercase (p) and a (q) in Wildcat Blue.

Xavier only knew what the color was called because of its use by the University of Kentucky football team. His home state football team, the University of Indiana, known as Hoosiers, was a significant rival of UK.

Titling his head to the side, he asked Katherine, "Why is there a tattoo on the screen? I do not have a tattoo. I would have remembered something like that throughout my lifetime."

Katherine threw a startled look at Xavier. "What do you mean you do not have a tattoo? What is that on your face and neck?"

Xavier started to laugh, "I will explain everything in a minute. Can someone bring me a washcloth or towels soaked with hot water and wring it out?"

An unnamed technician quietly stood up and left the room, returning with the requested items. Xavier paused for dramatic effect; the people in the room watched anxiously for what would come. With a slight upward quirk of his lips, Xavier placed the hot steaming washcloth on the left side of his face for the count of 15 Mississippi and then laid it down on his right thigh; he put his fingertips at the edge of his hairline and moved slowly down along his jawline.

A gasp ran through the room as his fingertips followed his jawline, creating a slight fissure between his skin and the tribal tattoo. In just a few seconds, Xavier's face was transformed from a man with a distinct tribal tattoo in his mid-twenties who projected a tough guy image to a young eighteen-year-old baby face kid.

"That is amazing," said Castor. "How did you do that?"

Xavier scanned the room, laughter lighting up his eyes. "Matt, our good friend, designed a new prototype of skin that can be created using a 3D printer with a design overlay that is waterproof, heat resistant, and mimics the exact skin tone of a person without the application of glue, cosmetics, and is guaranteed to last for 24 hours whether eating, sleeping, or participating in extreme sporting events. Once it starts to cool, the material clings to the individual's skin underneath without any visible lines or creases, making it appear as natural as the skin with which you were born."

"However, if you want to remove it, apply a heated wet washcloth directly to the skin you want to remove. First, heat the washcloth for 15 seconds in a microwave, then hold it on the skin for 15 seconds, and then feel for the slight buckle of skin to indicate the separation point. The last step requires slowly separating the two layers of skin. Matt was thinking of marketing it as Mir@15. But that was just an idea he threw around before I left to come to Chicago," said Xavier.

The silence in the room was eventually broken by a cough and throat clearing. Castor looked in amazement at Xavier's face. "Someone, please remind me later to suggest a partnership venture with Matt after everything returns to normal," said Castor. Everyone laughed as the tension in the room suddenly dissipated.

Once everyone was settled and back on track, a non-script gentleman across from him answered Xavier's previously forgotten question. "Let me introduce myself; my name is Dorian Grayson." Xavier struggled to suppress his initial reaction to hearing the name of Katherine's colleague. Dorian responded with a mild groan as if he could read his mind. "I know my mother was a big fan of Oscar Wilde. I am glad she made my first name Dorian instead of my middle name."

Xavier casually surveyed Dorian, noting that his five-foot-six-inch stature, dark brown hair, and dark-rimmed glasses did little to make him stand out in a crowd.

Leaning forward, Xavier rested his arms on the table and casually asked, "So, what is your middle name?

With an awkward tug on his shirt collar, Dorian responded, "Wilde."

The laugh that Xavier had previously attempted to suppress burst out of him. "You definitely don't look like a Wilde man to me."

Dorian also chuckled as he stood up and moved around the table; in his hand, he held what appeared to be a portable dark light device used to identify bodily fluids at crime scenes. Stopping to the left of Xavier, Dorian casually motioned to Adam to stand by the light switch. He asked,

"Katherine, do you have your compact mirror so I can use it for my demonstration?" Reaching into her purse, Katherine pulled out a gold inlaid compact mirror and handed it to him. He then instructed Xavier to wait until the lights went out and then angle the mirror just so that he could look at his left shoulder. "I guarantee you will be surprised by what you see," said Dorian.

Shrugging his shirt off his left shoulder, Xavier did as instructed; Adam then turned off the lights, and a hush descended on the room as Dorian aimed the black light at Xavier's exposed shoulder blade. The luminous florescent light provided an eerie glow; Xavier gasped as the image on the screen suddenly materialized on his left shoulder blade.

Xavier declared in an unsteady voice. "What the heck is that?"

"Well, that, as close as we can tell, is a tattoo, but that is where the similarities end," said Dorian. The image of the tattoo seemed to glitter and appeared translucent, as ripples of light made it seem as if it were a living, breathing thing. "Right now, we are still determining what it is. Based on the information provided by Xavier, we know that it had to have been created before his earliest memories and that it was done without his knowledge. We noticed the tattoo because we sanitized Xavier's clothes and body before running the remaining tests to eliminate cross-contaminates.

With a quick flip of the switch, Adam turned on the overhead lights in the conference room, illuminating Xavier's stunned features and making everyone shade their eyes as they adjusted to the unexpected increase in light. Dorian sat at the door as Adam moved toward the front of the room. Xavier barely registered Adam's words as he attempted to sort through the overwhelming revelations Castor's medical team had revealed.

Adam's voice gradually penetrated the fog surrounding Xavier's mind. "Right now, we have only figured out that the tattoo is made of ink currently unknown to us and is not listed in the FBI or the European database on ink pigmentation. The tattoo also has the same shimmering qualities as your bone structure, resulting from the inclusion of nanobots. However, where the nanobots in your bone structure are fused together and appear inactive, the tattoo nanobots are very separate and active."

Slowly, he removed his glasses and cleaned them on his white lab coat before replacing them and looking toward the screen.

"When we tried to retrieve a sample of the nanobots for analysis, it dissolved into a puddle of goo within 5 seconds of its removal from the epidermis leaving behind a small amount of ink. While we could not study the nanobots, I have a friend who agreed to look at a sample of the ink left behind and let us know if he learns anything new. I am optimistic he will succeed, considering he helped develop the method of laser desorption ionization mass spectrometry currently used to analyze carbon nanotubes."

Xavier sighed, "So that means we have learned nothing that could help us solve this mystery."

Laying his head on the conference table, he briefly considered giving up and running away to some unknown destination like Belize. He knew from his culture fair project in his high school Human Cultural Geography class that they spoke English and were friendly to Americans. He could even give tours of the Mayan Temples at Altun Ha or learn how to make chocolate at the Mahogany Chocolate Company in Belize City.

Then the thought of never seeing his mom and brother again eliminated the urge to run away. While Xavier loved his dad, he never felt as close to him as he did his mom and his brother. They always considered themselves the three musketeers. While Dad always joked that they were the three stooges to aggravate and rile up Mom, it was all done in good fun. Now he thought he did not even have that to fall back on.

Castor cleared his throat; Xavier raised his head while every person in the room stopped what they were doing and looked toward the man in charge.

"The best way to approach this problem is to break it into two distinct phases. The first phase will consist of Deralyn, Katherine, Dorian, and Adam continuing to analyze the data obtained from Xavier's medical reports and the tattoo. The second phase will involve having the tech guys create a digital profile of the doctor's likes, dislikes, movements, and potential habits to determine when and where we can access his files. The final phase will consist of an action plan based on the information we obtain from phases one and two."

Xavier spoke up; "I want to be on the team that accesses his files." Castor started to open his mouth, intending to say no, and detailing how dangerous it would be when Xavier interrupted. "Look, I know what we are looking for, and I can help identify which files are the public files and which are his personal files. A man like him would have two files: one you show the rest of the world and one with the information he wants to keep hidden. We need the correct files, not the other way around."

Castor nodded his head affirmatively as everyone pushed back their chairs, gathered their materials, and headed out of the Conference room, determined to unravel the mystery of Xavier.

The scientists did not question their immediate acceptance of a young man they had only known briefly. It only seemed natural to extend to him all the benefits and devotion customarily associated with family and long-term friends. Something about him made them want to help; it was not anything they could logically explain. Sometimes it almost felt like a compulsion, but many brushed that thought aside. Most passed it off as feeling empathy for a young man on the verge of losing everything.

After leaving the conference room, Castor led Xavier down a hallway that his father liked to refer to as a shotgun hallway because, as he often said, a bullet shot from the front door would pass through without hitting anything and exit through the back door or in this case the emergency exit located at the end of the hallway. Blaine, his dad, always compared Xavier's habit of running in the front door, grabbing food, and then heading out the back door to that of a bullet, racing toward its intended target, not hitting anything but still making his presence known.

After passing three gates on the left, Castro opened a plain, nondescript door labeled **BROOM CLOSET** in big, bold letters and underneath "Stargate mandatum." Once the door was opened, Xavier realized that the broom closet was an access point to a staircase leading toward what he assumed to be the basement area. Most historic homes and buildings in Chicago had some basement or sub-basement for heating and cooling apparatuses. However, that was where any similarities ended. The preconceived image in his head was nothing like what he imagined; it had an open floor plan. Massive Samsung monitors covered the basement's east and west walls. The northern border had what looked like a mirror that reflected and duplicated the brightness given off by the flickering of multi-colored lights from all the high-tech equipment in the room.

The reflective mirror was broken into two ginormous panels with an ornate antique double French door with lead glass panes in between. The door was beautiful and, in keeping with the theme of the 1920s building structure, gave almost no clue as to what was behind the doors. The hum of computers and the flickering of multi-colored lights momentarily disoriented Xavier, and the soothing sound of classical music gave it a surreal quality.

Castor laughed at the started look on his face, "Welcome to the broom closet or, as we like to call it, Stargate mandatum, which translates to Stargate Command. One of our founding tech members was a big fan of the television show Stargate Atlantis which ran from 2004 to 2009. I used to love to watch Stargate Atlantis. My favorite character was always Major John Shepard, mainly because he was tough and did things his way with little regard for paperwork and protocol. So, agreeing with the request to name the war room after a sci-fi television show was relatively easy."

"I think I remember that show as an option for episodes on Holocene," said Xavier. However, I never got to engage with it because Matt, Packer, and I were more into old Lucy re-runs."

Castor laughed; "from what I heard from Matt, you are the one who was obsessed with Lucy and Desi Arnaz."

"True," said Xavier, "but in my defense, Lucy is an artist of epic proportions." The sound of a person clearing their throat, followed by a cough that sounded suspiciously like the name Ethel interrupted the epic debate on Lucy's greatness as a comedian and an actress.

Castor turned towards a blond-haired, blue-eyed young man with ashen skin. Xavier could not decide if the pale skin was hereditary or because of an aversion to sunlight and the lower melanin production, a pigment responsible for darkening the skin.

"Ah, Sam, just the person I wanted to see," said Castor "I want to introduce you to Xavier. He will be working with us to help facilitate the creation of a digital profile we can potentially employ to gain access to some files we need."

Sam tapped his right ear and extended his hand, gripping Xavier's left hand and enthusiastically pumping it up and down.
Castor laughed, "Sam never does anything by half measure, and he is only allowed one cup of coffee a day; otherwise, we would be unable to keep up with him."

Sam laughed in response, "So true, but Castor forgot to mention that that rule also applies to the amount of Hershey Chocolate I am allowed to consume. I have a lot of natural energy, and stimulants of any type, such as caffeine and sugar, tend to ramp up my motor."

Xavier disengaged his hand and took a step back as Sam pivoted on his left foot and headed towards a partitioned area of the room containing multiple computers and monitors connected by cords and wires. The digital communication hub resembled a giant spider web capable of entrapping humans and insects. A shudder raced through Xavier as he imagined himself trapped, incapable of escaping the cords and wires connecting Sam to the outside world and modern technology. Xavier knew he was more of a people person, and the thought of never experiencing the wonders of life outside what you could view via a monitor was terrifying.

Even though he was relatively young, Xavier already had a bucket list of sorts planned out for his life, first starting with college, learning how to speak fluent Japanese, afterward visiting Japan, and then backpacking across Europe before starting graduate school and becoming a lawyer and one day being confirmed by the Senate as Chief Justice of the United States Supreme Court. He always loved history, especially during the time of the great Renaissance painters, philosophers, and artists. He embraced idea of becoming a Renaissance man like Leonardo Da Vinci, and Chief Justice Hansen had an appealing ring. However, first thing first, he needed to get his life back, and with that thought, he turned towards Sam and the computers that seemed to taunt him.

Sam sat at the computer; glancing over his left shoulder towards Castor, he asked the question on everyone's mind. "So, what is the game plan?"

Castor, looking expectantly at Xavier, "Well, what can you tell us about Dr. Proctor? Just remember, even trivial details could lead to a breakthrough."

Xavier excelled a breath and asked, "Well, do you have a piece of paper I can write on?" At which point Sam activated the holographic keyboard that hovered a few inches above the desk with green, red, and blue lights reflecting atop the desk. "No need; I can type one hundred words per minute while the average individual can only type between 40 and 65 words per minute. I can type even faster if I drink more than one cup of coffee, have an energy drink, or eat another candy bar."

"Wow, cowboy, no need to go crazy just yet," said Castor. "Let's look at what we find first before we pull out the big guns and start traumatizing Xavier and your fellow co-workers."

Those who worked with Sam regularly and heard Castor's comments broke into laughter. Sam refocused on the screen with a sheepish grin, waiting for his cue to start compiling research data.

Xavier did not know why, but on some level, Sam reminded him of a combination of Mathew and Packer. He was intelligent and efficient like Mathew but exuberant and playful like Packer. He missed his family and friends and could not wait until this mess was resolved. However, his intuition signaled that this situation would be challenging to fix and had the potential to be lengthy.

Castor turned towards Xavier, his body positioning and eye placement demonstrating his willingness to listen. "Start with the simple stuff, such as what your mother or Dr. Proctor and the nurse told you," said Castor. "Once we have compiled all the information you can recall, I will introduce you to a young lady who has been specially trained to help individuals access additional information via memory retrieval strategies. Let us start at the beginning by focusing on what you do, remember?"

Taking a deep breath, Xavier closed his eyes. He started repeating everything he could remember he had been told, no matter how small or outdated the information was.

"I remember the first time I told my mom I did not want to continue seeing Dr. Quacko. My mom mentioned that he was only one of three doctors qualified to treat my type of illness and that the other two were in Europe. The doctor in Denmark was a female, and the other was in Italy. I told my mom I wanted the doctor from Italy because I liked spaghetti and thought I could eat spaghetti after my appointments. Mom laughed and then told me no because Dr. Quacko had to travel from Chicago to see me and sometimes flew in from London for our visits," said Xavier.

Sam's fingers started racing across the keyboard in a mad dash to record everything being said as if losing one word would result in earth-shattering consequences.

"Good, we have a primary location in London followed by Chicago. What else can you remember?"

Xavier sighed; "I remember being told that my condition is referred to as PNH or Paroxysmal Nocturnal Hemoglobinuria, a scarce form of cancer that typically affects older individuals due to cellular degeneration. Dr. Proctor once told me that I was one of thirteen kids in the entire world who had been diagnosed with the same affliction. I also remember that when I snuck into my wake after my funeral, I overheard the doctor telling a woman he was with that they would grab some other kids. She acted like she was his boss. She threatened him and said that if he failed, he would receive a deadly promise."

"The doctor seemed very scared of the woman; honestly, she also scared me. I thought at the time she looked familiar, but I could not place who she was, but I know I had seen her somewhere before; I cannot remember when or where. I do not think she is an actor. She does not have that glamorous plastic look that is a dead giveaway that the person has had massive surgery. Also, her mannerisms are perfect, as if she had etiquette lessons early on in life. Overall, she comes across as very much aware of her own self-importance in addition to being greedy and power-hungry."

"Wow, the boy has some mad analytical thinking skills. Okay, that is a start," said Sam as his fingers flew across the keyboard. The light on the keyboard flickered with each keystroke illuminating the severe expression that marred Sam's pale visage. The rhythmic sound of the keyboard captured Xavier's mind. It produced a surreal feeling in his head, temporarily causing him to disassociate from the reality of his surroundings.

Castor directed his gaze behind Xavier. "Ah, here is the young lady I wanted to introduce to you," said Castor, placing a light kiss on her cheek as he wrapped his arm around her waist. "She is my second in command and the gatekeeper to all my secrets. I want to introduce you to my lovely wife, Pollux."

Xavier turned to look at the young lady in question. She was tall and slender, with ash-blonde hair framing her face giving her a fairy-like appearance. She wore black leggings, a white sweater dress with a strand of black pearls draped around her neck, and a knot resting at the midpoint of her long torso. Her eyes sparkled like gemstones, framed by coal-black lashes, with a light rose blush gracing her high cheekbones. She was stunning in her simplicity.

Her voice was smooth and mellow with a subtle undertone reminiscent of early jazz singers such as Ella Fitzgerald.

"Hello, Xavier. It is a pleasure to meet you," said Pollux. "My husband has talked about you nonstop."

Xavier had always heard that the eyes were the window to the soul until he looked into Pollux's green eyes; he had never put much store into the saying. She reminded Xavier of the young lady who performed the role of Clara in the holiday classic Nutcracker. She was an old soul in a young person's body.

Pollux watched him; her facial expression was impassive.

"My lovely wife was a former CIA hacker, behavioral coder, and deprogrammer," said Castor. "Her primary talents include reading body language, hypnosis, and memory retrieval. We hope she can help you retrieve some slight details that most people subconsciously store away during day-to-day interactions."

During Castor's introduction, Sam's rhythmic typing abruptly stopped startling those around him.

"Hey, CAS, I think I might have found something," said Sam.

His typing suddenly picked up speed, and the double monitors in front of him started to spew information at a dizzying rate as his eyes darted back and forth, rapidly digesting the information.

For just a moment Xavier wondered if he was human? He felt sick just watching Sam jump around rapidly from screen to screen; now he understood why Castor put a limit on his caffeine and sugar intake.

Sam's voice interrupted Xavier's thoughts. "From what I can tell, the doctor has a house in Chicago and London. The FFA has him booked on a flight to London on Wednesday with the return trip that following Monday. So that gives us five days to develop a plan. He has a clinic in Winnetka, a wealthy suburb in Cook County just sixteen miles north of Chicago. The name is derived from the Winnebago Indian word *winneba*, which translates to place of wild celery. Personally, I think it should be translated to a place of a lot of cash."

Castor tapped Sam on his right shoulder to refocus him away from the impromptu history lesson on Native American culture.

"Oh, sorry," said Sam. "The doctor has a residence and an upscale pediatric clinic at 750 Green Bay Rd Suite #1. The clinic is funded by a company named CITRUM. So far, from what I can tell, Dr. Proctor is head of the clinic, with ten employees under his supervision. Mason Todd Trudel is the CEO of CITRUM Industries and has a doctoral degree in Molecular Bio Engineering and Genetics. His great-grandfather was the former presidential Candidate Henry

Simon Trudel. His grandfather was Liam Mason Trudel, who married Rosalee Mason Todd, the granddaughter of former presidential candidate Dewitt Mason Cyder and descendant of Mary Todd Lincoln."

"Wait, why would an international pharmaceutical company like CITRUM be interested in funding a clinic specializing in sick children," asked Xavier.

Sam turned around to look at everyone and said, "Look, the company does more than just pharmaceuticals; they also have subsidiary companies that branch off into other areas of economic development. Their construction company Linctus Gratis LLC International obtained the Denver International Airport contract and completed it in February 1995. According to reports, it was two years past the due date and three billion dollars over budget." An image of the Denver International Airport in Colorado replaced the data stream on Sam's monitor.

If money is to be made or power to be gained, the Trudel family gets their share of the pie? Ironically, at one time, they were fierce political rivals; one favored the Democratic party, and the other favored the Republican party. Their love of money and power united them. Just like the old saying goes, opposites attract, especially in the case of the current Trudel family. There is even a rumor that the family has a secret book with dirt on the mover and shakers in every part of the government. It has also been said that working with them is a lifelong commitment, and those who try to leave either take their own life, die in accidents, or are enslaved by the cult-like atmosphere of the company."

Castor cleared his throat breaking the awkward silence following Sam's monologue, "Well, that is all fine and good, but let us focus on the task. Pollux, can you take Xavier to your office and work with him to dredge up additional details that might help us later in the mission? Sam will monitor the digital traffic to isolate the doctor's movement. I will contact two field operatives and establish twenty-four-hour surveillance on the clinic and his home outside Chicago."

Before Castor even finished his thoughts, Sam hunkered down over the keyboard and started typing; the sound of it mimicked the pitter-patter of rain hitting a tin roof during a rainstorm. The image of a man and a woman popped up on the dual screens in front of Sam; the male had the word "Felis" in bold letters underneath his image, and the female had the "Panthera" in bold letters underneath her picture as well.

The only thing Xavier could think of was that they must be code names or nicknames because Felis meant house cat, and the guy was anything but small. Panther referred to large cats, which did not mesh with the petite woman on the screen. Plus, whoever was stupid enough to give the male operative the code name house cat was either extremely brave or brain-damaged, depending on how you looked at it.

Pollux's hand rested lightly on his left elbow, pulling him away as she directed him through the doorway and to the right. The pitter-patter of Sam's keyboard and the sounds of multiple conversations gradually became softer and more muted with each step he took along the carpeted hallway.

Pollux's smooth, mellow voice broke the silence. "Xavier, my office is at the end of the hall; I designed it to provide a safe and relaxing environment for myself and others. I want to ask you some non-threatening questions and I will use minimally invasive exercises to help cultivate the process of retrieving lost memories. The first process I will use is hypnosis, and I will give you a list of words divided into common categories. In addition, I will incorporate visual, olfactory, kinesthetic, auditory, and gustatory stimuli to work in conjunction with the list of words. Using these different stimuli should trigger possible latent memories. Based on the response, the word provided can be adjusted to draw out additional details," said Pollux as she opened an unremarkable door and gestured for Xavier to precede her into the room.

Xavier's first glimpse of Pollux's office confirmed everything she had said earlier about it being designed to be relaxing and inviting. The wall directly opposite the door was painted with a light color, neither green nor blue but a soothing in-between. Dark green leaves and black inked stems created a calligraphy-styled image as it crawled across the lower right corner of the wall, branching up and across the border, only to end with a single green leaf touching the upper left-hand corner of the wall.

A burgundy chaise lounge with a cream-colored throw pillow was pushed against the wall. If his mom were here, she would have complimented the decorators' ability to use the chaise lounge as an accent piece bringing all the room's elements together. It reminded Xavier of his decision to redecorate his room after starting middle school. His mom told him that the key to decorating was to have two bold colors and one neutral color to bring everything together.

Now he owed his mom an apology because it turns out that she was right about so many things.

Xavier closed his eyes momentarily and silently wished he could be a kid again with no troubles or worries beyond anxiously anticipating that school would be called off because of snow and ice and Mom waking up Rosie, Newsprint, Will, and him to go outside to play. A memory imposed itself before his eyes reminding him of better days. Newsprint's black spots sharply contrasted against the iridescent white snow as he raced around the yard barking in ecstasy as he and Xavier dodged the hard-packed snowballs his brother rapidly assembled and threw with unerring accuracy. Will always got the best of him or seemed to know what tricks he would pull before he knew it himself.

Only after they had reached the first stage of exhaustion and hypothermia would Mom call them in and treat them to a piping hot mug of cocoa topped with whipped cream and peppermint chocolate shavings. They would eat chocolate cookies for breakfast while snuggling on the couch under multiple blankets in front of a roaring fire as Christmas songs from the Rat Pack hummed in the background. It was not the healthiest of meals, but like Mom always said, once or twice a year would not hurt anyone.

The funny thing about memories is that the sights and sounds can transport an individual back in time. He could almost feel the warmth emanating from the fireplace and smell hot cocoa in the air. The only thing that could make it perfect would be if his family and Newsprint were here. Xavier opened his eyes and realized that the warmth of the fire and the smell of hot cocoa were genuine and not a figment of his imagination.

A warm glow emanated from the multi-colored Tiffany lampshade placed upon a fragile-looking end table made of brown oak. To the left of the door on the wall was a matching custom-built bookcase with multiple first-edition novels, textbooks, and trinkets randomly dispersed amongst the leather-bound tomes, which provided a homey, lived-in atmosphere. The desk in front of the bookcase was more like a dressing table or table you would place behind a sofa in a living room. On the one hand, the cream color of the desk seemed out of place when you looked at it individually. Still, when looked at in its entirety, it brought everything together.

The wall opposite the desk had a faux fireplace slash heater which provided a warm crackling sound followed by simulated lighting to mimic a real fire. The painting above the mantle reminded Xavier of a street from Mackinac Island. He and his family visited the island once in October. It was beautiful with all the fall colors on display.

Pollux's voice interrupted his thoughts, pulling him out of the rabbit hole he found himself in. "So, what do you think of the decor?"

He tilted his head. He wanted to tell her that it reminded him of his mom and home, but he was unsure whether Pollux was a friend or foe. Clearing his throat, he looked her in the eyes. He decided to take a chance and follow his instincts. "I like it, but it makes me homesick for my family."

Pollux moved around the desk and gestured with her left hand towards the chaise lounge. "Why don't you have a seat, and we will start trying to see what we can come up with."

Xavier paused for a moment and moved towards the chaise lounge. He sat on the seat and pushed the throw pillow to the side. Leaning forward, he placed his forearms on his thighs, placing his head in his hands before looking up, and staring off into space at the painting above the mantel. Xavier's voice cracked as he asked, "How will you help me when I can't seem to help myself?"

Pollux eased down into her chair and placed her forearms on the desk, mimicking Xavier's movements. "Before meeting Castor, I worked at the Central Intelligence Agency in D.C., specializing in hypnosis. If used properly, it can aid in retrieving memories by activating cognitive mechanisms. However, it is not admissible in court, but since we do not plan to testify in court, it really does not matter."

Moving her hand across the top of the desk, Pollux repositioned an electronic perpetual motion desk toy to the space opposite Xavier's line of sight. The device had four purple balls, two silver balls, and a golden disk at the center point between each ball. It resembled a small Farris wheel you would find at the traveling carnivals set up in Mall parking lots across America during the hot summer months. The toy immediately captured Xavier's attention; he had not noticed it when he entered the room. Now it caught all his attention as his fingers itched to turn it on and get lost in the hypnotic blending of colors.

Pollux noticed his preoccupation with the device and flipped the switch on. Her smooth voice flowed over him like a gentle breeze; the stress and anxiety slowly trickled away as he swung his legs up and laid down on his right side with his ash-brown hair touching the pillow. He never once took his eyes off the kaleidoscope of colors produced by the now-moving Ferris wheel toy.

"I know you are feeling anxious about what we will be doing, but I assure you all I want to do is talk to you about your family and then just see where it takes us," said Pollux. "So, tell me about your family and what it is like around the holiday."

"My family is close-knit, especially with the age gap between my brother Will and myself. I have lived in Huntington, Indiana, lettered in Swimming, and suffered from a rare form of cancer since I was a kid. I Love playing virtual reality games, and I love my dog Newsprint. He is a cocker spaniel with black spots on a white coat, and funny enough, he has these shocking brown eyebrows. He is starting to get old and not as active as he used to be, especially since he has lost his eyesight," said Xavier.

With a flick of her wrist, Pollux motioned him to stop, "Good, that is a great start, but let's talk about what it was like attending your own funeral?"

Xavier looked at her as she sat behind the desk, just looking at him and not bothering to take notes as he spoke. "Why are you not taking notes, and how is this going to help if you forget what I said," asked Xavier.

Pollux's emerald, green eyes sparkled with suppressed mirth, her lips curved upward into a half smile.

"Well, remember how I mentioned I worked for the CIA because I was a child protégé. I am an expert in my field with a doctorate in Psychology, specifically memory retrieval. In addition to my academic credentials, I also have a photographic memory. Most people have what is known as an eidetic memory in which they remember what they read with great precision."

"Still, the retrieval time is longer than what you would see with someone with a photographic memory. Most people have some form of eidetic memory related to visual stimuli. A photographic memory is scarce, but some of the most notable figures in history, such as Thomas Edison and Charles Darwin, had it."

Shaking his head in amazement, Xavier laid back on the couch. He watched the purple and silver balls rotate around and around.

"Well, going to my own funeral was surreal; honestly, I never realized that I had made an impact on others. Some things I would have considered trivial seemed to have the most impact on others. I felt overwhelmed by the outpouring of love and grief. I also felt like the most horrible person on earth because I was not dead and was deceiving them into thinking I was. At one point, I wanted to be done with everything, curl up in a ball and hide. I saw how devastated my mom was and how solemn my dad and brother were during the service, and it broke my heart," he said.

Pollux removed a remote from the center drawer of her desk. She directed it towards the fireplace, turning off the heat but keeping the flickering lights of the faux flames on.

"So, out of curiosity, how did you attend your funeral without drawing suspicion to yourself?"

Xavier laughed, "Actually, my friend Packer came up with the idea to dress up in one of my old high school costumes I wore when I did the play Yankee Doodle Dandy."

Pollux interrupted him, "Please tell me you did not dress up like a World War II version of Uncle Sam?"

"No, nothing like that," said Xavier. "I dressed up as George Cohen and went to the service to pay my respects and see my family one last time before I left for Chicago. Mathew even made me a fake identification card with the name Joseph Christmas. Oh! That reminds me; my friend has an audio transcript of what was said at the visitation at my house. It may not help much because we used my mom's baby cam that she uses for my nephew Carter. We stuck it in the middle of an enormous flower arrangement in the front foyer near the staircase."

Looking again towards the Ferris wheel, as he liked to call the device, he discovered talking to Pollux was more manageable and accessible. Granted, having a relaxing conversation for over an hour significantly relaxed him and eliminated his doubts. Xavier now felt more comfortable talking to her about the events leading up to his arrival in Chicago.

Pollux again asked Xavier to close his eyes and look at the events like he was watching a movie and stop it when he got to a part that he felt he needed to stop and examine in greater detail. With the help of Pollux's gently guiding voice, he was able to provide descriptions of the events with a clear and concise efficiency that bordered on detached and unemotional.

Suddenly he stopped talking and opened his eyes to look at Pollux.

"Hey, the lady talking to the Dr. Proctor had a black Gucci handbag with a gold chain and buckle overlaid on red and green nylon. I am unsure, but the bag looked personalized with gold calligraphy embroidery in the top-hand right corner. I think it might have been initiated either RTM or RMT," said Xavier.

"Towards the end of the visitation at my house, when they left, they got into the back of a black BMW G99 with what looked like a red and teal Washington DC license plate. I did not get a good look at it besides the colors and the first two letters. I think it may have been D.C., but I am unsure."

Swiveling in her chair, Pollux picked up her iPad and rapidly started typing. Suddenly, she turned the device around to allow Xavier to see what was on the screen. A black BMW G99 sedan was displayed on the screen. She swiped to her left and pulled up a license plate that resembled his description.

Still, instead of being issued by the District of Columbia, it was issued by the United States federal government. Across the plate's top was a red ribbon with the word Diplomatic written on it. The United States of America's official seal was in the top left-hand corner. Under the ribbon were letters and numbers overlaid on a teal backdrop.

"Yes, that is what it looked like," shouted Xavier as he excitedly jumped up from the chaise lounge.

Pollux stood up, gesturing towards the door; she motioned to Xavier to follow her, "I think it is time we go tell

Castor and Sam about what you remembered and also get a copy of the audio transcript from your friend Mathew," said Pollux.

Xavier thought about the implications as he strode down the hallway; it seemed they were finally making headway, but would this be another dead end, or was it just dreaming on his part?

Walking through the Broom Closet, he realized Castor no longer stood beside Sam. Pollux moved past Sam's work area and went toward the mirrored wall on the opposite side of the room. Next to the mirrored frame was a door that resembled the structure that outlined the mirror. Xavier hesitated; at the same time, Pollux motioned for him to follow her into the room.

Once in the room, he noticed Castor sitting behind his desk with a lamp behind his left shoulder, casting a shadow across the desk and the floor. It almost seemed as if he had not heard them enter. Suddenly he stopped what he was doing and stood up, moving toward his wife with a half-smile gracing his lips. After embracing her and giving her a light peck on the cheek, he looked toward Xavier.

With his arm wrapped around Pollux's waist Castor smiled, his attention solely focused on Xavier. "So, before we get into whatever you discovered, let me tell you what Sam and I have been doing. My two best operatives are surveilling the clinic and the Doctor's house. Once it gets dark, Felis and Panthera will break into both addresses and do a preliminary search. Then Sam will run a detailed analysis of the Doctor's spending habits. Now, what have you folks discovered?"

Cancer: VII

Gesturing towards the chair in front of the desk, Castor moved back to his chair as Pollux perched on his right side.

Clearing his throat, Xavier started reciting the information he and Pollux had uncovered during their session. Castor stared off into space. Everyone in the room held their breath in anticipation; they did not have to wait exceedingly long before he grabbed a piece of paper and started writing on it.

After five minutes, he sat back and smiled, "I figured out who the lady was talking to the Doctor. It is Rosalee Mason Todd Trudel; she is the granddaughter of former presidential candidate Dewitt Mason Cyder; she later married the grandson of Henry Simon Trudel, and had one child named Mason Todd Simon Trudel, and earned a doctoral degree in Molecular Biology and Genetic Engineering from MIT. She also has diplomatic status due to her work as a special envoy, and her initials are RMT."

"How does that help us?" asked Xavier.

Before Castor could answer his question, Pollux moved from her position on the edge of the desk and started pacing back and forth in front of the two men. Her graceful movements were hypnotic, and her fierce look of concentration on her face foretold salient thoughts. "What if Dr. Todd is really the boss and not the Doctor who has cared for you all your life."

She then stopped and turned towards the two men and asked, "What if your diagnosis of Paroxysmal Nocturnal Hemoglobinuria is just a smoke screen to monitor your progress and development." Her pacing increased as if her steps correlated to her thoughts' speed. Suddenly she stopped and looked around at Castor, "Did Sam mention earlier that the Clinic was financed by CITRUM Industries?"

Castor laughed and looked at Xavier, "This is why I married her because she is the total package, beauty, elegance, intelligence, and suspicion. Plus, she is the only person willing to put up with my shenanigans. However, I am confident she married me due to the entertainment value I bring to the relationship."

Pollux smiled indulgently towards her husband. "Back on task, I will see about contacting some of my former CIA and Justice Department friends. Some may have heard the scuttlebutt around the office and can pass along some valuable information about the Trudel family." She turned towards the door and made her way out; her entire body radiated focus and determination to solve this new puzzle.

Xavier looked at Castor and asked, "What do I do in the meantime?"

"That is simple, my dear Watson," replied Castor. "You will take additional tests to see if you really did have cancer the Doctor said you had, and then you can spend your downtime helping research CITRUM and the history of the Trudel family. It is not a coincidence that Dr. Proctor and the Trudel family are working together. We need to proceed cautiously because, with her diplomatic position as an Envoy for the United States, she has diplomatic immunity. If she is involved, we want to wait and accidently tip our hand and have her go underground before getting the necessary information."

Later, Xavier felt a sense of Deja Vue again as everyone assembled at the conference table. Still, this time around, instead of multiple unknown participants, there were only two. He suspected that these two individuals, a man, and a woman, were the infamous Felis and Panthera he had heard so much about over the last three days.

He wondered if the time had come to move against the Doctor and his cohorts. He itched with every fiber of his being to be doing anything that would help him regain his life and be with his family. The room started to get quiet as Castor was the last to enter before the guard at the door closed it, and an audible locking of the door from the outside echoed through the room.

Castor's voice broke the silence, "First thing first, many of you are wondering why we locked the door, and it is because we want to make sure no one interrupts us or is privy to what is about to be disclosed in this room. I would also like the two newcomers to introduce themselves to the group."

The first person seated to the left of Castor stood up, her hair was jet black, and her almond-shaped eyes implied a mixture of Asian ancestry. In contrast, her deep brown eyes gave her a porcelain doll look. She barely stood five feet tall, and looking at her, you would think she was only 15 years old, if that. Her outfit consisted of faded blue jeans with holes located in areas of her anatomy that foretold wear and tear rather than fabrication. The black military boots had a zipper on the outer side for easy removal.

The shoes reminded him of the type Packer's dad wore when he was on duty at the firehouse. The black leather jacket also showed signs of wear and tear from usage rather than by design. The coat covered a simple white T-shirt with the message, "*I see Stupid People*." The statement alone made Xavier smile. The young lady's voice, however, did not match her youthful appearance. Instead, it implied an ability to intimidate and invoke fear in those who made the mistake of double-crossing her.

"Everyone calls me Panthera," she said before sitting back down.

The following individual seated to the young lady's right dramatically differed in mannerisms and appearance. He stood straight and tall and appeared six feet four inches tall with the build an NFL defense linebacker would envy. His extremely short hair was worn in a style made popular by military personnel, with silver sparsely sprinkled through his jet-black hair. His face was smooth and unlined, directly contrasting with the silver running through his hair. His glacial grey eyes complemented his black suit and red power tie. While Panthera projected a youthful, laid-back appearance, the male projected a strict military bearing.

In an exact repeat of Panthera's introduction, he stood up. He stated, "Everyone calls me Felis," before he sat back down and directed his attention towards Castor. Both newcomers were people of few words.

"Thank you," said Castor. "Now, let's open the floor first to the doctors and move around the table clockwise."

The first to stand up was Katherine, the specialist for neurology, orthopedics, and spinal cord injuries. With a wave of her hand, the room darkened, and the screen behind her lit up.

"After speaking with Castor, Dorian and I went back and looked at your test results to specifically verify or eliminate the diagnoses of cancer made by Dr. Proctor. Once we started looking at the test results, we determined that at no time do your cells or physical structure show obvious evidence of ever having cancer of any type. If anything, your cellular structure shows almost no signs of aging beyond what you would expect for an eighteen-year-old. There is evidence of some mutations, but at this time, we do not have enough information to determine if the mutation is a result of evolution or manufactured."

Dorian smoothly made the transition from Katherine to himself as the main speaker. "We also noticed that the tattoo on your left shoulder changed slightly as we conducted additional tests. My friend, who studies different types of ink, determined that one part of the mixture is man-made, and the other is composed of a rare mineral known as Ringwoodite. The minerals range from bluish to smoke-gray and are found in a solid state like quartz. He cannot identify the secondary mineral that acts as a binding agent for the nanobots and the dark blue color. He hopes to eventually identify the secondary component."

The following person in line to speak was Felis; however, unlike Dorian and Katherine, he chose to remain seated as the lights in the room were gradually increased to allow the occupants of the room plenty of time to adjust to the sudden brightness.

"Castor asked Panthera and me to establish 24-hour surveillance on the Doctor's home and the clinic. During the first eight hours, nothing really happened at the home or the clinic. Then everything changed around 10 pm when the Doctor, his nurse, and a young lady appeared. The young lady in question was carried into the house by one of the Doctor's goons, a man with short blond hair and a bad attitude."

"That would be Hulk Hogan," said Xavier.

Felis nodded his head in acknowledgment of what he had said. "Right now, we are unsure if the young lady was asleep, drugged, or unconscious. We do know that she is not a willing guest in the house based on the presence of heavy-duty zip-tie handcuff restraints like the type used by the military and law enforcement. Also, we noticed that the room she was taken to was on the second floor and had bars on the window. In addition, there was evidence of infer-red motion detectors placed strategically on the windows and the doors."

Felis looked towards Panthera. Their silent acknowledgment of each other illustrated their comfort with one another.

She picked up where he left off; "so far, based on surveillance, the analysis of the blueprints, the call logs, and the security layout of the house, the best chance we have of getting into the house undetected would be through the storm cellar located at the back of the house."

Saying this, she unfurled what looked like house plans to a McMansion; the blueprints detailed a four-story house with a full basement and a completed attic.

Xavier noticed that the back of the building had a storm cellar under the kitchen, with a staircase next to the walk-in pantry. The rest of the undersection of the basement appeared to have only one access point. The open floor plan extended from the back of the cellar wall towards the front section of the house. The access staircase leading from the main floor to the basement was located next to a private office with a bathroom behind the stairs' wall. It was a little confusing, but it screamed, "Look at me; I am an evil scientist; I am up to no good."

Panthera continued with her briefing, "the guard dogs can be incapacitated using animal sedatives. Once in the cellar, we can move towards the upper floors. The cook and the maid both have the same day off, as does the chauffeur; during the days they have off, the Doctor likes to spend time at his favorite hotel and private club in the city. We suspect the goon will stay behind to attend to the young lady; we plan to sedate him and the girl. While we suspect the girl is being held against her will, we need to minimize any potential threats of discovery and to the organization."

Xavier interrupted and pointed towards the open area of the basement located behind the cellar. "What is that?"

Panthera responded quickly, "That is the Doctor's personal laboratory, and as far as we can tell, it is impenetrable. It has the same type of door as a bank vault, requires a passcode, a retina scan, and has a time lock device which makes it near impossible to access."

Once she finished her sentence, Castor picked up where she had left off.

"So far, we plan to go in under darkness; everyone must prepare for the worst-case scenario. I want the doctors to have a full surgical team, and a triage unit prepared just in case. Felis, Panthera, Xavier, and I will be going in to retrieve the girl and important files. Pollux will stay behind and manage the logistical operations. Sam will provide technical assistance via the communications devices created by him and his team."

Everyone started collecting their stuff and heading toward the door. Castor's voice stopped Xavier in his tracks. "We will be heading out at midnight tonight; I suggest you go get some sleep and meet us in the command center at 10 pm, and we will get all suited up and do a last-minute run-through of the checklist before we leave."

Nodding his head in acknowledgment, Xavier headed towards the temporary quarters he had been assigned to once it had been verified that he was not a significant threat to the organization. It seemed like just yesterday he was celebrating the holidays with his family and counting the days to the end of the school year and the start of college in August. If someone had told him that he would be involved in shady dealings, forced to run for his life and pretend he was dead, he would have suggested they get psychiatric help or called the police and demand they be arrested.

The command center was humming with energy as Xavier walked into the room. Everyone in the group wore identical black boots, pants, and t-shirts with tactical jackets. Felis, Panthera, and Castor were checking the tranquilizer guns when a technician came into the room with hamburger balls in plastic wrap. Castor directed the technician to give the hamburger balls to Xavier. He then placed them into the small messenger satchel slung across his shoulders.

He silently wondered if they would use the hamburger as a distraction, put the sedatives in the hamburger, or shoot the dogs with the tranquilizer. Regardless of how they did it, he hoped it would work. He did not relish getting up close and personal with a couple of Doberman Pinchers. The screen in front of the group displayed a 3D image of the layout of the house and grounds. The moving red dots indicated the path the dogs and their handlers traverse.

 "Will we have to knock out the handlers and the guards," asked Xavier.

Sam spoke up before he could ask another question. "The handlers leave the dogs to roam free after midnight, and the next shift does not take over until 6 am. I tapped into the dogs monitoring collars so we could keep track of them once the handlers left. I developed a program that will replicate the biosignatures of the dogs so that the remote facility that monitors them will not realize they have been sedated."

Castor spoke up, directed everyone in the group to head out the doors, and instructed them to load up into a black Mercedes Sprinter van parked in the back alley with its motor running. The frigid winter air created a plum of white smoke from the exhaust pipe that drifted upward toward the dark-tinted windows. When the back panel doors opened, Xavier noticed the driver was dressed in the same manner as the group members.

However, he did not remember being introduced to the individual. Considering his size and demeanor, Xavier knew he was not the type to be overlooked or forgotten. He looked once in the group's direction; his eyes scanned the area, refocused on the street before him. The temperature within the van seemed to drop five degrees in direct proportion to the driver's indifference. Once everyone was loaded in the truck, the mood shifted from optimistic to solemn and morose. Nobody talked; each was absorbed by his or her thoughts and anxieties or, in the case of Panthera and Felis, their mental preparations.

Sitting on the benches that lined the van's interior, Xavier felt highly nervous about the mission. He prayed with all his heart to Saint Francis that he would not be a liability and potentially get others hurt. His complexion in the dim lighting reflected his internal turmoil, and the green hue of his skin worsened by the minute. To distract himself, he thought about all the hours of training he had put in for the upcoming Regional Swim competition in Indianapolis.

While he had not been practicing as usual, he was still nominally in shape. During the fall sports season, he would practice six days a week and participate in various swim competitions until the end of February. While he was not as muscular nor as tall as Felis and the driver, he knew he could move fast, especially when the adrenaline kicked in and his muscle memory took over. He just hoped it would be enough.

The doors shut, and the van started moving into the night; the smooth hum of the motor complemented the silence of the streets; only the moving shadow of the truck produced by the streetlamps indicated that they had been there. Xavier shut his eyes and thought about everything that could go wrong, but then he felt someone hugging him. He opened his eyes and looked around, noting that everyone was in their place, seated and belted in. Did he imagine the warm embrace; was he going crazy?

He shut his eyes again when he felt the warm embrace and heard a voice say, "Everything is going to be alright." He again opened his eyes, looking towards the others to see if they had spoken to him. However, their faces remained grim and unreadable as they were absorbed in their thoughts. "Had they heard the voice, or was it just in his head?" While he could not locate the source of the reassurance, he suddenly felt more confident and hopeful that he would make it through the night and eventually find his way home to his family.

The van stopped abruptly about a block from the Doctor's home, far away from any streetlights that could reveal their presence to anyone or local busybodies. The group disembarked and crouched down low, moving along the hedges that lined the wrought iron fences separating the stately homes from the pedestrian roadways. Felis moved like a black panther, smooth and graceful. Castor, second in line, appeared to be moderately more experienced than he had realized. Xavier was third in the line, and compared to the others, he felt noisy and clumsy. Panthera was the last member of the team; she acted as the anchor, and her job was to cover the rear and guarantee they were not interrupted or detected. She was even more stealthy than the two men, moving with the grace of the large cat she was named after.

Felis suddenly stopped and held up a fist motioning everyone to follow his lead. Pointing to the bag containing the hamburger balls, he motioned him to come forwards and throw them onto the front and side lawn. In one smooth motion, Xavier stood up, threw the balls as far as he could, and rapidly resumed his position behind the shrubs. Castor crouched behind the two men as Panthera continued to cover their flank. He then tapped Xavier on his left shoulder and Felis on his right.

He held up the monitoring device that signaled the altered path of the dogs and their handlers. The dogs had decided to investigate the hamburger balls. Castro's hand started counting down the distance between them and the dogs. Five, four, three, two, one, and now the dogs were so close that if anyone in the group took a deep breath, they would alert the handlers to their presence. It was a good thing that the group used scent neutralizer spray to eliminate or camouflage their natural body odor.

The dogs started pulling on their leashes, dragging their handlers along as they discovered the hamburger balls hidden in the lush grass. The two handlers dropped the leases and let the dogs sniff around as they withdrew cigarettes from their pockets and lit them up. The taller blonde handler took a long drag of the cigarette and blew out rings of smoke while the dark-haired handler stood by, smoking a cigarette minus the tricks. The childish antics of his colleague left him looking unimpressed.

Suddenly the two Doberman pinchers started to wobble and grew unsteady on their feet. They lowered their body to the ground and put their heads on their paws. The two men looked at each other in puzzlement. The blonde-haired guard moved towards the dog closest to him, "Get up, Major;" then, looking at his sibling, he said, "Get up, Captain." Neither dog even twitched; both men moved closer to the dogs when suddenly their heads jerked up as they heard a slight whistling sound. However, it was too late to evade the tranquilizers once they registered the sound as a potential threat. Their falling bodies barely missed the sleeping dogs.

Xavier felt relieved; as a dog lover, he did not want to see the two Dobermans hurt because the dynamic idiots landed on them. Moving forward, Felis and Castor checked to ensure everyone was soundly asleep. After confirming they were both out for the count, they dragged the two unconscious men towards some shrubs and pushed them out of the direct line of sight. Turning his head towards Panthera, he asked, "Do you want me to move the dogs as well?"

With a negative shake of her head, the compressing of her lips, and the pointing of her two fingers towards Castor, she indicated they needed to remain silent and move towards the house.

The group gingerly moved towards the right side of the house parallel to the driveway and out of sight of the bay window on the second-floor landing, in case anyone was watching. The insects and the nocturnal animals held their breath, creating an eerie, unnatural absence of sound. Once Felis reached the storm cellar door, he stopped; then motioned the others to line up along the side of the house.

One by one, the group moved toward the bottom of the cellar steps; the light was non-existent once the door had been closed behind them. Indivdually, the four group members activated their blue light wands to help them see without risking exposure. Together they moved towards the panel outlined in the ceiling of the cellar; access was achieved using a slender staircase that seemed too rickety to support the weight of the entire group at once.

Each person crept up the staircase and lifted the panel, silently climbing through until the whole team was squished together shoulder to shoulder in the secondary walk-in pantry meant for one or two people at the most. Easing the door, Felis listened for footsteps or any sound alerting them to possible exposure.

After a few minutes, it became evident that no one was around, yet they still cautiously proceeded. Standing in the kitchen surrounded by modern conveniences and state-of-the-art appliances, Xavier found it hard to imagine that the house's owner was a sadistic monster who tortured children.

The team tiptoed through the kitchen towards the door; once through the door, Xavier was stunned by the sight of the twin staircases that spiral down from the second floor. Each staircase was constructed from pure oak, polished to a high glossy sheen with a hint of lemon in the air. The wooden face of each step was engraved with intertwined ivy leaves and vines extending from the bottom of the stairs to the top of the stairs, along the railing between the two staircases, and back down to the main level of the house.

In between the two staircases was a circular wooden oak frame hung from the ceiling by stainless steel chains. In the center of the circle was a stained-glass image of God extending his forefinger to man transferring knowledge from himself to humanity. Behind the artwork was a wall decorated with recessed lights mounted strategically to allow for year around illumination of the stained-glass masterpiece. Xavier knew that the amount of craftmanship and detail that went into the piece must have been equal to that of the Renaissance paintings he had seen as a kid. He had no doubt that the work belonged in a museum.

Felis and Xavier headed up the left staircase while Panthera and Castor went up the right side of the stairs; each moved as silently as possible. Once both groups reached the top of the landing, they stopped suddenly; Xavier thought he heard something falling on the carpet, but it could be just a figment of his imagination. Felis motioned for him to get behind him; the door closest to him opened, making a booming sound as it hit the wall behind it.

Out stepped a goliath of a man. His face looked like he had been on the receiving end of one-to-many blows to the head. His nose was slightly smashed; his face had numerous visible scars, creating a roadmap starting from one side of his face to the other. Grotesque was the only word that could be used to describe the newcomer to the party.

Before Goliath even registered that intruders were in the house, Panthera shot him with a tranquilizer. One dose should have been enough for any other person of average size. The mountain of a man rushed towards her and Castor, giving no indication that he had been drugged.

Simultaneously, Xavier and Felis realized that bringing this guy down would take more than one dose. They started shooting him with additional tranquilizers. Even then, he struggled against the effects of the drug until his menacing determination was extinguished by the massive number of sedatives in his system.

His falling and the subsequent noise from his body impacting the floor reminded Xavier of the philosophical argument, "If a tree falls in the woods with no one around, does it really make a sound? He now had his answer, it did!"

Castor and Panthera used hand signals to convey that they would return to the first floor and search the Doctor's private office. Nodding affirmative, Felis motioned for Xavier to step around the sleeping giant as he searched for the key to the girl's bedroom. Moving past the snoring giant, Xavier noticed a puddle of drool spreading out beneath his head. Oh, gross, he thought. He pitied the person who had to clean the carpet.

Moving silently along the hallway wall, noise from the far room became more audible the closer they came to the door. Finally, after positioning himself on the left side of the door frame and Felis on the right, they could discern what was happening behind the closed door.

The young lady was pacing back and forth from the door to the far side of the room. Her ranting and raving got louder and more descriptive the closer she got to the door and then faded away as she turned toward the opposite side of the room. Felis motioned towards Xavier; by hand signals, he outlined the plan.

He would unlock the door and push it open, allowing Felis to rush in and sedate the young lady. At the same time, Xavier would cover his back, watch for potential threats, and neutralize it if necessary. Both waited for the young lady's voice to recede as she turned and headed toward the opposite side of the room. He quickly inserted and turned the key; pushing the door open, he watched Felis spring into action.

The girl barely had time to turn around before being tranquilized. Felis rushed to grab her, placing his hand over her mouth to muffle her screams. Her struggles against her captor proved ineffective against his brute strength; all it did was circulate the sedative throughout the rest of her body in a timelier manner. Unexpectedly her body went limp as the sedative made the need for restrain a moot point. Lifting the young lady into his arms, Felis headed along the dark hallway toward the nearest staircase.

One of the first things Xavier noticed about the young lady was her beautiful auburn red hair that hung over the side of Felis' arm, gently swinging back and forth in step with the rhythm of his body as he walked down the staircase. It was so long that it almost reached the floor, even with the curls. From what he could tell, she was about five feet seven inches tall with a slender but curvy build that he found appealing. Her skin was devoid of color; the only hint he had that she was still alive was due to the dark red color in her rosebud-shaped lips, as the rest of her was pale like newly fallen snow.

Xavier was not one of those guys who felt he needed to date someone shorter than him or stick thin. He always believed that a girl should look like a girl and not like a boy in disguise or like a life-size version of a Barbie doll. If the truth be told, he would have loved to date the daughter of the actress who played Wonder Woman in the 1980s, but that was just a dream. Upon reaching the first floor, Xavier and Felis met up with Panthera and Castor coming out of the Doctor's office; It looked like they had raided the kitchen for appropriately sized containers to haul the files from the office. Both produce boxes were full of files.

Felis handed the young lady off to Xavier, "I will signal to the driver to bring the van around to the front door," he stepped out into the night and disappeared before anyone could acknowledge what he had said.

Xavier stood there holding the unconscious young lady. He could not help but notice how she smelled like a combination of vanilla and peppermint and wondered if it was because of the perfume of her body wash. The smell reminded him of the vanilla sugar cookies and peppermint tea he liked to drink during the holidays. Shaking his head, he reminded himself to pay attention. Maybe they could get to know each other later once it was determined what role she played in this elaborate, messed-up drama he called his life. In about five minutes, the van pulled up to the front doors. The heavily laden team loaded their precious cargo into the truck and pulled off into the night as Goliath, the hell hounds, and their handlers continued to dream the night away.

The following day after everyone had gotten a few hours of sleep, the crew reassembled in the conference room to discuss their options. Castor stood and called the meeting to order as Felis, Panthera, Xavier, and Pollux sat drinking coffee to wake up after their long night of breaking and entering. Sam leaned back in his chair, balancing on the back two legs; his constant fidgeting and booming voice was annoying, to say the least. He, of all the people in the room, was the only one not drinking coffee, and that was more of a form of self-preservation for the others in the group. Even after a long night of data processing, Sam was still more awake than the others; at the moment Xavier's lack of sleep made it where he secretly dreamed of duct taping Sam to his chair and stuffing a gag in his mouth to silence his obnoxious chatter.

Castor's first words to the groups did more to wake them up than numerous cups of coffee ever could.

"Now comes part II of the plan; I want Felis and Panthera to interrogate our guest; I then want Sam to investigate everything little scrap of information they get from the young lady."

The image of the young lady appeared on the wall behind him as Castor continued his monologue, "I will be in the command center tracking the Doctor and Rosalee Trundle link. At the same time, Pollux and Xavier will start reviewing the files and looking for anything that may help us."

The door to the room opened upon the completion of his last statement, and two nameless technicians entered the room carrying the two produce boxes containing the files from the Doctor's private office; after setting them down in the middle of the conference table, they left as quietly and as efficiently as they had entered. Once they had left, Castor again asked if anyone had any questions. With a shake of their collective heads, everyone jumped up and left the conference room as if the hounds of Cerberus were nipping at their heels.

Once the others had left the room, Castor walked up to his wife and gave her a peck on the cheek as he headed to the door. "Let me know if you find anything; I also instructed the kitchen to make up some cold-cut sandwiches and soup for lunch so that we can provide updates on what we find."

After Castor left the room, it felt to Xavier as if all sound had followed him.

Pollux continued to look at Xavier, pushing one of the two boxes across the table. She asked him, "Would you like something to drink before we review the files?"

Xavier nodded affirmatively and responded, "That would be great."

Pollux left the room as Xavier started thumbing through some of the files; he noticed the files were labeled according to zodiac symbols instead of people's names.

There were twenty-six files with two folders per zodiac sign. Half of the files had a large, thick black X next to the file name, and the other half had a zodiac name with a bold red star. The first file he decided to look at was labeled "Virgo X." Inside was a birth certificate. The first birth certificate had the name of the child. Parents names were blacked out and only showed that a male child was born on October 1, 1968, followed by a death certificate in 1970 due to sudden infant death syndrome (SIDS). Then under that was another birth certificate for a male child, also with the names redacted and dated October 1, 1972.

For a moment, Xavier wondered if the second child from 1972 was a relative. Even more puzzling was another death certificate for the birthday but dated March 14, 1974; the cause of death was also listed as SIDS. After the death certificate, there were a series of notations, one he recognized as the word written on the picture he found behind his mother's filing cabinet, **XEROX**?

He looked up as Pollux entered the room with both of their drinks, his being a can of Coke and hers a glass of good old southern sweet tea. Xavier motioned her over and showed her the contents of the folder he was previewing. "It seems like it is a jumbled mess, but I can't shake the feeling that the birth certificates might be from one family," said Xavier. "I wonder if they are doing genetic research of some type?"

"That is great; let me start looking in my files, and let's see what we both can find and then we can share it with Castor when everyone gathers for lunch in about two hours," said Pollux.

The two started browsing through the files, each making notations on a legal pad beside their work area. The clock on the wall provided the occupants within the room with a method for measuring the passage of time.

Just when they were about to call it quits and break for lunch, their stomachs started growling and churning, reminding them that the only substance they had that morning consisted of either coffee, Coke, or sweet tea. Standing up, both Xavier and Pollux started to stretch out their cramped muscles when the door opened, and in walked Castor.

Panthera, Felis, and numerous kitchen helpers followed; one helper had a big pot of steaming hot tomato soup, and another carried a platter containing a mountain of golden-brown sandwiches oozed with a combination of melted Cheddar, Provolone, and Swiss cheese. The combination of the smell and sight of the food made Xavier's taste buds salivate. His stomach started growling, suggesting a Pavlovian response. The last two helpers to enter the room carried a platter containing soup bowls, saucers, spoons, and linen napkins for everyone. While the final individual held a container of sweet, iced tea with matching glass goblets.

Xavier rushed to move the folders to the credenza under the flat-screen television in front of the room; hunger motivated him to complete the task as fast as possible. The kitchen staff moved quickly and efficiently around the table, setting items before everyone, and exiting the room once their trays were empty. Once the door closed Xavier sat down and helped himself to the heavenly creation's place before him. For the next twenty minutes, no sounds were made beyond those associated with the clinking of spoons against the bowls or the clinking of glasses against plates. You would think the silence would be awkward and stifling; instead, it conveyed a sense of camaraderie and acceptance.

After everyone had finished and the remnants of lunch had been removed, Castor suggested that everyone provide a summary of what they had discovered since the group had disbanded to tackle their assigned tasks. Felis went first as he was seated to the right of Castor. He clicked the remote for the projector, and the image of the young lady from the estate of Dr. Proctor appeared on the screen. He outlined the demographic information obtained during his and Panthera's interrogation of the subject.

Her name was Colleen O'Conner, her current age was seventeen, and she was born to Mary Margret Bryant and George Lyle O'Conner from Hershey, Pennsylvania. Further conversations and research established that she was an only child, and her father worked as a Mechanical Engineer for the Hershey Chocolate factory. Mary Margret, the mother, worked as a junior accountant for the same company.

According to the young lady, she was home doing homework in the kitchen, waiting for her parents to get off work. Apparently, they would often ride to and from work together. She heard a noise and suspected the neighbor's dog might be terrorizing her cat again; she got up to investigate. As she walked down the back steps, she claimed that someone grabbed her and placed a cloth over her mouth and nose.

The next thing she remembered was waking up in the locked room at the estate and demanding release. She stated that she was under the care of the same Doctor as Xavier and had also been diagnosed with PNH. She also did not know that the house belonged to Dr. Proctor. The young lady confirmed that she had been under his care since she was old enough to remember. Panthera nodded in agreement with Felis' assessment of their session with Colleen.

The following person to provide a summary was Sam. As with the two before, he confirmed everything that was said previously but was able to add some additional details, such as the fact the electronic signature and carbon footprint of the family was non-existent until the time of Colleen's birth. Any information before that time was either inaccessible or did not exist electronically, which was surprising given the prevalence of the digital age. Sam could not find any trace of where the O'Connor's were born, went to school, or married before moving to Hershey and having Colleen.

Jokingly Sam said, "Whoever covered their tracks should work for the FBI Federal Witness Protection Program."

Sam also added that it seemed neither of the parents had gone to the police to report Colleen missing. Instead, they told the school that Colleen would be visiting a sick uncle in California and asked if she could complete the last few months of her senior year via homeschooling. It was extremely puzzling, especially since the O'Connor's seemed to be a very loving family, according to Colleen. Everyone looked at Sam in confusion; everyone was thinking, "Why would two loving parents hide the fact their child had been kidnapped from their home?"

He then added a second layer to the mystery by mentioning that four days after Colleen was taken from her home, both her parents died in a freak accident where their car went off a cliff known as the Devil's Slide, located fifteen miles north of San Francisco, California. The couple's car was discovered three hundred feet down from the top of the cliff along the Pacific Coast Highway #1, and both individuals were pronounced dead at the scene. According to Sam no one was sure why they were in California after the kidnapping of their daughter, nor why twenty-four hours later, a family court judge in San Francisco County named Dr. Proctor her legal guardian.

Before Xavier could start his summary, Castor made a comment that stopped everyone in their tracks. "Colleen does not know that her parents are dead yet. After completing this round table discussion, Pollux and I will inform her of their passing. I feel that we must get what information we can from her before she is incapacitated by her grief over the death of her parents. So, after we finish this meeting, Pollux and I will temporally be unavailable to everyone. Colleen has the potential to be a great asset, but we need to handle her carefully now. Does anyone have any objections, asked Castor?" Everyone shook their head while maintaining their silence.

Xavier was the next person to provide a summary to the group; he started detailing how he had discovered that the files were labeled according to zodiac signs rather than individual names. Each zodiac sign had two folders; the zodiac signs with a bold, black X next to the name contained two birth certificates and two death certificates with the name redacted with thick black permanent marker. The folders with the Zodiac sign followed by a bold red star had two birth certificates, one death certificate, and the name redacted in bold black permanent marker.

He hypothesized that the folders with the bold black X indicated deceased test subjects due to the inclusion of two separate death certificates. However, the bold red stars consisted of current test subjects because there seemed to only be one death certificate, so the second birth certificate must apply to the current test subject. He also hypothesized that the birth certificate might belong to members of a particular family. This would indicate possible genetic mapping or testing centered upon one specific group of individuals.

Another thing Xavier noticed was that specific folders had an infinity symbol in the upper right corner with a number. The Zodiac signs were also paired with another Zodiac sign, such as Sagittarius being linked with Aries, and each had the infinity sign followed by a number. The pattern was also repeated with Virgo and Gemini. However, their infinity sign had the number two next to it. The entire setup reminded him of the animal husbandry studies and eugenics research conducted by Nazi Germany during World War II.

Pollux was the last person to present her summary of information, and she agreed with Xavier on his hypothesis for dividing the folders. However, her portion of the files was a little more difficult to decipher since the material required a key to break the code. She mentioned that she would like to do some background research on the Doctor and his family and see if that could help her break the code and decipher the materials in the files.

Castor cleared his throat, looking at the guard at the door, "Please bring the young lady here." Everyone looked expectantly towards the door.

Xavier's breath caught in his throat when he saw her enter the door. Her copper-red hair cascaded down her back in beautiful waves of red and gold. When he first saw Colleen, her complexion lacked color. Still, now her cheeks were tinged with a soft pink blush that complemented her overall appearance. Her rosebud lips were compressed together, reflecting her apprehension. This time instead of smelling like vanilla and peppermint, she smelled like a mixture of peaches and vanilla. Xavier could not tell which he liked better. The electric blue sweater, short sleeves, faded blue jeans, and sparkling white tennis shoes made him think she looked like the stereotypical girl next door.

Temporarily the welcoming smile turned to a frown when he realized that after this meet and greet had ended, so would her life as she knew it. The death of her parents would be devastating to most people, especially if they were a close-knit family like hers. While his parents were still alive, he felt empathy for her because he knew what it was like to have everything you know, and love turned upside down through no fault of your own; bad things did happen to good people.

"Ladies and Gentlemen, I would like to introduce Colleen O'Connor," said Castor as he gestured for her to sit between Xavier and Pollux. Moving to the indicated seat, she pulled out the chair and sat down, waiting for someone to challenge her right to be there.

Meanwhile, Xavier could not believe his luck; however, sitting next to her made it difficult to concentrate on what was happening. Colleen's voice was not what he had expected; instead of being soft and fragile like her appearance, it was solid and firm, revealing an inner strength she would need from this day forward.

Sitting next to Pollux and Xavier did little to ease the nervousness and anxiety that came off her in waves. Colleen took a deep breath and leaned forward with her hands firmly pressed together between her knees to hide the shaking of her hands.

"I want to thank you for helping me escape that house. I am not even sure why they grabbed me; besides being a straight "A" student on the Speech and Debate Team and the Mock Trial Team, I tend to live a quiet life. I have a few friends, and my teachers and parents agree I have the gift of gab. However, neither of my parents is well-known or wealthy," said Colleen.

Xavier looked at her and smiled, and said, "It's going to be ok; we will figure it out together." Without thinking, he reached out with his hand and patted the hand she had placed on the table before his comment. When his left hand touched her right hand, Colleen and Xavier gave a startled cry of surprise.

They started to reach for their left shoulders as pain raced across their shoulder blades and seemed to burn for five agonizing seconds. Leaning their heads simultaneously on the conference table, they struggled to understand what had just happened. Everyone in the room crowded around them as the combination of all their voices garbled their words of concern. The group moved back and gave Xavier and Colleen space as they lifted their heads and expelled a simultaneous sigh of relief.

Castor was the first to ask, "What happened?"

Xavier took a deep breath and looked at Colleen and said, "Ladies first." With a slight nod, she stated, "I felt a sharp pain across my left shoulder, and it felt like I was burned with a hot poker."

He nodded his head in agreement. "I also felt like my skin was on fire. But the fire seemed like it was spreading past the point of my tattoo," said Xavier.

Castor moved around the table, picked up the phone receiver, and asked Dr. Dorian and Dr. Kathrine to come to the conference room. The other group members assumed their original seats while glancing with concern towards the two teens. Once the door opened to admit Katherine and Dorian, Xavier noticed that Dorian again had the blue light device in his hands and that Katherine had her stethoscope hanging haphazardly from her white medical coat.

Her right hand had a black medical bag with the initials KGM. What was it, he wondered, with women and their need to personalize their accessories? Wait a minute, he thought, his gaze swinging back and forth between Dorian and Katherine. Were they married? Could the G be Katherine M. Grayson? It made sense that they would be a couple; it simplified things on the dating front.

Katherine went over to check Xavier first; she monitored his heart, took his pulse, and asked him to look at the light as she studied the dilation of his pupils.

"His pulse is slightly elevated, and pupils are also dilated, possibly a response to pain. So, have you had this reaction before she asked?"

Shaking his head, no, he remained quiet out of fear of disrupting the process. Once Katherine was done, Dorian motioned to Xavier to pull his shirt up above his shoulder blades until it rested on the back of his neck; the blood rushing to his face signaled his discomfort and embarrassment with the situation, mainly because Colleen was weirdly looking at him. Upon noticing the blush on his cheeks, Dorian realized he was embarrassed and suggested taking him to the next room to look at his shoulder. Getting up to follow Dorian, Xavier was silently thanking God for his timely suggestion.

The door closed behind the two, and Katherine moved over to Colleen and started doing an initial assessment as she had done on Xavier. When Katherine asked Colleen if she had had any problems with her shoulder before, she said "no" in response.

She stared at Katherine apprehensively; fear and worry were evident in her eyes. "Is my cancer back," Colleen asked?

Katherine looked towards Castor, and he nodded, affirming her unspoken request before she could respond to the question. Turning towards Colleen, she said, "I would like to do complete medical work on you before answering that question. It should give us a better idea of what happened with you and Xavier."

Castor then stood up and dismissed everyone. Pollux also stood and gathered her materials in preparation for leaving; however, before leaving, she decided to remind Castor that she expected to see him at five o'clock sharp for dinner. He kissed her cheek and assured her he would be there promptly. Pollux smiled; she knew that did not give her much time to dig into the doctor's family background. She also needed to work on deciphering the coded notes before the next meeting. Smiling to herself she reminded herself that she always did like a challenge.

The following day everyone gathered around the conference table and ate a hot breakfast in what had become the new norm for the group; Xavier noticed that the gang was all accounted for except for Colleen, who was conspicuously absent. He looked at Dorian on his left and asked, "Where is Colleen?"

After wiping his mouth and placing the linen napkin on his lap, Dorian responded, "Castor and Pollux broke the news about her parents to her last night after we finished all our tests. I was told she took it hard and refused dinner last night. I highly doubt she will be here for breakfast."

Before he had completed his assessment of the situation, the door opened, and Castor, Pollux, and Colleen walked in. Her eyes were still red-rimmed and puffy from the lack of sleep and excessive crying. Xavier hastily stood up, pulled out the chair next to him, and gestured for her to sit down.

She gave a weak, watery smile as she sat down and reached for a cup of milk and two pieces of dry brown toast. An intelligent choice, Xavier thought, considering how long she had gone without eating. He, however, had no qualms about devouring the feast set before him and placed a little bit of everything on his plate; eggs, toast, bagel and cream cheese, scrambled eggs, and white gravy with sausage on the side, followed by a large glass of freshly squeezed orange juice minus the pulp.

The silence in the room was comfortable and non-threatening as everyone satisfied the demands of their stomach. Once he had almost completed his feast, he turned his head and momentarily looked around the table, wondering how he got so lucky to find the people he needed to help him.

His gaze lingered on Colleen; his mind was full of unanswered questions. How she fit into all this mess? Why did he and Colleen experience pain in their left shoulder when they touched it? What did it all mean? Would he ever honestly know what all this was about?

His musing was interrupted by a soft touch upon his sleeve. Instead of repeating the pain he had experienced when she first touched him, he felt a warm, peaceful feeling of contentment envelop him. He had never felt this strong sense of peace and serenity, even with his family and friends. It made him momentarily forget all the non-stop worries that seemed to circle in his head like a record player set to repeat. Looking towards Colleen, he waited for her to speak.

"Is it Xavier," she asked? Her soft-spoken whisper made him wish for things that, as a stranger, he had no right to expect, much less wish for in the secret recess of his mind and heart. He wondered if they would go their separate ways after everything was said and done or just remain friends; nothing more, nothing less. Part of him felt like a weirdo for having such a crush on a girl he just meet while another part felt a connection he could not deny.

"Yes," he said. I just want to say that if you need anything, let me know."

Her pensive expression was the only sign indicating she understood what he meant.

Just then, Castor stood up and raised his goblet of orange juice into the air. "People, before we move on to the conversation of what we have learned and where we go from here, let us raise our glasses and welcome Colleen and Xavier to our little band of deviants. Together we will decipher the clues surrounding Xavier's past. In addition, Colleen, while you are new to our merry band of misfits, you are more than welcome to call this place home and us your family until you decide you don't need us or want us." Everyone laughed at Castor's attempt to lighten the mood.

Colleen lowered her head as a slight blush tinged her cheekbones. Her shyness only made her seem more adorable to Xavier. The kitchen serving staff started to remove all the empty dishes, glasses, and silverware; they silently weaved in, out, and around everyone. To Xavier, it seemed like a graveyard had more noise than the conference room at that moment in time.

Once the kitchen staff had cleaned away everything and left the room, Pollux stood up and broke the prolonged silence.

"Through a little reading between the lines, researching the doctor's family, with Sam's data algorithm and Dorian's assistance, I determined that the files were written based on a cryptography code. A key is required to enable others to read the materials. Not to bore anyone or make it too complicated, but I discovered during my research of the doctor's family he had severe mommy issues that would rival those of the famous serial killer Edmund Kemper mommy issues. I also learned that the doctor's undergraduate degree was in Greek and Roman literature. Once I discovered that it made sense that the key was somehow embedded in the Athenian tragedy ***Oedipus Tyrannus***. It is now possible to translate the files and dig deeper," she said.

Pollux turned towards the screen and activated the monitor, and Sam dimmed the lights in the room. The screen displayed what looked like an astrology chart, but instead of twelve signs, there were thirteen signs and symbols. Still, none of the images looked like the symbols commonly attributed to the zodiac signs.

Xavier raised his hand and tilted his head to the side. Colleen thought it made him look like a curious little puppy. He looked more like a dog than a cat person; he was too friendly and forthcoming toward others to be a cat. If she had to pick a dog breed for him, she would choose either an American Cocker Spaniel, an English springer spaniel or maybe a cute little beagle. She could imagine him with a puppy with some unusual name, playing fetch in the park surrounded by other people enjoying warm summer days full of sunshine and laughter as they made memories.

She could not understand why she felt so drawn to this young man she had never met until 24 hours ago. The connection between them was getting stronger the more they interacted. The only time she did not feel overwhelmed by grief about losing her parents was when she was near Xavier. Just being in the same room with him seemed to mute the intense grief she was experiencing; it was the only time she felt like she was not losing her mind and drowning in sorrow.

Colleen's thoughts were interrupted when Pollux asked, "Yes, Xavier, what is it?"

After clearing his throat, he lowered his hand and asked. "Shouldn't there only be twelve zodiac signs, and the sign or symbols depending on how you look at it, are different from your standard astrology chart."

"I agree with your observation. However," said Pollux, "the Babylonians started with thirteen signs, and it was decided to exclude Ophiuchus. The date for this sign is from November 29 to December 17. Individuals born under this sign are believed to have a great sense of humor, eagerness to learn, and a strong attachment to family life and values. The zodiac symbol consists of a man represented by a U with a squiggly line representing a snake through the middle." Suddenly, she stopped and looked towards Xavier; "how many did you say Dr. Proctor tell you were diagnosed with PNH in the world?" She asked.

Xavier temporarily looked confused, "he told me that only thirteen individuals in the world had PNH." He could tell when everyone else in the room started to think the same thing he was based on their facial expressions.

Pollux shook her head, affirming the conclusion everyone had come to, "It is suspicious that of the thirteen patients with PNH, all of them are his patients. Especially since two other specialists in the world could potentially treat these individuals. Additionally, everyone one of the thirteen patients has been going to him from the time they were a few months old until they reached the age of majority. The "Zodiac Thirteen," as they are referred to by their charts, have either just turned eighteen or will do so in the next six months to a year."

Sam took Pollux's place as she sat down, "While Pollux was uncovering a gold mine of information, I went through the audio recording of the baby cam that Xavier had placed in the flowers at the memorial; lucky for us someone moved the flowers from the church and placed them in a separate area of the house for the family to do with as they may."

"Well, I can tell you," said Xavier, "that most of the flowers will be dead within a month, if not quicker, my mom is notorious for having the black thumb of death. Knowing my friends, I guarantee there will be a betting pool on how long they will last once she starts caring for them. I should have Matt and Packer put some money down for me," said Xavier.

"Dude, morbid much," responded Sam. "No, seriously," said Xavier, "I am not exaggerating my mother's ability to kill plants. The woman is great with children and animals but not so much with plants."

Ignoring Xavier's last comment, Sam continued with his presentation of information. "The audio from the baby cam gave a little more information, but we are unsure how it fits in with the rest of the current information. The doctor was overheard talking to Rosalee Trudel, who told her that Xavier's development had followed the standard guidelines previously established by subject Leo. He also mentions that, just like Leo, he estimated that the new serum they had developed would simulate the extreme stress needed to trigger the emergence of his talents. The rest of the audio confirms what Xavier had told Castor and Pollux," said Sam.

At that point, he handed the remote off to Dorian as he left his seat and walked up to the screen. The image of the tattoo from Xavier's left shoulder appeared on the left side of the monitor, followed by the commonly accepted Gemini symbol on the right side.

Dorian looked towards Xavier, "Before I summarize our findings, I want to mention that as I looked at the files and helped Sam and Pollux, I was reminded of your tattoo. After comparing what we could determine by decoding the doctor's notes and the information on the charts, we determined that the tattoo symbol on your left shoulder matches up with the Gemini sign on the astrology charts. This also verifies that you are one of the thirteen patients we call the "Zodiac Thirteen," said Dorian.

Xavier was startled by the knowledge imparted by Pollux and Dorian's discoveries of his being one of the Zodiac Thirteen patients. The screen transitioned to another image of a tattoo similar to his. Still, on the right, the zodiac sign bore the label Scorpio.

At that moment, Dorian turned to Colleen and made a surprising statement. "The patient labeled Scorpio also has a similar tattoo on her left shoulder, and we have been able to ascertain that the subject is a female approximately 17 years old, born November 25."

Colleen's startled reaction to the date alerted Xavier that the date meant something to her. Watching her face, Xavier intuitively realized she was also one of the Zodiac Thirteen.

He felt terrible for her because her life was about to get crazier than she could imagine. He wondered if that was why he felt such a connection to her, and did she also feel the same weird connection? If so, would she welcome being involuntarily tethered to him? He knew that once Pandora's Box was opened, there would be no turning back from the path destiny had plotted for them. Life was so much easier when he only had to worry about scoring well on college admission tests and picking out what he planned to wear to his senior prom.

Dorian's following statement confirmed Xavier's suspicions. "Colleen, you are patient, Scorpio," said Dorian.

Her brow furrowed in confusion as she looked at the others in the room. "Wait, we may share the same birthday, but that doesn't mean I am patient, Scorpio," she said in surprise.

At that moment, he replaced the previous image with another image; Instead of just one, it looked like a combination of the Scorpio image merged with the tattoo from Xavier's shoulder. This confused Xavier as he struggled to decipher the possible meaning behind merging the two tattoos.

Dorian's response shocked Colleen into silence. "You do have a tattoo based on the notes in the folder; it is in the same place as Xavier's. We, Pollux, and I theorize that your tattoo looked like the original Scorpio tattoo image but that somehow when you and Xavier touched, it produced a merging of the two tattoos," he said.

This last statement startled Xavier; did that mean his tattoo had changed in response to meeting Colleen, as did hers? How did something like this happen, and would there be negative repercussions?

"No, I do not have a tattoo; I would have known about it," said Colleen.

Her words reminded Xavier of his initial denial of having a tattoo; he, too, had been confused and scared. To ease her discomfort, Xavier reached for her right hand and turned her towards him. The heat of his body and the soft, gentle touch instantly calmed her tumultuous emotions and thoughts. The sense of warmth and security she felt with him was becoming addictive. She silently wondered how she would cope with him returning to his life once everything was resolved. Would she become a footnote in the next chapter of his life, ignored and forgotten?

Xavier cleared his throat and continued to hold her chilled hands in his warmer ones; his grip was gentle and reminded her of cold winter days sipping hot cocoa and relaxing on the couch under a multitude of blankets in front of a crackling fireplace.

"Colleen, the tattoo was put on you as a small child. The tattoo is undetectable unless you use a specific type of blue light and know where to look for it. I also have one on my left shoulder. I was unaware of its existence until Dorian and Katherine discovered it by accident," said Xavier.

"While we currently do not know the true purpose of the tattoo or the significance of the tattoo location. We know more now than when I first came to see Castor. I also know that we will keep looking and digging until we discover what is going on and eliminate the threat the doctor may pose to us," he said.

As Xavier comforted Colleen, Dorian relinquished the floor to Castor. "Xavier is correct about what he said. We are going to keep searching for answers," he said.

The screen again changed, bringing everyone's attention back to the front of the room. An image of a woman Xavier had never seen before graced the screen; she had long black hair cut in style reminiscent of a young schoolgirl with bangs stopping along the upper ridge of her matching black framed glasses. Her brown eyes radiated intelligence: they were medium brown and resembled the honey commonly found in the Midwestern United States. Flecks of gold and green broke up the dark color of her eyes and hinted at a compassionate nature.

Her slender build would have made her look malnourished if not for the white doctor coat she wore, adding bulk to her petite frame. Her black turtleneck sweater made her complexion appear washed out and lifeless. A person could not help wondering if her appearance resulted from ignorance of current fashion trends, supreme indifference to her appearance, or a combination of both.

Castor continued the briefing, "During the raid on the estate and the subsequent rescue of Colleen, I placed monitoring devices among some of the doctor's things."

He then explained how the listening devices were designed to remain dormant until certain words were spoken. The inactive feature enabled the devices to stay undetected by potential scans. Instead of transmitting data via radio waves, they piggybacked any individual's wireless phone network within one hundred feet of the device.

The more wireless phones available, the less likely anyone would be able to pinpoint the location of the devices due to their jumping from one wireless phone to another. Then if any information were needed to be sent back to the individuals monitoring the devices, it would be hidden within the network IP signal to avoid detection.

After receiving the transmission, it could only be decoded using a crypto key known to the individual who placed the device. The owners of the machines could also remotely reprogram the units to wake up more often by including other word choices. This allowed for fine-tuning the device and enabled battery conservation while eliminating the need to peruse useless data.

Turning towards the screen, Castor said, "This is Kendra Parodine, an associate of Dr Procter. She also works for the CITRUM industry. Based on the conversations we recorded after we rescued Colleen, we determined that she was likely the individual Colleen's parents were planning to meet in California after their daughter's abduction. Based on her bio, she is a geneticist specializing in embryo development and genetic mutations. It is currently unknown what she is working on because of the high level of security clearance associated with it."

"We summarize that it may involve a government contract or be related to industrial technology research and development. We also know that Dr. Procter hates her passionately and desperately wants to take over her position as head of research and development of CITRUM. Pollux and I agreed that we needed to find a safe way of contacting   Ms. Parodine; this would require Colleen to see her personally. However, at this time, we need to put this mission on the back burner until after we have infiltrated the Clinic and retrieved some additional files," said Castor.

Virgo: IX

Sam, unlike the others, chose not to stand up; instead, he outlined his plan for infiltrating the Clinic from his seat. Leaning forward to address Xavier and Colleen he outlined how between the help of Pollux's off-the-book contacts at the CIA and his hacking abilities, he was going to create a fake identity and background under the name of Samuel Murray. He planned to apply for the position of Central Sterile Manager at the Clinic.

The previous manager's mother was ill and was being admitted to hospice care and was taking a brief leave of absence. Sam, as temporary CSM, would oversee all the surgical technicians in the facility and maintain state-mandated sterilization records according to OSHA standards. Once it was safe, Sam would insert a program that would covertly make duplicate copies of all computer files.

Castor briefly interrupted Sam, "after the program's installation, I will pose as the official auditor from OSHA and notify the Clinic that Sam's credentials had been previously revoked due to failure to comply with government standards. Sam will protest that his previous employers and the government are out to get him. Any objections made will make him seem irresponsible and incompetent while providing him with a way to leave the job without raising suspicions."

Xavier raised his free hand while still clutching Colleen hand.

"What will Colleen and I be doing while Sam is infiltrating the Clinic," he asked.

Colleen smiled, pleased he had included her in that statement, which made her feel less alone. Intellectually she knew she was not alone, but it felt that way emotionally. In retrospect, she knew she would never wish these circumstances on her worst enemy; having someone close to her own age and going through a similar experience made it slightly easier to cope.

Even though she was staying in one of the bedrooms in the same Condominium as Xavier, she had spent most of her time crying and feeling sorry for herself after Castor and Pollux told her about her parents' death. The grief was still overwhelming but manageable when she was close to Xavier.

Later when she was alone and capable of managing her emotions, she would examine these new feelings towards Xavier. Who knows, she thought by the time everything was all said and done, she might come out of this with some new friends.

Castor's response to Xavier's question was not one Colleen had been expecting to say the least.

"Xavier, I want you and Colleen to start training with Felis and Panthera; you must be able to defend yourselves if you will continue participating in future missions. I know it will take years to get as good as Felis and Panthera, but I don't doubt they will be able to whip you into shape at least enough to defend yourself and help with some of the less risky assignments."

While everyone gathered their stuff and headed out of the conference room. Colleen and Xavier hung back, allowing everyone in the room to leave before them; just as they were ready, Panthera and Felis walked over to them. Both teenagers looked at each other in apprehension.

Xavier rarely felt this discomfort; everything in school had always come easy to him. But in hindsight, he had to admit he only had to make a little effort to achieve the AB honor roll. Even the ACT exam in school had been a breeze. All Xavier ever wanted was to go to college, join the Navy and travel the world, come back home, go to graduate school for Law, become a famous attorney one day, and even get an appointment to the United States Supreme Court as Chief Justice. Instead, he was about to be tormented by Castor's professional security advisors. If asked to pick which advisor was scarier, it would be difficult to pinpoint which one.

Panthera was the first to speak, "Colleen, you will be working with me learning how to defend yourself, and Xavier will be working with Felis. The curriculum we developed will play upon your strengths and minimize your potential weaknesses. By the end of the day, Felis and I will work out a detailed schedule covering fitness, nutrition, self-defense, military strategy, and anything else we deem fit; exhaustion will become the norm for both of you. So, I suggest you enjoy yourself for the rest of the day, and we will see you tomorrow at 3:30 am."

Just as he was getting ready to leave, he was stopped by Felis' unexpected comment.

"Xavier, you will also be placed on a high protein, low carb diet so we can build up your core strength and tone your frame. Training is important but so is nutrition and so we will focus extensively on the four main components."

Xavier groaned mentally and prayed that he would survive the various levels of hell he was about to experience at the hands of his new trainer.

"This will be your last supper, so to speak, so you may want to enjoy some carbs before tomorrow," Felix said. The slight smile he gave seemed ominous; as he slapped Xavier on his shoulder causing him to lose his balance; this was definitely not a good omen.

Colleen and Xavier took this last statement as a form of dismissal. They walked towards the corridor, leading them back to their rooms. Upon entering the Condominium's living area, Collen moved towards the island in the kitchen area and set out two plates, glasses, and silverware before turning towards the refrigerator and retrieving a cherry-covered Cheesecake.

Xavier pulled out one of the breakfast stools and calmly accepted a piece from her. His mind was not really focused on the Cheesecake; instead, all he could think about was that he would be unable to coast through the training as he did with many things in his life.

"Cheer up, I know it will be rough, but you should not worry. I have faith in you," said Colleen. "When I first came here, I was a total mess, and while it may not seem as if I noticed anything beyond my grief, I did. I noticed that you were calm and collected during the briefings. Then there were the snatches of conversation I overheard from others. I have no doubt that you will do what is needed to make it through to the end."

Xavier looked at her in surprise; his fork hovered halfway to his mouth, the Cheesecake all but forgotten.

"You must believe in the patron saint of lost causes, St. Jude," he said before devouring the cherry cheesecake. A smile graced his face belying the seriousness of his statement.

"Yum, this is really good," he said as he savored another bite with his eyes closed to maximize the taste and texture; it was indeed a slice of heaven.

Colleen smiled and said, "What would you like to do tonight, what with it being our true last night of freedom? I thought we would watch a movie or some retro flicks. I like Abbot and Castello and Jerry Lee Lewis, or if I am in a particularly sour mood, I watch I Love Lucy."

Xavier laughed, "I love Lucy; my friend Matthew and Packer tease me constantly about my obsession with the red-headed comedy queen. That is why I always secretly fancied redheads." His eyes widened in surprise as he abruptly stopped talking. "Did I say that last part out loud?"

A pink blush slowly moved from the bottom of Colleen's neckline towards her forehead, deepening in color as it progressed. Turning her head, she coughed to disguise her discomfort with the conversation's direction. Ignoring the whispered question, she continued talking as if she had never heard it.

"Then that is settled; you go find I love Lucy, and I will make us some popcorn and fix us some drinks in preparation for our movie marathon," she said.

Xavier thanked his lucky stars and took off into the living room, hoping he had not ruined his chances with Colleen.

Xavier's first thought was that the morning could have looked more promising, especially when you were required to get up before dawn. Felis and Panthera woke the two teenagers up at 3:30 am; both were highly embarrassed when they realized they had fallen asleep together on the couch watching I Love Lucy sometime during the night.

He imagined that they must have resembled a litter of puppies with limbs going every which way and, in some cases, defying the laws of physics. It was gratifying to know that Colleen was just as out of it as he was, and the best thing to do was to pretend it never happened.

The exercise room the two teenagers were led to did not resemble the image in their heads. When someone mentioned an exercise room, you imagined a 10 x 12 room capable of fitting a full-size bed and dresser with a small end table. Instead, the room seemed cavernous; if asked, Xavier would estimate it was the size of a high school gymnasium, just without the bleachers.

On the left of the doorway was a fully functional NordicTrack Fusion CST Pro with free weights and a weight bench next to it. To the right of the door were a treadmill and stair-climbing machine. Just in front of the door, located on the far wall, was an indoor rock wall that extended from the base of the floor to just a hand-width distance from the ceiling rafters.

In case the treadmill and stair stepper was busy, there was a red tape outline circling the gym's perimeter, the distance between the inner red tape line and the out red tape line created a running lane for those interested in working on their cardio endurance. The piece de resistance of the entire gym was the sparing ring in the middle, cordoned off with padded poles and ropes with padded inlays on the floor no more than one inch thick. The slim padding provided enough cushion to allow for physical contact sparing, martial arts, and boxing based on the need of the individual or collective training schedules.

Each section of the gym was currently occupied by individuals wearing generic Navy-blue t-shirts and gray shorts like the ones provided to him by Felis. Xavier was grateful that most of the occupants ignored his entrance as they continued to train or exercise. He hoped with all his heart that his introduction to self-defense would include something other than sparing, martial arts, or boxing, especially if Felis was his opponent. With a sigh, he turned and walked towards where Felis was standing watching two other individuals fight hand to hand each determined to immobilize the other.

Xavier asked Felis, "What are we going to do first."

Felis gave him a sinister smile, followed by a chuckle that had the potential to develop into an evil laugh. "Well, I think the first thing we will do is assess your level of physical fitness."

Xavier felt slightly relieved only to wish he had not gotten up this morning when Felis pointed to the red running lane along the gym's perimeter and said, "Twenty laps should do it.

" Now Xavier knew he was genuinely going to be made to suffer. Timidly he asked, "What about warming up before I start running?"

Felis laughed and chose not to answer his question, motioning him with his right hand to get started.

As Xavier started to run, he noticed Colleen entering the gym with Panthera next to her. He wondered how she had the same amount of sleep as he did, but she looked better than he did this morning. He heard Panthera tell her to start running, minus the evil chuckle. Slowly Colleen began to gain on him; she was faster than he thought. After about five minutes, she ran alongside him with a bright smile. She was enjoying the run; with a shudder, he reflected that he would rather have swum laps instead of running any day of the week.

"Don't you love running? I could do it daily; I used to run mini marathons in Pennsylvania. My mom would sign us up for the Rock n Roll mini-marathon series, and we would pick each run based on whether we had ever visited the city before," said Colleen.

With a distinct grimace, Xavier responded. "I am more of a swimmer and less of a runner. I do not particularly appreciate sweating and smelling like body odor. The great thing about swimming is that you do not do either, or at least not to the point you notice."

Just as he completed that sentence, Felis bellowed for them to stop socializing and pick up their pace. Both teenagers abruptly clamped their mouths shut and kicked it into gear. Instinctively Xavier knew they would be lucky if they found time to talk again, get a hot meal, or get extra sleep before everything started the next day again.

On day twenty-one of Xavier's training sessions with Felis, he finally started feeling confident about his ability to care for himself in a worst-case scenario. He still did not like running, but he had now learned how to use basic self-defense moves such as boxing and Ju Jitsu. The key to using this form of martial arts was to know when to use ground fighting techniques, grappling moves, or submission holds. His ability to defeat Felis was still in serious doubt but not so for the average thug.

Xavier excelled the most in analyzing and assessing his opponent's weaknesses. One of the first things Felis taught him was that strategy was just as important as physical prowess, if not more. The public announcement system interrupted his train of thought as Castor made the announcement to assemble for the weekly afternoon meeting.

Walking towards the locker room, Xavier could not help but notice the changes those three weeks had brought for Colleen as well. She seemed more confident; her friendship with Panthera had progressed to the point that it looked like they were now sharing clothes. She had slimmed down and toned up in all the right places. If he were honest with himself, he would have to admit that his feelings for her were getting stronger each day.

Most days consisted of running from 3:30 am to 5:00 am, sparing from 5-8 am, lifting weights from 8-12, and having lunch at 12:30 pm. Then later, all trainees would come together to receive instruction in strategy and advance military tactics and other academic materials. Once class was dismissed, there would be an updated meeting in the conference room, followed by supper and an hour of socialization before crawling into bed due to extreme exhaustion. Through it all, Xavier had little time to wonder how his parents, Will, and his friends were handling his death; instead, he focused on making it step by step, inch by inch.

Once everyone had assembled in the conference room, Castor started the meeting by welcoming Sam back from his undercover mission and congratulated him for successfully accessing and copying the digital files without being detected. Sam stood and bowed in recognition of the accolades attributed to his completion of employment with Dr. Procter. After Sam sat down, Castor informed the group that Sam's work uncovered a gold mine of information related to the Zodiac thirteen.

The room exploded into a frenzy of noise as those in the room started talking loudly; their voices overlapped in excitement; Castor held up his hand, signaling for silence. Once everyone had settled down and redirected their attention to him, he asked Sam to outline some pertinent information.

Sam again stood up and directed everyone's attention to the screen as a map of the continental United States popped up on the screen with a miniature replica of Xavier's and Colleen's tattoo marking Chicago, Illinois. Looking out towards the audience, he detailed how the records were used to locate what states the other twelve lived in, the age range, and the gender of each patient.

However, they did not know everyone's name or address; instead, they were labeled based on their Zodiac sign. Both Castor and Sam agreed that the next step was identifying the legal name and addresses of the other eleven individuals. The red tattoo pins represented the males, and the blues represented the females. Sam continued to explain that according to the files, there were seven females and six males, with two in Florida, three in California, one in Wisconsin, one in New Mexico, one in Maine, two in Iowa, and one in Montana.

The following slide showed a graph tracking the approximate age of everyone, with the female known as Leo being the oldest at the age of twenty-three and the youngest being Colleen at seventeen. The age gap between the Zodiac thirteen patients was based on seven years with a ratio of 10 to 16. The presentation ended with an image of each zodiac sign with the age, birthday, gender, and state location listed underneath.

While Sam activated the lights and turned off the presentation screen, Castor turned to address Colleen and Xavier. "While you two have been training and working on your abilities and strategy, we have pinpointed the best location for Colleen to meet with Kendra Parodine without alerting those at CITRUM."

Pollux, at this point, started to detail the biographical information obtained from her numerous off-the-book contacts at the CIA. Based on the information provided, it was determined that Dr. Parodine was a widow whose husband and daughter were killed due to a house fire a week before Christmas in 2014. Before the fire, she attended a Genetic conference in Denver, Colorado. At that time, she was approached by headhunters for CITRUM Industries.

She turned down their offer of employment based on her desire to enable her husband to keep a job he loved and allow her daughter Angelina to have a secure home life and school environment. The local fire Marshall ruled that the fire resulted from faulty wiring in a set of old lights that came with the original Christmas tree.

My contacts speculate that the fire may have been arson. Still, once the Fire Marshall had submitted his report, the remains of the home were demolished due to the potential hazard it represented to the children in the neighborhood. Within a week of the information being filed with the district attorney's office, the Marshall came into a significant amount of money, suddenly retired, relocated to Belize, and later died in a hit-and-run accident in the capital city. The accident has yet to be solved, and the only description provided by witnesses included a massive male with blonde hair cut close to the scalp.

Dr. Parodine did not accept the position with CITRUM right away. Instead, she worked with her previous employer for another five years. The medical reports my contact forwarded to me detail her battle with depression, extreme weight gain, suicidal ideation, and post-traumatic disorder; (PTSD). The loss of her child and her husband almost destroyed her.

Then, for some unknown reason, she relocated to California and accepted a job with CITRUM Industries. She works twelve to fifteen hours daily, lives alone, and shuns human contact and relationships. She has no pets, plants, or anything beyond work, so arranging to meet with Colleen's parents after her abduction is suspicious. Pollux proceeded to sit down and turn over the floor to Castor.

"Colleen, this is why we think that the only way we can get Dr. Parodine to talk to us is if we send you and Xavier to speak with her," said Castor. "While we do not know why your parents wanted to see her, we know she had dropped everything to meet with them. She paid for both of their funerals and arranged for everything in your house to be packed and stored."

"What are you talking about?" asked Colleen. Her stunned expression demonstrated her surprise and puzzlement at the new turn of events. Things were happening so fast that when she thought she had a handle on everything, a new development would result in confusion and chaos. She missed her quiet and peaceful existence with her parents, friend, and cat Michelangelo.

Castor folded his hands in front of him; looking at Pollux for assistance, he motioned for her to answer the question.

"Well, from what we know, your mom and dad had no other family except for you. According to your parents, she was to be the executor of their estate if they passed away before you reached eighteen or if there were no direct heirs. Since you are still seventeen, according to the state of Pennsylvania, she was made your guardian and executor. However, Dr. Proctor was also appointed your guardian in California, and it looks like he did not inform the court of your parents' request for guardianship to be given to Dr. Parodine," said Pollux.

"Wait," said Colleen, panicking, causing her voice to raise two octaves above her usual tone. "I don't want to live with that psychopath or with a woman I never met, I lost my family, and I am just now feeling like I have found people I can call friends and possibly family as well."

Colleen with each passing second, became increasingly agitated and emotional to the point of dissolving into tears.

Xavier patted her on the left shoulder directly over the tattoo. A warm, soothing feeling traveled from the top of her left shoulder blade to the rest of her body, slowly eliminating the panic and fear that threatened to overwhelm her and reducing her to a basket case.

He leaned in close and whispered in her ear, "No one is trying to force you out or make you live with a total stranger. The only thing Castor and Pollux are asking is that we see her, get a few answers, and figure out the next step towards solving the enigma of the Zodiac Thirteen."

Colleen gave a tentative smile and nodded to acknowledge what he said. "Well, now that everyone is up to speed with what is happening, please locate either Pollux or me to discuss your next assignment. However, I would like Felis, Panthera, Colleen, and Xavier to stay behind and work out the travel details for the trip to California," said Castor.

Everyone stood up, collected their materials, and left the room, each heading to their respective work areas within the facility.

Once the last of the stragglers left the room and shut the door, Castor turned towards the rest of the assembled individuals.

"I have spoken with your trainers, and from what they have shared with me, it is agreed that you two should be able to meet Dr. Parodine, provided you have the appropriate support structure in place. So, both trainers will travel with you, and we will message the good doctor requesting a meet and greet."

"Colleen, we need to send the doctor something to prove you are contacting her. I think a picture of you holding today's newspaper and a lock of your hair should be enough to convince her of the message's authenticity," said Pollux.

"I also suggest you go and pack the appropriate attire, so you do not stand out in the crowd. Include some clothing that will make you less visible in an emergency. Everyone must be ready by this Friday to fly to San Raphael."

The teenagers and the adults immediately started discussing possible strategies for the upcoming trip. Together they started brainstorming ways to get a message to the doctor after reviewing surveillance information obtained by an unknown operative in her Condominium and at her place of employment. Everyone knew it would be difficult to make contact considering the extent of her social disconnect from others and her being a severe workaholic.

Castor chose that moment to provide Xavier with individual instructions to reapply the tribal tattoo on his face when in San Raphael and pull his hair back, so he was not so easily identified.

On the day of their flight, Xavier and Colleen waited next to their trainers by the curb in front of the Clinic; their matching black duffle bags were packed with everything they would need for the next four days. A black Cadillac from the Kratos collection slowly moved into place along the curb in front of the Clinic. The black tinted windows made it impossible to determine the number of individuals in the vehicle and who was driving unless you stood directly in front of the windshield. None of the doors had a lock in the handles, and the rims of the tires were a solid black and perfectly matched the rest of the vehicle.

Based on a conversation Xavier had with the person in charge of maintaining and purchasing the fleet of cars used by Castor and his company, he knew that the vehicles were well-equipped to handle any situation and could act as a mobile command center with continuous Satellite access for Biophones and internet usage. Castor's company figured out a way to guarantee internet access 24/7 by using a relay system with an antenna embedded into the paint of the SUV extending from the front bumper to the back bumper. The unique makeup of the paint also provided camouflage by reflecting the surrounding environment's images onto the car's skin through a coating of specialized paint, an industrial trade secret manufactured at an undisclosed facility in the southern part of Alabama.

The middle partition of tinted glass that separated the driver from the back was designed to act as a self-contained laptop with a holographic keyboard keyed to the individual person's Biophone. The entire car was a workaholic's dream come true, designed to provide a continuous working environment. However, if a person did not want to work but decided to take the day off and relax or surf the web, they could do that through a voice control command system.

Most technicians referred to the car by its nickname B2 after the story's title, "Beauty and the Beast." The vehicle's ability to withstand a bomb, gunfire, and surface-to-ground missile made it a beast. The classical and understated design of the vehicle's outer shell revealed its beautiful and classical appearance. The name fits the vehicle's capabilities and appearance with a capital T.

The forty-one-minute drive from the Clinic along East Marquette Road to the Midway Airport, a private airstrip used by Castor's company, consisted of a detailed briefing on mission guidelines and need-to-know information. It had been decided during the last meeting that the best way to travel undetected was under the guise of a nuclear family. The stated purpose of the trip was to allow the two teenagers an opportunity to complete a college visit to the Dominican University of California.

The arranged meeting between Colleen and Dr. Parodine was outside San Raphael at an out-of-the-way location. The group would stay at CiderLane Farm and Cottage, along Highway 1 in Tomales. The site was chosen because it had a little cottage where they could wait; the farm was isolated and provided an elevated landform to watch for suspicious activity. It would minimize the chances of either Colleen or Xavier being recognized by those employed by Dr. Proctor or CITRUM. The farm also had a back entrance they could use if the need arose.

The message for Dr. Parodine had been placed in a supply box of packaged food from the food delivery service Home Chef. Included with the instructions for food preparation was an encoded video with a pre-recorded message explaining the reason for the meeting and a picture of Colleen holding a newspaper with the current date and additional information on how to respond to and receive details of the proposed meet and greet.

The four-hour and forty-minute flight would see them arriving at the CiderLane Cottage around supper time with plenty of time to eat, bathe, and prepare for the meeting scheduled for Sunday at noon. Panthera and Felis planned on getting friendly with the proprietors to cement their cover story. Afterward, the group would continue their stay until Monday to complete the proposed college visit, explore one or two more tourist sites, eat dinner, and catch their flight to Chicago at around six.

Xavier looked out the window as Colleen slept in the seat beside him, resting her head heavily on his shoulder. The warmth of her rhythmic breathing started to lull him to sleep; only by focusing on the tiny specks of civilizations down below was he able to resist the sandman's hypnotic pull and avoid anxiety-filled dreams. He had never traveled this far from home without his family, which made him nostalgic for family trips.

He vowed that when he has reunited with his family again, he will never take them for granted. He would stop complaining about the many family memories his mother insisted on making. It made him realize that people only appreciate what they once had only after you no longer have it. The sudden heaviness in his heart threatened to suffocate him.

In an attempt to distract himself and break the cycle of morbid thoughts he looked around the cabin. The plane was beyond anything he had ever experienced, with the seats made of genuine leather and the ability to transform into a recliner. A projector screen was placed in front of the cabin door leading to the cock pit with surround sound speaker capabilities. The plane also had the same capabilities as the B2 and could work as a mobile command center.

Panthera and Felis sat across the aisle just opposite them, their heads bent together as they spoke to each other in softly whispered tones. Repeatedly they dissected the plan, reviewing each detail and checking for potential mistakes. Looking at the two trainers, he was struck by the oxymoron they represented, especially as it applied to their names. Xavier looked at Felis and Panthera, his curiosity overriding his common sense; he just had to know.

Xavier moderated the volume of his voice to keep from waking up Colleen.

"How did you acquire your unique code names," he asked.

"Felis, your name refers to a small, domesticated house cat. While on the other hand, Panthera's name refers to big cats such as leopards and panthers. Whoever chose your code names had a wicked sense of humor, or they were highly sadistic," he said with suppressed laughter.

Panthera smiled and chuckled as Felis face palmed himself and made a defeated groan. "Go ahead, tell him; I know you are dying to tell him the story," said Felis.

Moving the files and important papers to the adjacent seat, she launched into a tale that made all the hell Felis put him through during training well worth it. According to Panthera, they both went through the academy together. However, you would never know it because Felis looked older than Panthera, what with the liberal amount of gray hair he supported.

Mentally reminding himself to focus on this once-in-a-lifetime story, Xavier listened as she continued her narration.

"Everyone was gathered in a central location on the first training day, waiting for the instructors to arrive. As with any event, some individuals felt the need to act like posers and brag about their physical and mental prowess to make others feel inferior. Somehow or another, the braggarts started making bets on who would be first in the class and who would be runner-up," she said. The reference to the battle of David and Goliath morphed into a panther versus a house cat,"

"The instructors had, by this time, snuck up on the noisy cadets and decided to have a little fun. They put up a chart with randomly assigned numbers and tracked each point the cadets earned. In the meantime, a betting pool started between the cadets and the rest of the facility, trying to predict who would acquire the code name Panther and who would become the house cat. As you guessed, I won the cadet competition and was named Panther, but I added an A to make it more feminine, and Felis was runner-up."

Felis momentarily paused, piping up, "Don't forget to tell him how you rubbed my nose into my defeat. You bet on yourself; that is not fair. "

"Oh, phish posh, I did no such thing," said Panthera. "I cannot help that I won a couple grand in the betting pool. All is fair in love and war, darling."

Xavier tried to hold in the laughter; his eyes watered from the struggle to maintain his composure and not hurt Felis' already damaged pride. The sudden movement of the plane signaled an end to the four-plus hour trip. It motivated him to return to his seat in preparation for landing. The change in altitude and cabin pressure woke Colleen before Xavier even had a chance to completely fasten his seatbelt. The discomfort associated with the elevation change was an effective method of waking up sleeping teenagers.

Turning away from him, she stretched out her arms and torso. Looking over her shoulder toward him, she smiled and said, "I hope I didn't drool on you. I do that if I sleep sitting up or in a semi-upright position. I have only flown once, so I am more comfortable sleeping in a car than on a plane."

Before he could respond to her comment, his stomach crawled into his chest cavity as the plane's engines scaled back. The pilot began to turn towards San Rafael's private airport runway and gradually made its descent. While he did not mind the take-off and flying in the air, he had a problem with landings.

The mental image of plunging to the earth in a heaping mass of burning twisted metal and debris occupied his every waking thought at that moment. With that in mind, he reminded himself of something he learned from his mom; when you panic, people get hurt, and giving into fear kills your spirit of adventure over time. Closing his eyes and gripping the arm rests he forced himself to face one of his deepest fears, crashing.

The sound of Xavier's hysteric-induced giggle only did more to endure him to her, this man-child she had learned to trust and confide in as a friend and an opponent during their routine sparing matches. The closer the plane got to the ground, the more excited and anxious Colleen became.

She hoped Dr. Parodine could fill in some of the gaps surrounding her parents' life before they moved to Hershey,

Pennsylvania, and answer why they were in California rather than looking for her or the people who kidnapped her.

What was the big mystery surrounding her and the health condition she had been treated for since she was a child? She feared opening Pandora's Box because she dreaded unleashing additional confusion and chaos into her already fragmented life.

She also stressed about the possibility of the doctor revealing something that could alienate those individuals she now called friends. Xavier was luckier than her because he still had family who would gladly accept him back no matter what he said.

While Colleen was not jealous of Xavier, she was swamped by the fear of being left with nothing. She was barely hanging on by a thread. She would have nothing if she lost her new friends; her parents were dead, her school friends had already moved on with their lives, and her cat was probably somewhere homeless and starving to death. The only thing she could do would be to plan for the worst, hope for the best, and continue to pray.

As the pilots applied the brakes and aligned the plane parallel to the airport hangar, the wheels bounced up and down on the asphalt. Once the plane stopped, Felis stood up, opened the door, and lowered the steps. The pilot exited the cock pit and mentioned to the adults that there was a rental vehicle waiting for them, parked along the right side of the hanger.

He also informed them that a courier would deliver the keys in a few minutes. Everyone stood up, started retrieving their bags, and followed Felis down the steps.

Libra: X

A gentleman in blue jeans, a t-shirt, and a baseball cap walked across the space, separating the plane from the hanger. He carried a manila envelope in his right hand and had one single blue rose in his left hand. After saying hello to Felis and the kids, he handed him the envelope with the keys and registration for the rental. He then turned and extended the single flower towards Panthera with a twinkle in his eyes.

"Jake, what are you doing here?" asked Panthera. She accepted the flower and buried her face as she inhaled its glorious perfume.

"Well, I own the rental company, and when I realized that you would be in town, I thought I could personally deliver the vehicle and ask if you would like to have dinner, do a little small talk, and maybe catch up on old times," Jake said.

The pleasant smile she bestowed on him seemed to irritate Felis. "That would be great, but we are only in town for a few days. We are taking my niece and Felis' nephew on a college visit to the Dominican University of California," Panthera said.

"Oh, well, if you change your mind, my number is in the envelope along with two sets of keys, and just so you know, to get the other eleven blue roses, you have to first go out to dinner with me," he said as he turned to leave.

Felis looked on with a frown as Panthera laughed at the guy's silly antics. Xavier could tell that did not think he much of Jake, and he wondered, could a little jealousy be mixed in with his dislike of the man? He did not know the guy well enough to pass judgment, but he did know and trust Felis. Plus, that story Panthera told about her and Felis gave him better insight into their relationship.

In a way, it made him want to play matchmaker. He knew he needed to talk with Colleen first and get her perspective on the whole thing. Girls tended to be better at matchmaking than boys. Xavier wondered if Panthera and Felis were still single because they were too busy with work to see what was right in front of their faces.

The kids picked up their duffle bags and followed the adults toward the rental vehicle. He was severely disappointed when he saw the rental car, a powder blue CoNserv hybrid, a successor to the Ford Prius and just as lacking in the get-up-and-go factor as the original Ford Prius from the early 2000s. Xavier did not know if his disappointment was because he was starting to get used to the luxurious lifestyle with Castor or what. He doubted Felis would even fit in the vehicle without removing the driver seat, but he could be wrong.

He and Colleen silently laughed when they saw the expression on Felis's face after he realized that the rental car was not the SUV he had been expecting.

The look he directed towards Panthera said it all as she raised her hands in surrender. "Do not blame me; Sam was the one who made the reservations for the car and the cottage."

Both kids, at that point, lost the battle to contain their glee and doubled over at the waist as the peals of laughter rang out, blending with the sound of planes landing and leaving the airfield.

Opening the trunk, everyone piled their stuff in as Felis angrily gestured for everyone to get in the car. After everything was secure, Felis slammed it close. Once in the car, Felis punctuated his displeasure by slamming the driver's side door.

Panthera looked over at him, her eyebrow raised as she spoke. "Do not take it out on the car; I am sure Castor would be upset if he had to pay for any damages to the vehicle."

Felis started the car and shifted into gear, but when he put his foot on the gas pedal, the get-up and go was non-existent. Now Xavier understood why all the cars Castor owned were supped-up SUVs.

Feeling frustrated, Felis said, "When I get back to the clinic, I am going to buy enough red bull and Coke slushies to fill an old-style iron claw foot tub, and then I am going to drown Sam in it."

Everyone except Felis burst into uncontrolled laughter again as they envisioned the scene. "That means you would have to catch him first, and you know how he is when he drinks coffee or Red Bull," said Xavier.

Once the laughter died down, he realized that the camaraderie and anticipation reminded him of what he felt with his family when they went on their annual vacations.

The trip to the small town of Tomales was forty minutes north of San Rafael along Highway One. The drive did not bother anyone except Felis, and that was because he was driving scrunched up with his knees higher than the steering wheel. Sam was going to get it when Felis got back to the clinic.

Xavier continued to watch the passing scenery as the little Ford Prius did its best to assume the role of the little engine that could. The sound of the ocean was something he had yet to experience. The crashing of the waves was hypnotic, and the lush green grass was mesmerizing. Highway One consisted of rolling hills and bluffs, the road at times came perilously close to the cliff edge. During those times, Xavier could distinguish the white foam as the waves battered the rocks along the shoreline.

The temperature was perfect, neither hot nor cold, and the gentle breeze from the water carried hints of flowers, salt, and other unidentifiable smells. He now understood why so many people flocked to California. Suddenly he realized this would have been the perfect place to wear his numerous Hawaiian shirts.

His mom always teased him about all the Hawaiian shirts he liked to collect and wear. He remembered how Packer, Mathew, and he kept spare Hawaiian shirts in a school locker so they could wear them every Thursday. The tradition started the first week of his freshman year and continued every Thursday until his death. He chuckled when he remembered his mom asking why he was trying to set himself apart from others at school, and he told her he wanted to be a leader, not a follower, and those who threw shade on Hawaiian shirts were losers. Ironically by the time his senior year rolled around, the rest of the school started embracing the trend. Who knew he would one day become a trendsetter?

The sound of the tires transitioning from asphalt to a gravel drive pulled Xavier out of his reminiscing; His first look at the CiderLane Farm and Cottage showed it to be quaint and cozy. It was the type of place his mom and dad would have loved to stay. The green welded wire fencing separated the property from the main highway. Yellow-red marigolds mingled with the bushy, overgrown grass, and the open cattle gate welcomed visitors to explore the apple orchard and purchase fresh organic cider made on the farm. Directly ahead of the open gate sat a long gray rectangular building with either skylights or solar panels on the roof. Xavier suspected that was where the apples were processed and packed for sale to locals and visitors alike. The sounds of cows mooing in the adjacent field to the right of the gate illustrated that this was a working farm and not some tourist trap.

Xavier and Colleen decided to stay in the car and continue looking around, each lost in their thoughts. Panthera and Felis left, searching for the main house or office, whichever came first. After the adults had completed registration and obtained the keys, they headed towards the cottage a short distance from the main house.

The first thing he noticed about the place as they approached was the weathered gray appearance of the structure's wood and the weathered gray planks that lined the walkway. On the opposite side of the planks, the proprietors planted grass, accented by white baby's breath, yellow butter cups, and desert mallows in shades of brilliant orange to watermelon red, intermingled with clumps of giant wild rye grass. The cottage was gorgeous and gave off peaceful and relaxing vibes.

The inside of the cottage surpassed the outside and was not as he had expected. Not only was it elegantly decorated, but it had two bedrooms. He had only expected one room at the most. He anticipated that he and Colleen would be roughing it with sleeping bags in front of the fireplace in the living room. However, now he knew that he would be sleeping in comfort instead. He just needed to scope out the rooms and figure out who was sleeping where. The main bedroom was simplistic in its rustic appeal. It had a king-size bed and an original hand-crafted quilt with matching throw pillows ideal for a romantic getaway.

Kitty corner from the end of the bed was an ornate cherry wood armoire with a matching end table next to the bed as you entered the room. An old black rotary phone sat on the end table. The walls were decorated with pictures of the local flowers gracing the landscape outside the cottage. The second bedroom was the same, just smaller, and instead of a king-size bed, it had a Queen. Xavier suspected that he and Felis would get the giant bed because of his ginormous size.

The Jack and Jill style bathroom was situated between the two bedrooms, with only one access point from the outside of both bedrooms. The bathroom looked more modern than the rest of the house, but it still processed an old-world charm. The bathroom was a blinding white compared to the rest of the house. White Subway tiles decorated the walls of the enclosed stand-up shower stall. Outside next to the shower stall was a tiny white porcelain pedestal sink with a bronze faucet, handles, and a white commode. The burgundy towels, the fixtures, and the bronze pedestal lights with tulip-shaped globes above the sink provided the only color in the bathroom. The floor also had white subway tiles intermingled with a burgundy tile with a hand-painted gold flower accent.

The living room was also simplistic and beautiful, with polished hardwood floors and a stone fireplace built to be flush with the wall in front of a burgundy-red loveseat with cream-colored accent pillows on each end of the couch. To the right of the fireplace was a matching cream-colored wingback chair with a burgundy throw blanket draped over the back of the chair. Matching floral landscape pictures decorated the walls, and a wooden bookcase to the left of the fireplace had a collection of local tourist guidebooks, books on the native plants and animals, as well as a few picture books on landscape photography and the history of Apple Cider and the development of the cider press.

The kitchen also contrasted sharply with the rest of the house's rustic appearance, layout, and design. Guests could talk with others and had a direct line of sight from the living room into the kitchen. A large stainless-steel double-door refrigerator dominated the north side of the room with a window above the kitchen sink. The cabinets were a blinding white with bronze knobs, and a dark black walnut glazed butcher block countertop with a checker black and white backsplash.

A matching black walnut table was strategically placed halfway between the kitchen and living room but still close enough to provide a surface area to chop vegetables and work and a place for evening meals. Two bronze high-top stools were on the side closest to the living room. Under the side nearest to the refrigerator and the sink were two saddle seat bar stools hidden under the table should they be needed later.

The east side of the kitchen was designed to maximize the natural light from the sunrise, with double French-style doors leading to the backyard. Beyond the cottage was a relaxation area with four lime green Adirondack chairs and a well-used fire pit. Entertainment was provided by Mother Nature via a small pond with a multitude of momma ducks and their babies frolicking in the water. Swimming was also an option, with a wooden dock for guests to sit on and dangle their feet or jump into the water. Xavier found it to be very peaceful and relaxing. Sam may have been goofing with the CoNserv, but he got it right with the CiderLane Farm and Cottage.

Unloading the vehicle and the bags was completed with military efficiency and precision, the type only former soldiers and those in the field could achieve. Felis brought in the bags, and Panthera put away the supplies the proprietors had left on the table in preparation for their arrival. Colleen was the first to start moving loads into the bedrooms; she moved her and Panthera's stuff into the room with the queen bed. So, Xavier assumed correctly that the boys would take procession of the king's bed. He prayed that Felis did not snore like a freight train like his dad, or he would be sleeping in the fetal position on the loveseat in the living room.

After moving all the stuff into the bedroom, he returned to the kitchen. He watched Panthera start putting the fresh vegetables into the bottom crisper drawer in the refrigerator. From what Xavier could tell, the farm cultivated more than just apples; they also produced cucumbers, broccoli, carrots, onions, potatoes, and squash.

He hoped and prayed that the farmers supported organic farming practices, not veganism; his love of meat products was a deal breaker. Ironically, his mother always told him she would give any girl he brought home a chance, even though she thought no one was good enough for him. But the hard rule in the Hansen family was no vegans; vegetarians, yes, but no vegans because, as mom said, she would not be made to feel guilty when her body required high levels of protein and Iron, nor would she give up her ice cream, milk, and cheese.

Once everything was put away and everyone assembled in the kitchen, Panthera asked, "Who will be the chef for the next few days?"

Felis and Colleen started looking around, avoiding eye contact as if afraid that looking at her would signal their willingness to be the cook. Xavier let out a resigned sigh, he knew how to play this game, and if he played it right, he would not have to do the dishes for the entire time they were here.

"I will cook dinner, but the rule is the person who cooks does not wash dishes or cleans the kitchen afterward."

No one volunteered to cook or asked him if he could cook so that alone told him that their level of expertise in the kitchen probably consisted of making peanut butter and jelly sandwiches. Everyone looked at each other in relief, not realizing they had just been suckered into KP detail. Xavier's mom always said he could cook any recipe, but cleaning as you go was not one of his strong points.

"Time for everyone to leave the master to his work," he said as he peaked his head into the refrigerator, looking for some meat to add to the vegetables he already had. After verifying that he had steak and brown rice in the pantry, Xavier started working on making Hibachi steak with stir-fried veggies and fried rice. He always enjoyed eating Japanese food and associated it with spending time with his mom and brother Will. While thinking about it, he still had that burner phone; he needed to contact Mathew and Packer and let them know how things are going and check on his family.

The smell of dinner wafted through the cottage; those in the living room were optimistic that dinner would not be a disaster based on the heavenly scents from the kitchen. Once the food was done, Xavier asked Colleen to help him set the dinner table. In celebration of their progress so far, he poured the chilled sparkling apple cider the owners had left as a welcome gift into wine glasses he had discovered hidden behind the regular glasses in the back of the cupboard.

He loved sparkling cider; his mom would buy six bottles for Thanksgiving, Christmas, New Year's Eve, and Easter. She would then hide three in prominent places because she knew Will and Xavier would steal at least one each for themselves and one for baby Carter; they then would sneak off and play video games and drink their non-alcoholic sparkling cider. Mom was wise to their antics because she would hide the other three bottles where no one would ever find them in preparation for the holiday dinner. He missed those days; if an outsider had observed the activities in the cottage, they would have believed that mom and dad were relaxing as the son cooked the meal and the daughter set the table.

Dinner was a surprise for everyone at the table except for Xavier.

Panthera was the first to comment after taking a bit of the Hibachi steak. "Oh my, this is delicious," she said.

Followed by a round of nodding heads and moans as the others were too busy eating and less inclined to vocalize their approval beyond the bare minimum?

Xavier started to feel the heat in his face and took a sip of cider to give him something to distract himself with, just as Colleen asked him a question. "How did you learn to cook Japanese food?"

He smiled and swallowed the cider before attempting to respond to her question. "Well, I have always enjoyed cooking with my mom. Sometimes I would wake up at night and could not sleep, so I would search for recipes to try. My mom had only two rules: first, no 2 am wake-up calls to taste test food, and second, ensure the kitchen was spotless before she woke up the next morning. Once I learned to follow those two rules, I could experiment, provided I did not go hog wild. I now know how to make Japanese food and Cheesecake from scratch using the water bath method, which was not easy. But my true masterpiece is my homemade Egg Nogg with butter rum. It is the only time mom allows alcohol inside the house besides communion wine on Sunday during Mass."

Felis wiped his mouth with a paper napkin. "From now on, if we go on any missions that require cooking skills, you are forever assigned to feeding us poor plebs that cannot boil water without burning it."

Everyone at the table burst into laughter, and the festive mood lasted through the rest of the meal. When the food was all gone, everyone but Xavier got up and started cleaning up the mess in the kitchen and at the table. Xavier smiled; he knew he had come out on top with the deal he had made before making dinner.

However, he did not feel guilty about conning everyone until Colleen stuck her tongue at him. With that one little gesture, he decided to earn some brownie points with everyone by helping the others even though he was under no obligation to clean up since he did the cooking.

"You know you don't need to help," said Panthera. She had not seen Colleen childishly sticking out her tongue at him as he relaxed in his chair at the table.

"I know, but I figured that the sooner we get done, the sooner we can discuss the details for the planned meeting with Dr. Parodine," said Xavier.

The remaining time was spent working in companionable silence as everyone started pitching in and helping wherever needed. In no time at all, the kitchen and the table were spic and span. Now was the time to sit in the living room, turn on the gas fireplace and hash out the details.

Xavier sat down in the rocking chair facing the fireplace. He watched the flames flickering as he listened to the conversations flowing around him. Felis sat in the wingback chair, and the ladies curled up on the loveseat and covered up with multiple throw blankets to ward off the chill of the night. Once the fireplace had been started, Panthera took command of the room and outlined the plan for the upcoming meeting. The adults agreed that every alarm should be set to five am so there would be time for a shower, breakfast, and travel to Ross, California. They would then attend Sunday Mass at St. Anselm Catholic Church. The zig-zag travel arrangement was designed to throw off anyone who tried to follow them and add a layer to their cover story.

Prior to mass Felis and Panthera would conduct a brief surveillance of the area and map out escape plans in case they needed to bug out, especially when driving a CoNserv. Xavier would apply his tribal tattoo and pull back his hair, making him look older and unrecognizable should any of Dr. Procter's stooges be watching and sit with Colleen giving the appearance of being a couple. Panthera continued her summary; according to the response to the original message, Dr. Parodine suggested meeting after mass. She was a long-standing church member, and it would not look out of the ordinary for her to talk to guests or new members as a designated Chairperson of the Welcoming Committee. Now that everyone had eaten and the plan's details were shared, it was time to turn in and rest before the 5 am wake-up call.

Xavier moved all but one throw pillow off the couch and curled up in a fetal position. Felis' puzzled expression proceeded his asking the obvious question, "Why are you sleeping on the couch?"

He turned his head, gazing past his shoulder to look at him, "Well, I assume your snoring is proportional to your size. So, I would rather save time and sleep on the couch."

Colleen started to giggle, and Panthera nodded in agreement as she tried to smother her laughter.

Felis huffed and went towards his assigned bedroom. "That's fine by me; I have room to spread out and plenty of blankets," he said. The door closed with a bang.

Xavier looked toward Panthera, "did I hurt his feelings?" he asked. She shook her head no as she and Collen headed towards their room, calling it a night.

The following day the smell of dog poop woke Xavier up; he knew no dog was in the cottage. The only other time he had smelt that odor was whenever his dad ordered coffee from Hawaii. He did not know what it was, but something about organic farming methods made the coffee smell as bad as dog poop. While he passed on the coffee because of the scent, he ate two homemade muffins and fresh fruit the farm owners had left on the front porch.

He noticed that Colleen picked at her muffin and ate extraordinarily little. At the same time, Felis and Panthera nursed their cups of coffee. He realized that for Colleen, a lot was riding on this conversation with Dr. Parodine, and he wondered if this would be his reaction when the time came for him to get answers. Would he handle it similarly, or would he lose what little of his sanity he still had left?

St. Anselm Catholic Church was structurally different from the other churches Xavier attended; the architecture was reminiscent of the style found in Bavarian countries such as Germany and Austria. While most Catholic churches in the United States were tall and majestic, this one was compact and rounded compared to the average church.

The building was an amalgamation of wood, brick, and plaster, with a squat-like turret on the left and right side and a taller turret directly behind and to the left of the shorter turret. The inside of the building was just as unique, with dark brown-black wooden beams in the shape of geometric triangles of all sizes acting as a structural support system for the vaulted ceiling.

The floor was a red carpet with twenty-five rows of wooden pews on each aisle. A wooden circular step marked the transition from the carpet to the platform where the altar was placed. Behind the altar, between two round windows, was a solid wooden panel made of polished driftwood on which the gleaming white figure of the Crucified Jesus Christ hung. Six lit candles rested on a credenza just under the feet of the statue of God's son. Overall, the church appeared warm and inviting; Xavier now understood why Dr. Parodine felt more comfortable meeting in the Lord's house.

Panthera and Felis took seats in the last pew closest to the confession box as Colleen and Xavier moved to the sixth pew towards the front on the right side, as instructed by Dr. Parodine's message. Both nervously waited for the service to start knowing that she could change her mind and not show up at any moment. Just as Xavier was beginning to think that they had been stood up, a dark-haired woman with a white scarf draped over her hair, like how Jackie Kennedy wore it when she went incognito after the assassination of JFK.

The woman he assumed to be Dr. Parodine quietly asked if the seat next to Colleen had been taken. They both whispered a quick no and moved over to allow her to sit. The service started without disruption and followed the standard format Xavier had come to associate with attendance at a Catholic Church.

The great thing about being Catholic was that biblical reading and traditions were always the same no matter where you were in the world. Catholics had the unique ability to feel at home in any church regardless of location or language. It made sense because the word Catholic, translated from its original form, meant universal. Once the service was underway, and after the Eucharist had been completed, Dr. Parodine motioned for them to head towards the exit mingling with parishioners heading out to assume the end of service duties.

Along the way, Felis and Panthera covertly followed the teenagers and the doctor, always maintaining a safe distance to avoid detection without putting Xavier and Colleen in immediate danger. Dr. Parodine directed them to enter the church playground area and motioned them to sit on the weather-stained picnic bench under the pavilion and away from prying eyes. Once seated, Xavier looked at the woman they had traveled so far to meet. Kendra Parodine had dark brown hair and brown eyes, was about five feet seven inches tall, weighed about one hundred and fifteen pounds, and looked much like the actress Sandra Bullock.

She had that pleasant girl-next-door vibe. Looking at her, you would never know she had a Doctorate in Biology and a Ph.D. in Genetic Theory. She wore black dress slacks with black pumps and a red blouse, matching silver rose bud earrings, a bracelet, and a necklace set. The embroidered roses on her head scarf perfectly matched her jewelry. Her hair was pulled back away from her face in a messy bun that was all the rage among the younger generation. Her skin was smooth and unblemished, with a light trace of blush gracing her cheekbones and a little mascara and lip gloss for the finishing touch. If asked to guess her age, he would have said she looked 35 to 40 and probably had a husband, a teenager, and a dog waiting for her at home. However, the reality of the situation was far different.

Colleen sat next to Xavier with one hand under the table, gripping his with the strength of a momma bear defending her young cub. No one spoke, and the silence weighed heavily on everyone.

He knew that it was up to him to break the oppressive silence. He gestured towards himself, "I am Xavier, and this is my friend Colleen. We think you knew her parents, or at least we hope you knew her parents."

Dr. Parodine took a deep breath, her eyes filled with unshed tears.

"I was your mother's college roommate; we were thick as thieves. I first met your mom when we were freshmen at the University of Alabama. Originally, we were not supposed to be in the same room. Still, your mother had a little bit of a temper back then and did not take kindly to her current roommate, having her boyfriend over all the time and locking her out of her room. So, she requested a room transfer, and she was assigned to be my new bunkmate. Your mom and I became best friends, and I even set her up with your dad. I was at their wedding as the maid of honor, and I was named your godmother by proxy. For that reason, I was named as your guardian in their will and why I am the executor of their estate."

She stopped for a few seconds as the tears started rolling down her cheeks, "I am the reason they are dead; I am also the reason why my husband and only child are dead."

Her sobbing shook her entire body as she struggled to regain control. Xavier and Colleen looked at each other in shock. Colleen's face wore a mask of confusion. Neither knew what to say or do. They feared that if they said the wrong thing, they would lose the opportunity to get answers to their questions.

Colleen leaned forwards and retrieved a red handkerchief from her front pocket; Xavier wondered where she got it and why she was carrying it. Colleen paused, looked at him directly, and said, "Just in case."

Xavier wondered how she knew what he was thinking.

Once she had stopped crying and gained a small measure of control, she looked at both teenagers and said, "I shouldn't be talking to you about this; I don't want to see you get hurt. I only showed up to ensure Colleen was safe and tell her I put her stuff in storage and have her cat, Mr. Kitty."

Colleen's exclamation of surprise and happiness told Xavier just how much the thought of her cat being homeless, and starving had bothered her.

"Actually, his name is Michelangelo, but I guess Mr. Kitty will do for now," said Colleen.

Xavier feared she was going to leave after her last statement; "no, wait, we need to know what you know, and If you are worried about our safety, then we have a couple of friends we want you to meet, and I guarantee they will keep us safe," he said.

Colleen stood up, pulled out another red handkerchief, and started waving it.

Xavier knew he needed to ask her about them after they were done with the meeting because no girl he had ever met had one, much less required two red handkerchiefs.

The three occupants at the picnic table watched Felis and Panthera walk towards the group as if they had materialized out of thin air.

Dr. Parodine tensed up in fear until she saw the welcoming smiles the two teenagers directed toward the newcomers. Once they reached the picnic table, Panthera sat next to Colleen on her right, and Felis sat next to Xavier on his left. Both adults intentionally sat next to the kids to provide additional protection and give the doctor an illusion of freedom to leave if she decided to end the meeting. Xavier introduced the new group members and gave them a quick rundown of the information they had already obtained.

Colleen's next question was asked quietly, calmly, and reassuringly. "Why did you say you were the reason they were dead?"

Dr. Parodine sat still for a few seconds before answering the question.

"I need to give you some more background information before I tell you why I think I am the reason they are dead. As I said, I majored in Biology at the University of Alabama. During my graduate work, I studied Genetics. I made a revolutionary breakthrough in stabilizing the genetic decay in animals that had been cloned. The formula I developed had the potential to help slow down the decaying of cells as we age, prevent mutations that cause cancer, and make it possible to genetically reproduce livestock without the risk of cell degeneration. Livestock would never again be susceptible to disease or genetic mutations."

"When I went to graduate school, I published my findings and was awarded a Ph.D. in Theoretical and Applied Genetics. Around that time, my husband got a job as a firefighter in the county we lived in, and I became pregnant. My daughter Angelina was born, and I started working for a genetic laboratory specializing in livestock cloning. The same company acquired the rights to the first cloned sheep named Molly. I worked at the company for about five years. Then during a Genetic Symposium in Denver, Colorado, the head of CITRUM Industries approached me about possible employment."

Dr. Parodine shifted in her seat as if uncomfortable with what she was about to reveal; with a quick look around to ensure no one else was around, she proceeded with her narrative.

"I turned them down because I did not want to uproot my family. My husband was moving up in the ranks at the fire department, and Angel was happy and making friends in her class. After speaking to my husband on the phone about the offer I made my decision, I then requested a wakeup call from the hotel concierge, and I went to bed."

"While I slept safe and sound in the hotel, I was unaware they had died in a house fire and did not find out until the next morning. The police report stated that the fire broke out about five minutes after I had spoken with my family. The fire moved incredibly fast for an electrical fire, and the neighbors said the house was fully engulfed in less than five minutes," she said.

Closing her eyes in sorrow, Dr. Parodine continued in a monotone voice.

"The fire marshal claimed it resulted from faulty wiring on the Christmas tree lights and that the fire alarms near the main bedroom malfunctioned. Until recently, I never thought about what caused the fire or why brand-new smoke detectors failed until I started working at CITRUM. Then I remembered something the head of the company said to me in Denver before the death of my husband and daughter. The woman asked me something to the effect of what would I sacrifice to have my loved ones back? I did not really think anything about it one way or another," she said.

"It wasn't until I started treatment for PTSD that I remembered bits and pieces of what happened before my family died. I remembered how Brody, my husband, checked the fire alarms religiously. I also know the fire detectors worked because before I left for Denver, I helped test them and replace the dead batteries. I think the fire was set deliberately; Brody was so well trained he would have detected it before it got out of control. He was passionate about fire safety, highly trained, and had the uncanny ability to detect a fire by smell alone. So why did he not wake up at the first smell of smoke?"

Panthera was the first to break the silence when she asked, "Do you think they had something to do with the fire?"

Dr. Parodine shook her head, "In the beginning, no, I did not, but it was not until recently that I started questioning the events that led to Angelina's and Brody's death. I did not go to work for them right away. After my family's death, I was in no shape to change jobs because I was battling depression, PTSD, and suicidal ideation; all I wanted was to join my husband and child. Then one night, I went to sleep, and I had a dream that changed my life and the direction of my research. In my dream, I accepted that I could never have my daughter and husband back. However, I realized I could still help others who lost loved ones because of comas, those who had dementia, and those who had traumatic brain injuries."

"I realized that if I could figure out how to map the neurons in the brain, copy memories, and transfer them back to the individuals, no one would ever lose their loved ones if they continued to live and breathe. I decided to work for CITRUM Industries because they had the funding I needed and the most modern research and development facility outside of a university or government facility. I knew I had found a new purpose in life. I then devoted all my time and energy to figuring out how to map out the brain and copying the memories of those at death's door. The machine and the program created were patented and known as Brainbow KT."

Felis was the first person to break the stunned silence, "so were you successful?" he asked.

"Yes," she said, but let me backtrack briefly. The mission statement CITRUM gave me stated that my research aimed to develop technology that would allow for the duplication of thoughts and memories in individuals suffering from cell degeneration due to age and traumatic brain injuries. The official name given to it was the Xerox Project."

Xavier's startled exclamation interrupted the flow of the conversation as he stated, "I found a piece of paper with that word written on it in my mother's handwriting behind a picture. Does that mean Colleen and I were test subjects, and someone out there has a copy of our memories, feelings, and thoughts?"

Parodine shrugged her shoulders, "I don't know. I used the idea of labeling neurons with various color codes in different brain parts. After fine-tuning the process, I adapted it to map neurons and used an algorithm to convert the colors and code into visual and auditory images. Theoretically, it could transfer knowledge from one individual to another. I only ever tested it on one subject, a chimpanzee. If there were any human trials, then I was never a part of them. After the success with the primate, I started thinking about how the technology I created made me feel as if I were playing God, and I started to realize the potential harm someone could do if it got into the wrong hands."

Taking a deep breath to center herself, she continued, "That is when I told them I would quit. I then had a visit from Roselyn Trundle, who told me that if I quit, they would be unable to protect my friends and me from future accidents such as house fires and car accidents. I then started to suspect they were behind my husband and daughter's death. After my conversation with her, I was removed as lead researcher on the Xerox Project. Executive authority was transferred to Dr. Proctor and another geneticist named Dr. Melham. Then right before your parents called me, I told my boss I planned to relocate and gave my two weeks' notice. I mistakenly thought that since the death of my family, there was no way they could truly threaten me into submission. Then less than 24 hours later, I was notified that you ran away, and your parents died in a car accident on their way to see me. I still do not know why they were on their way to see me; they never emailed me, called, or even left me a message letting me know they were coming."

Colleen took a deep breath and tried to get her temper under control; she temporarily forgot she was still holding Xavier's hand in a vice grip.

Gritting his teeth from the pain, he said, "Colleen, you're hurting my hand."

Sheepishly she released his hand and placed both in her lap. "Oh, sorry, I forgot I was holding your hand," she said.

Colleen looked at Parodine, "I did not run away; I got home from school and heard a noise. I thought it might be the neighbor's dog going after Michelangelo. I went outside, and the next thing I knew, someone grabbed me from behind and put a smelly cloth over my nose and mouth. When I woke up, I was in some strange house under lock and key until these guys came to my rescue."

Panthera picked up where Colleen left off as she said, "The house we liberated her from was Dr. Proctor's residence, and while we were there, we snagged some of his files and deciphered some of the information, but we were hoping you could give us something else to go on. Maybe tell us why Procter's goons grabbed Colleen?"

Shaking her head in bewilderment, Parodine said, "Colleen's parents and I lost touch after my husband and daughter died. I mistakenly thought Colleen was over seventeen, but my memory of the eight years after my family died is fuzzy and distorted. Working was the only thing that helped me get through my grief until I was finally diagnosed with PTSD and started taking medication. Colleen, I am not even sure why your parents were coming to see me. I did not know I was made your legal guardian until I was contacted by a private attorney who learned of the accident in the local newspaper."

Felis was the next to ask a question. "Do you, by chance, still have any files related to the Xerox project? Even one might tell us where to look for additional information."

Sadly, I do not; I can ask a friend who worked on the algorithm for Brainbow KT; he still works in the technology section of the company. I will need to contact him in person. When do you plan to leave?" She asked.

Panthera replied, "We are leaving later tomorrow, but could you meet us at the Dominican University of California? We told the owners of the bed and breakfast place that we were taking the kids on a tour of the University."

While the ladies conversed among themselves, Felis took the time to research eating options at Dominican. "How about we meet at Caleruega dining hall at noon, and we can get any last-minute information you may have," he said.

Everyone agreed to meet up tomorrow at the University. Still, for the safety of everyone involved, it would be better if everyone went their own way and kept it down low for now. Xavier had a lot to think about since talking to Dr. Parodine or Kendra, as she insisted on being called. The adults and the teenagers piled into the car and left to look for a place to eat lunch before returning to CiderLand Farm and Cottage. Along the way, they picked up some t-shirts and souvenirs to cement the image of a family on vacation. The car was deathly quiet as everyone processed the information they had learned; gradually, the stillness in the car lulled the teenagers asleep, leaving Panthera and Felis alone with their thoughts.

Back at the bed and breakfast, the kids woke up as the tires met the gravel drive; yawning and stretching his arms, Xavier asked, "Who wants to go play in the pond and chase some of the ducks?"

Everyone laughed, and Felis looked at him and said, "Are you sure you weren't a cocker spaniel in your past life?"

Later Felis sat on a blanket next to the picnic basket the owner of the bed and breakfast had assembled for them and watched as Colleen, Panthera, and Xavier chased each other and fell to the ground in a heap as they laughed and played. If he closed his eyes and listened, he could picture them as a family enjoying a typical college visit. Just as he was ready to fall asleep, the sound of angry ducks squawking broke the spell; Felis opened his eyes and noticed them giving the laughing trio the stink eye, threatening to flog them with their wings like disapproving parents scolding young children. For the rest of the day and evening, the four enjoyed their stay and built memories to sustain them through the upcoming hardships.

The next afternoon Xavier and the gang waited for Dr. Parodine at Dominican University's Caleruega Dinning hall; when Kendra came in, she looked flustered and not as well put together as yesterday. Her hair was in a ponytail covered by a black baseball cap; dark sunglasses obscured her features; she wore a black t-shirt with South Laguna Beach written in white cursive. Her jeans were a faded light blue and worn in places from excessive wear rather than from strategic placement by fashion gurus. Her expression conveyed fear, worry, and something Xavier could not identify. She moved towards the round table where the group sat eating breakfast; she weaved in and out of tables packed with students, avoiding collisions with others with the expertise of an Indy 500 Nascar driver.

The noise in the cafeteria was loud enough to block anyone from snooping and listening to their conversation but low enough that they could still converse. The tension radiating from Kendra seemed to increase as she sat down and removed her sunglasses. Her eyes were red and puffy from crying, and the stress was evident in every line of her face.

Everyone at the table held their breath; no one bothered to say good morning because it was apparent in her every movement that it was not a good morning. Before saying anything, she reached into her Black messenger bag and retrieved a manila folder. She placed the folder on the table and looked at Xavier and Colleen.

"Yesterday when I told you I did not have access to any files, I was telling the truth," Kendra said.

"I was talking to my friend from the technology department. He mentioned that Dr. Crocker had recently replaced his old standard company-issued desk with a French 19th Century Louis XV St. Mahogany, Tulipwood, And Ormolu Bureau Plat Desk worth about twenty-nine thousand dollars. I located where the old desk was moved to and looked at the desk to see if one of his flunkies had missed something. Well, my hunch paid off, and I located three pieces of paper scrunched up between one of the bottom drawers between the back of the drawer and the back panel of the desk. I put everything I could find in the folder, along with the three pieces of paper I found."

"Then last night after I went home, I had an unexpected visit from the attorney handling the estate of Colleen's parents. He mentioned that they had only recently changed their will in the last two months. The lawyer also had a letter they had written at the same time as their will. It explained that I needed to keep Colleen away from CITRUM but did not give any details. Along with a copy of the will and the letter, there was a notarized deposition provided by your parents stating that Dr. Proctor confessed to killing my family and should anything happen to Colleen's parents, or they die unexpectedly that, the police should investigate CITRUM and Dr. Procter and Dr. Melham. I didn't know Colleen's parents even knew Proctor or Melham."

Xavier reached across the table, pulled the folder towards him, and looked at Colleen; with a slight tilt, he mentally asked if she wanted to open the folder instead. She shook her head and placed her hands in her lap. He looked at the folder briefly, then towards Felis and Panthera; neither seemed inclined to take the lead. Opening the folder, Xavier was disappointed when he realized the information in the file was based on a young Asian American woman in her mid-twenties. According to the file, she was also one of the Zodiac Thirteen; her sign was Leo. The only other thing listed about the young lady was that she was gifted and talented in leadership and a chess master.

The third sheet in the file consisted of a memo written by Rosalee Mason Trundle to Dr. Proctor one week before Xavier's death. The memo stated that Xavier's development was progressing faster than anticipated and that his unique talent would soon manifest if it followed the standardized timeline.

Xavier stopped reading and looked up in surprise, "I don't have a special talent? I was classified as gifted and talented in Leadership and Language Arts in elementary school, specifically in drama and writing."

Kendra looked at him and said, "Keep reading; I think this is what you were looking for when you came to see me. The file had a notation in red ink in the left side margin reminding Dr. Proctor to update XMD and place it in a secure location T001G. According to my friend, XMD refers to the master disk and the project name Xerox. He also mentioned that the company keeps a master disk separate from the facility mainframe. CITRUM is paranoid about industrial espionage, hackers breaking into the system, and the potential for whistleblowers releasing classified proprietary information."

Xavier looked at the rest of the memo and asked what "T001G" meant?" He showed the notation to the others; no one knew what it meant. "Maybe," Kendra said, it is a clue as to where to look for the master disk."

The memo and the sworn statement revealed the personal involvement of Rosalee Mason Trudel, CITRUM, Dr. Proctor, and Dr. Melham in what was starting to look like a significant conspiracy out of George Orwell's book 1984. Still, what stood out the most was the request for Dr. Proctor to burn a disk with current information on the Xerox

Program and have it overnight mailed to a secure location. The memo was specific enough to let them know they were on the right track but vague enough that the conspirators could claim ignorance. He figured they had already received the master disk based on the memo's date. For every step they took forward, they moved two paces back, only to run later to keep up with the influx of new information.

Kendra said, "I also want to mention that my friend told me that the master disk is broken into three segments. To read everything on the disk, you need to locate and place all three disks together. Each disk will give you a small amount of information, but it will be hit or miss on the contents."

Panthera looked at Kendra, "I understand how important the memo and the sheet on Leo are, but that does not explain why you appear so stressed out, and it looks like you have been crying to the point that your face and eyes are so swollen you had to cover them up with sunglasses."

Kendra lowered her head; tears pooled in her eyes; looking up towards Colleen, she pulled a crumpled piece of paper from her pocket and smoothed it out on the table before speaking. "I mentioned that I found three pieces of paper, and two of them I showed you already, but the third one is why I look the way I do."

Kendra pushed the paper toward Colleen and waited for her to finish reading it. After Colleen had finished, she passed it along to Felis to read; she still did not understand why it was so important.

Felis' startled glance made Xavier think that he understood the importance of the information, and it was confirmed by Panthera's reaction as well. By the time Xavier read the paper, he knew something significant was about to be revealed.

Kendra's following words confirmed Xavier's suspicions. "When I read that paper, I realized that Colleen's parents were not coming to see me but were going to see Dr. Melham, who took my place after I refused to work on the Xerox Project. I started thinking about why they would want to see him since I was sure they had never met. I then realized that Colleen's parents had met Dr. Proctor through me at the funeral of my husband and daughter. I am still at a loss of why my best friend from college would be meeting with Melham and Proctor. A small part of me always thought CITRUM may have killed Colleen's parents the way they did my husband and daughter. However, when I read the sworn statements written by your parents, I knew that CITRUM killed my family and they no doubt killed Colleen's family. When I thought about it I realized I am the reason why four people I loved with all my heart are dead." The tears in her eyes rolled down her face as she struggled to maintain her composure.

Panthera patted her hand; "Listen," she said, "You are not responsible for their deaths. You are responsible for helping us determine why Colleen and Xavier are in danger and helping us find the rest of Dr. Proctor's patients. Also, look at it this way if we can stop CITRUM, we can hold them responsible for the death of your daughter, your husband, and Colleen's parents." Kendra nodded her head in agreement as Colleen mimicked her movement as well.

Felis' decided at that moment to mention that Kendra might want to take some vacation time and leave the area so that CITRUM could not silence her. He suggested that she did not want to get caught in the middle when they tried to gain access to the master discs. Kendra nodded in agreement and pushed back her chair, and gathered up her stuff; before leaving, she looked at Colleen, handed her a business card with a private email address on the back, and mentioned that if she ever wanted to reach out and talk about her parents after everything was said and done, she would be more than happy to speak with her. Colleen smiled gratefully and placed the card in her pocket as she watched her last connection to her parents walk away and temporarily out of her life.

The flight home to Chicago differed from the ride to California primarily because they had more questions and information to hash out before landing. Xavier thought about everything he now knew about the investigation into Dr. Proctor. He realized that if they could get their hands on even one portion of the master disk, they would be one step closer to finding the answers he was looking for and bringing down CITRUM.

The plane's wheels touched down on the runway, breaking the melancholy atmosphere that permeated the air as everyone gathered their bags and strode towards the door. It was not until the plane had coasted to a stop that Xavier realized that Chicago and the people at Castor's facility had slowly wormed their way into his heart. He was starting to think of them as an extended family.

Xavier had never felt so relieved when Castor's SUV pulled alongside the plane. The worst part about not being able to go home was the feeling of not having something to anchor you in place when everything else in the world descended into chaos and confusion. For now, he could only think to follow Abraham Lincoln's example and keep moving forward; if Lincoln could walk four hours from Hodgenville to Elizabethtown, Kentucky, he could cope with homesickness. While Lincoln had his faults, being a quitter was not one of them.

Xavier could not wait until he returned to the Clinic and filled everyone in on what they had discovered in California. Walking into the conference room, he noticed Sam sitting next to Castor. He wondered how long it would be before Felis paid him back for the CoNserv incident in California. He knew that whatever payback Felis planned would be big, bold, and bad. Once everyone was seated in the conference room and had organized their materials, Castor took charge. Panthera was the first to give her report. She ran down everything said during the meet and greet with Dr. Parodine and provided copies of the documents to everyone in the conference room.

Castor and Pullox asked clarifying questions and seemed satisfied with the answers. Once the debriefing had been completed, Castor directed everyone's attention to the screen behind him. "Ladies and gentlemen, I would like to direct your attention to the screen; during your time in California, Sam intercepted some of the phone calls between Dr. Proctor and Rosalee Mason Trudel, but it has been pretty much a hit or miss," said Castor.

Sam advanced the slide to display an artist's rendition of the master disk based on the descriptions overheard between Procter and Trudel. "The calls I intercepted verified the existence of a master disk, and from what I could piece together, each of the three pieces is located in different locations. The next slide displayed a diagram of the separation between the three parts, so everyone knew what to look for when they were separated and how they fit together."

Pollux then stood up to provide additional research obtained about Dr. Proctor. Xavier listened as she detailed how his mother neglected and abused him after his father's death. According to the nanny who worked for the family, Procter also had a sister who died of accidental drowning at four years old. The nanny hinted that the little girl's death resulted from something Dr. Proctor had done. There was a three-year age difference between them which would have put him at the age of seven at the time of the accident. She also mentioned that after the little girl's death, she was relieved of her duties, and as far as she knew, no one was ever employed to take care of the little boy. Numerous individuals who went to school with him detailed hearing his mother criticize him for being a boy and repeatedly telling him she wished he had died rather than his sister.

Pollux finished by stating that the inheritance Dr. Procter received upon his mother's death covered the house's upkeep and paid property taxes. Employees who worked with the mother until her death received a generous gift of 200,000 per person. The rest of her money was used to create an endowment scholarship in her daughter's name. The mother also deeded the house to the Chicago preservation society. However, she made it possible for her son to live there until the end of his life.

Xavier thought of his mom and realized he was fortunate to have such a loving mother. Life could have been so much more complicated and unpleasant if he had Dr. Proctor's mom as a parent. However, that did not mean Proctor had the right to destroy other people's lives and play God.

Once Pollux had sat down, Xavier directed his question to the room at large. "Has anyone figured out what the notation in the memo's margin means?"

Sam smiled, "Yes, we might have figured out what T001G means. When I first noticed the five numbers and letters, I quickly realized they were too short for longitude and latitude coordinates. Then I started thinking it was a phone number and moved towards the theory that it might be a zip code. Once I settled on the idea it might be a zip code, I decided to use a simple transcription code. I matched the (T) up with the number 20, then figured the 00 must equal because two Os would make the numbers too long to be a zip code. I assumed one equaled a 1, then translated the G into a 7; this would create the following zip code 20217, located in the region of Washington DC. To ensure we did not miss anything, we looked at the 00 as actual zeros rather than representing a 2, then identified another potential location, 80017, in Denver, Colorado. Right now, we are not sure which location holds the key to the 1st master disk. With a few more days, we might get another clue either from research or from the wiretaps we placed on the phone lines leading to the offices of Dr. Procter, Roselyn Trundle's office, and Dr. Melham's lab."

Castor smiled and directed his attention to the person walking in the door; for the second time, Xavier was star-struck by Deralyn's beautiful features and how she held herself with majestic dignity and composure. She was like an expensive and elegant vase you coveted, but once you acquired it, you were too afraid to let others handle it out of fear it might get broken. Xavier paused momentarily and then looked at Castor. "How will we know what to look for or even what might be the next potential clue?"

Deralyn responded to his questions with a slight smile on her face. She gestured with her right hand towards the door, "Well, we now have two new additions to the team. I think they will be beneficial and much appreciated." Castor also smiled without saying a word. Xavier suspected he was up to something; he just had no clue what it might be.

The door opened, and in walked Matt and Packer, Xavier jumped up and rushed toward his two best friends, and they grabbed each other into a group bear hug. The grunts and groans punctuated how much the three boys missed each other and how glad they were to be back together. Moving backward, Xavier examined his two friends and noticed subtle changes in their appearance. Mathew shook his head; his out-of-control curls were gone; his hair was cut close to his scalp while his long full lashes framed his vivid green eyes. Even with the dramatic change in appearance, Matt's intelligence still revealed itself. He wore a warm cotton plaid red and black lumberjack shirt, faded blue jeans, and black scuffed military boots.

Packer had also changed his appearance; gone was the baby-faced kid who loved the Green Bay Packers. Instead, he now supported a well-kept beard and mustache. He also wore faded blue jeans, but instead of a Packer jersey, he wore a black Carhartt jacket over a black t-shirt. Both boys looked older than eighteen years, as evident underneath their eyes. He noticed signs of extreme fatigue and stress, with fine lines creasing the outer corner of their eyes. If Xavier had passed them on the street, he would not have recognized them until much later, only if they had spoken to him.

"How did you guys get here, and what are you doing," asked Xavier. "Wait, my mom and dad are ok? What about Will, Carter, and Lynda?" Matt held up his hand to stop Xavier's word vomiting and took the lead, pointing towards

Castor. "Ask him why we are here because he is the one who contacted me and told me you need us to come help."

Castor stood and shook Matt's hand before pulling him into a full-body hug. Matt turned towards Xavier as Castor started addressing the first of his many questions.

"Well, I knew you were homesick, and I thought you might need some cheering up. I also know that Matt is a whiz kid with computers, and based on the amount of data we need to analyze, I thought it would be better to have two kid geniuses. From what I can see, Sam needs some friendly competition."

Felis looked at Sam, "Just remember, I plan to pay you back for the CoNserv incident." Sam's indignant huff made everyone in the room laugh.

Gesturing towards Matt, Felis made a point of looking Sam in the eyes. "I promise your competing against Doggie Howser will be a piece of cake compared to what I do to you," said Felis.

Sam visibly gulped as everyone else who knew about the rental vehicle fiasco laughed in anticipation of the fun and games to come. The room's mood was especially jovial compared to some past strategy meetings before missions. Each person moved towards their now permanent seat around the conference table and adjusted their materials, waiting for the last person to join them before moving to the next agenda.

The door opened, and a man that Xavier had never seen before walked in. The man was of mixed ancestry, either Hispanic or African American; he was about six feet tall and weighed about one hundred and ninety pounds, four or five pounds. He wore a black t-shirt that stretched across his sculpted muscles and made every male in the room wish they had his physique unless you were Felis. His black slacks with black wing-tip shoes did little to draw attention away from his rugged good looks. Soulful dark brown eyes hypnotized the audience and only accented his clean-cut goatee.

The unknown visitor confidently walked towards Castor and offered his hand and smiled in greeting. Then pulling out the only empty chair a short way down the table, the man known as Wilson made himself comfortable. Looking at the individuals assembled within the room, no one would have known that some of them had known each other ranging from a day to a couple of months. For some individuals, it was years.

"Hello, Wilson. I am glad you could make it on such short notice, said Castor." He gestured to Wilson silently, indicating he currently had the floor. Wilson directed everyone's attention to the screen and put up a picture of two locations. One looked to be in Washington, DC. He then informed the rooms' occupants that the wiretaps were at CITRUM's ex-CEO Dr. Roselyn Trudel's home and office. He identified two places to look in connection with the deciphered zip code.

The first picture he put up on the screen was easy to recognize if you knew how to interpret the clues in the background. The cobblestone sidewalk and the late Victorian architecture from around the 1860s suggested the northeastern part of the U.S. The lower 1/3 of the building was made of pure white stone. The remaining two-thirds of the house consisted of traditional red brick with a compact spiral cement staircase and a black wrought iron rail along the edge of the eight steps leading to the front entrance.

Packer, the resident historian, raised his hand, "is that Ford's Theater in Washington D.C., he asked?"

Wilson nodded in affirmation and placed another image on the screen; this one was a little more difficult to figure out. The building resembled a Lego toy assembled by a toddler or a preschooler. The building had five levels, with the first floor made of wall-to-wall glass allowing for a visual inspection of the number of people in the lobby at any time. Floors 2-4 looked like they were made of blue coffee straw stir sticks laid vertically across the glass base of the building.

The final level of the building looked like it had a two-way class with a layer of smoked glass above and below it. The final touch on the building's design was the red straw-like pillars that connected floors 2, 3, and 4 and accented the blue stir sticks. If someone had asked Xavier what the building was used for, he would have said to manage the Lego Corporation or serve as a modern aquarium like the one in Newport, Kentucky.

Xavier remembered enjoying going to the Newport Aquarium with his mom and brother. One of his mom's former students worked at the Aquarium, and she had given them a behind-the-scenes pass and took them to see the stingray and play with the penguins. He had even had the chance to feed the stingrays, scuba dive in the tank, and watch how the tanks were cleaned each week.

After the Aquarium, Xavier and his parents visited Northern Kentucky University. He loved the campus and knew where he wanted to go to law school. Most kids wanted to attend the more prominent and prestigious law schools, but he wanted to attend a school that would not break the bank and had a small-town feel. The Salomon Chase School of Law had a program to allow individuals to work and study via a hybrid system of online classes and direct instruction. That day he felt like he had his entire life mapped out. It was a great day for not only him but for the family.

Wilson's voice pulled him out of his reminiscing; "This picture is the International Spy Museum, and it is the second possible location," he said. "The first image of the Ford Theater could be the target because of the history of the place with Dr. Trudel's ancestor Mary Todd Lincoln. Another reason could be the symbolic meaning of the fact that John Wilks Booth believed he was destroying tyranny with the assassination of Abraham Lincoln.

After completing his last statement, Xavier said, "I think the segmented disk is at the International Spy Museum."

Castor tilted his head and looked at him before asking the obvious question. "Why do you think it is the ISM, he asked?"

Packer laughed and told the room at large that it was because Xavier wanted to play with spy toys and techie gadgets. In a sing-song voice, he started to sing the theme song "Secret Agent Man."

Everyone broke out in laughter over the boy's shenanigans. Shaking his head, Xavier said, "No, it is because it would be too easy to find it in Ford's theater."

Turning his head towards Packer, he placed his thumb on his nose with an open hand and said, "Nana nana boo boo."

The group collectively laughed at the byplay between the two boys. "Plus, everyone knows that in spy movies and real life, it is never that easy," said Xavier.

Wilson redirected everyone's attention to the screen; "I agree with Xavier's assessment about the possibility of the disk being located somewhere in the ISM building. Based on the exhibits listed on the website at the ISM facility, we believe that the fifth floor may be the best place to start searching for the disk. Matt nodded his head in agreement and said, "we can use a portable X-ray Fluorescence (XRF) gun to identify the piece we are looking for because most C.D.s have an outer metallic reflective layer made up of aluminum, lead, and silver."

Just as Xavier was going to ask what an X-ray Fluorescence gun was Matt spoke up and said, "An XRF gun provides compositional and purity analysis of any object using an infer-red laser. Think of a scanner from the Wal-Mart self-checkout station, it is portable and could increase our efficiency rate and save valuable time while minimizing the manpower required to complete a comprehensive search."

Xavier felt like things were back to normal with Packer and Matt by his side for just one moment. He felt a little less alone and a little less homesick.

Wilson sat down as Castor pushed out his chair before outlining the three-prong process for identifying and obtaining the three pieces of the master disk. Xavier, Panthera, and Felis, according to Castor's master plan, would be tasked with scoping out the locations. Once the disk was located, they reconvened and planned to acquire it. Xavier would have to pull back his hair into a ponytail and apply the tribal tattoo made by Matt. The change in appearance would also apply to both Panthera and Felis to prevent anyone from CITRUM identifying them.

Matt then spoke up and mentioned that he had brought some special effect inventions and past costumes from previous school musicals from Huntington North High School. The idea was to dress Panthera and Felis as an older married couple, not too old, because their range of movement and agility would give them away. Xavier's disguise would consist of dressing as a nomadic college student traveling across the United States during his gap year and exploring the history and culture of his forefathers.

Xavier knew when they started out that Matt planned to transform their appearance, but he did not realize just how dramatic of a change it would be once everything was said and done. Felis looked like a middle-aged man. His sparsely sprinkled gray hair now dominated the once jet-black hair making it look like a mixture of salt and pepper.

It reminded him of his dad, and the homesickness became more robust and persistent than at any other time. Instead of a suit and tie, Felis now wore a faded grey Washington DC tourist sweatshirt and faded blue jeans with generic white tennis shoes. Panthera's appearance was also radically transformed as well.

She was dressed in the same manner as Felis, but her once beautiful hair was now covered by a shoulder-length wig similar to her partner's salt and pepper locks. Matt had also added some age spots and wrinkles on the outer corner of her eyes. Combining all three added ten years to her age and surprisingly made her seem to resemble Felis. Xavier had always heard that the older a couple got and the longer they were together, the more they started to resemble each other. He wondered if Felis and Panthera realized they had feelings for each other or if they were ignoring the chemistry between them. Would they ever move past being partners and explore the possibility of being a couple?

The line leading into the ISM building was extended and static; Xavier could tell that this was one of the more popular tourist destinations in D.C. just by the number of individuals standing in line waiting for the doors to open. Felis and Panthera were situated at the back of the line.

They ignored Xavier's presence as if they did not know each other. The line started to move a bit at a time, and every so often, it stopped as the individuals purchased their tickets and submitted to a cursory search of their bags. His train of thought was temporarily derailed when he realized that his backpack would be searched upon entry.

Felis provided an unexpected diversion by bumping into the white table used to place bags on to facilitate the search process. The table wobbled only to start falling slowly, knocking over the two men standing behind the table. While the guards struggled to lift the table and set it right, Xavier used the distraction to discreetly remove the XRF gun from his bag and move it to the small of his back. The line started to move forward again after everything was put to right. Xavier prayed that he would pass the guards without the XRF gun being detected.

Once past the guard checkpoint, he stopped before the museum directory detailing the exhibits on each floor. Based on the directory listings, the fifth floor looked like an exhibit organized around the themes of Briefing Center, Stealing Secrets, Making Sense of Secrets, Covert Action, and Mata Hari, the Dutch dancer, spy, and Ian Fleming's James Bond. Xavier had always liked James Bond movies, especially those with Roger Moore or Pierce Bronson. Still, as for Mata Hari, he barely remembered anything about her. He thought he may have covered the topic in Advance Placement World Civilization taught by Mrs. McClean. However, he was unsure if he was awake or sleeping, the funny thing is Mrs. McClean always suspected he was sleeping, but she could never prove it.

The building was designed in a semi-corkscrew progression, moving gradually from one level to another. Each exhibit seamlessly flowed into one another and was more interesting than the next. Rather than stop and participate in the activities on the lower levels or interact with the other patrons, he briskly walked up to the fifth floor. Xavier was the sole patron on the fifth floor; the exhibits immediately captured his attention. He temporarily forgot he was supposed to be scanning for the disk.

Removing the XRF gun from the waistband of his jeans, he started scanning for the metal alloys that could provide them with additional answers. Just for a moment, Xavier wished Colleen were with him. She could turn any boring and mundane event into something fun. He could just imagine her creating a fun game. It would be based on something silly like pretending they were getting married and running around and scanning every item as if they were putting them on a wedding registry until they fell into a heap from laughter.

The XRF gun barely made any sound as he was scanning the items. If Felis had not shown him the infrared light it emitted while scanning, he would have doubted it was working correctly. He continued working his way from one exhibit to another until he got to the Mata Hari exhibit. Temporarily he stopped scanning as he refreshed his memory on who she was and how she lost her life at the hands of the French government.

The evidence used to convict her was flimsy at best. The French claimed she had revealed to the Germans the identity of a double agent working for the Germans and the French in 1916. She was executed as a spy and used as a scapegoat for all the mistakes made by the French government and the French military during World War I. Seemed awfully convenient for the French and inconvenient for Mata Hari.

Suddenly the XRF gun started to emit a low-level beep like what a Geiger counter would emit the closer it got to radioactive materials. He waved the device over each part of the exhibit, dividing it into four quadrants as he was taught in his high school Criminology class when they talked about crime scene investigations. Quadrant A was located to the upper left, quadrant B was on the upper right side, quadrant C was beneath A, and quadrant D was beneath B.

The gun remained quiet as he progressively moved from Quadrant A to B. It was not until he moved into quadrant C that the device again started to emit the beeping tone that signified the presence of the materials he was looking for. Still, where it was located exactly was not yet evident. He continued to slowly search the area using both the gun and his right hand by running it along the edges of the objects. Randomly he would look over his shoulder to verify he was still alone.

His hand moved smoothly over each object when suddenly he noticed a sharp poke to his right index finger, and at the same time, the XRF gun started beeping like crazy. He quickly shut it off and moved away from the exhibit as two random patrons and a security guard walked up the spiral ramp, their talking alerting him to their presence long before he saw them.

He knew it was time to alert Felis and Panther to his discovery. Now that he thought about it, he realized that if a portion of the disk was hidden in the Mata Hari exhibit, it made sense in a weird but logical manner.

Mata Hari was talented and very progressive in her lifestyle and innovative in her unique ability to craft a new identity after the old one had been stripped away by an abusive ex-husband and a harsh patriarchal society. A small part of him felt a slight kinship with the long-forgotten spy. He also thought he was creating a new identity after Dr. Procter and his goons stripped him of his old identity and way of life.

Walking down the ramp, he casually looked for Felis and Panthera; he knew they were assessing the security arrangements and creating a plan to infiltrate the facility after everyone had gone home. On level four, he spotted both and walked over to the exhibit titled "Spying that shaped history" and started reading the information provided on the placards detailing the trial and execution of Julius and Ethel Rosenberg, who were accused of giving the

Russians the secrets of the nuclear weapons designs and other U.S. military secrets.

After a few minutes, he looked at another section of the exhibit. He casually bumped into Panthera as planned and gave the prearranged response to signal that he had located the object. "Pardon me; I tend to be clumsy and don't often look where I am going," said Xavier. She quickly responded with, "No problem." He asked, "Do you know where the bathrooms are located?" With a nod, she replied, "They are located on the first floor near the exit sign to the right of the ticket booth."

He turned towards the door-marked exit and walked down the stairs to the first floor. Upon exiting the stairwell, he went into the restrooms. He used the facilities, washed his hands, and stalled for time before heading out of the ISM building. Being in Washington D.C. seem surreal, especially since the last time he had been here was to attend in 2041 when Mackey O'Bannon (R) was sworn in as the 50th President of the United States of America.

Xavier started walking towards the L'Enfant Bar and Grill, waiting for Felis and Panthera to join him for lunch. He was grateful that Castor was footing the bill for the trip because, based on the look of the hotel and the restaurant, he figured the cost of the stay would be a little pricey. The National Mall Hotel by Hilton was a swanky upscale facility, and the restaurant was rated five stars. Xavier remembered something his mother once told him about eating at these restaurants.

She always said that you could tell how expensive the restaurant would be without looking at the menu based on three things: first, the heavier the silverware, the more expensive the food. Second, examine the type of napkins they used; cloth napkins increase the cost. The final telltale sign was whether the water glasses were genuine crystal.

His mom also showed him how to test if the goblets were genuine crystal by filling them up with water, dipping his finger in the liquid, and then running his finger along the rim; if it made a high pitch sound, then it was real. Based on these three things, he knew that the bill would be beyond his price range as a soon to be broke college student.

The L'Enfant Suite, where the group was staying, was located next to the Chef de l'État suite, also known in English as the Presidential Suite. Both occupied the entire top floor of the hotel. Each suite had a unique black diamond speckled card that provided the holder with unlimited access to the facilities offered by the hotel at any time, regardless of whether it was closed to the public. A chef and a waiter were assigned to work in the bar and grill after hours to man the kitchen and provide one on one service.

Those who worked during the off hours were well compensated for their time. Many of the waiters and waitresses knew that working just one of these shifts could provide them with tips equal to or above what they earned working in one month, so there was no shortage of volunteers. Xavier thought it was awesome that the hotel was built atop an esplanade. In this extended, open, level area, people walked for pleasure. A parking structure and a highway were situated underneath the hotel along the southwestern quadrant.

He stood before the podium with the sign stating, "Please wait to be seated." It seemed like forever before the maître

d' arrived, and he seemed to sneer at Xavier's choice of
attire, he asked if he was a guest in the hotel. Xavier
casually pulled out his black diamond-speckled hotel card.
He mentioned he was staying in the L'Enfant Suite with two
of his colleagues.

Suddenly the maître d' became extremely helpful and
apologetic; the man practically tripped over himself and
stuttered in a panic. Xavier asked for three seats, preferably
a booth in a remote area, to maximize privacy. He followed
the maître d at a leisurely pace, all the while reflecting on
how just mentioning the name of the suite radically
changed the behavior of the snobby little man.

His mom had always told him that the actual value of a
man was not what was in his bank account but what was in
his heart. He could tell the little man was not raised with the
same Midwest values as he and Will. The booth he was
directed towards could easily seat up to five people. He was
in a corner near the back of the restaurant to the right of
the kitchen exit. Slowly perusing the menu, he patiently
waited for his companions.

About ten minutes later, Xavier looked up from his menu
and noticed the maître d' escorting Felis and Panthera
towards the table; again, he wondered if they realized how
much they complimented each other. He placed the menu
on the table and waited until they were alone before
speaking up.

"So, did you enjoy your trip to the museum today?" He
asked.

Felis just looked at him and grunted; Panthera smiled and
laughed as she swatted him on his left shoulder. "Mr.

Grumpy Pants enjoyed it; he just doesn't want to admit it," she said. "I also enjoyed the Mata Hari exhibit, especially the old pictures and the letters retrieved after she died."

Panthera moved around Felis and slid into the booth, ensuring ample room between her and the two guys. Neither talked as they shook out the cloth napkins and arranged their silverware and water glasses in the same manner and format. They then perused the menu in silence only to place them on the table as the waiter in a hunter green polo shirt and black slacks approached with his tablet.

Once their selections had been conveyed to the waiter, they handed over their menus. They patiently waited for him to exit the vicinity.

After the waiter had crossed the room to the wait station to fill their drink orders, Xavier turned towards his friends. "Speaking of the Mata Hari exhibit, I found the item we are looking at in that exhibit. I do not know specifically where? I have a general idea, but I did not want to be too conspicuous and alert anyone to what I was doing," he said.

Panthera was the first to respond to Xavier's statement.

"That was the smart thing to do, especially since Felis and I agree that acquiring the needed supplies to access the building may take a few days. While we were scoping out the security and location of the cameras, we noticed that some security technologies were higher tech than what was necessary for a cultural museum that housed exhibits that monetarily would bring low payout if ever stolen."

"I agree," said Felis.

"The museum technology should only consist of cameras, alarms, and security guards; instead, there is a retinal scanner, a palm scanner, and laser beams only on the fifth floor. So that tells us that something on that floor is important to someone. Now the first thing I will do is reach out to a friend working for the Defense Department as an independent contractor. Maxis is a security specialist, and I can pick his brain on the best way to acquire the portion of the disk without possibly injuring anyone or causing massive damage."

Xavier leaned forward with his elbows on the table; he knew if his mom were here, she would pip him upside head and remind him that he could be trashy or classy, not both. Just the thought made him take his elbows off the table.

"Wait will we get in trouble for damaging the exhibits; it is one thing to break into a house to rescue a Colleen who had been kidnapped by Dr. Proctor and his goons. It is another thing to vandalize a facility; I want answers but not enough to be charged with felony breaking and entering," said Xavier.

Panthera shook her head and laid a restraining hand on Felis's forearm; looking at Xavier, she calmly explained that Castor had a plan to minimize the risk of being charged with felony breaking and entering if they should be caught.

"Castor as a member of the board of directors and as a person who donates a large sum of money to the International Spy Museum each year, has the authority to hire independent contractors to test the security system. He will argue that enough money is being allocated to security measures at the next board meeting if we are caught.

He will then propose to funnel additional funds into the educational budget instead of giving more to the security budget. The charges will be dropped, and our arrest will be expunged from our records. I promise nothing will be destroyed or taken other than the portion of the disk, and we will replace it with a replica created by Sam," she said.

Felis picked up where she left off stating, "the mission will take three days; we have already completed the first day of reconnaissance. The second day will require getting into the facility, measuring, and photographing the object, and sending the information to Sam to produce the replica. Then the last day will consist of removing the disk and switching the two items, followed by a hasty retreat to Chicago. Only those individuals who know of its existence and location will realize that the portion of the master disk is even missing, and that is only if they try to physically access the information on it."

Xavier could not one hundred percent eliminate his worries. Still, he acknowledged that Panthera and Felis had never lied to him before. They were more like the older sister and brother he had always wanted rather than an instructor or mentor. It was time to have faith that everything would work out for the best. What was that old saying his mother liked to say something to effect plan for the worst and hope for the best.

The heavy atmosphere was broken by the arrival of food; in all the confusion, Xavier had forgotten that they had placed their order, much less that it had arrived. However, before everyone started eating, Xavier said a silent prayer that he and his friends would be successful in their endeavors and that no one would get hurt or killed.

The remainder of the meal progressed in silence as everyone dug into their chosen entrees and enjoyed the rest of their food and drinks without worrying about paying for the meal out of their own pockets. One nice thing about working with someone as wealthy and powerful as Castor was that they had an expense account to pay for meals and lodging. After dinner, everyone agreed to meet in Panthera's hotel room after showering and changing.

Xavier, as a former swimmer, prided himself on his ability to get dressed fast. His mom used to hate how at competitions, he and his friends would deck change with just a towel in a remote corner of the pool deck. She always scolded him and told him it was inappropriate to not change in the locker rooms, but he and his friends felt that it took too much time away from flirting with the girls from the other schools. He remembered when one of his friends thought it would be funny to grab his face and place his thumbs over his mouth to kiss him.

Xavier did not know that the young lady he was interested in was standing behind him about 25 yards away with her friends, watching the two of them. He was so mad when he realized what his friend Allen had done. The girl afterward assumed they were a couple, and he was too embarrassed to correct the assumption.

He stopped suddenly and wondered where that memory came from. He did not know anyone named Allen, yet the memory seemed so natural, and something about the memory made him uncomfortable and anxious. Putting the question aside, he pushed away the memory to focus on the here and now.

The L'Enfant Suite had a beautiful view of the Potomac River and the newly revitalized Wharf District; the 1,379 square feet of space was equivalent to the size of a small three-bedroom house in the suburbs. The living area consisted of a sofa and two chairs with matching ottomans in front of an electric fireplace with a 65-inch flat-screen television above the mantel. A private dining room with seating for eight provided plenty of space to entertain, eat meals or conduct meetings.

A secondary seating area and a fully functioning wet bar encouraged impromptu gatherings around a small table with four bar stools. The master bedroom had a ginormous king bed with an oversized wooden work desk, a comfortable reclining chair to relax in, and a 65-inch HDTV with casting capability to stream content; it was designed to be a home away from home.

Upon checking into the hotel, Felis had offered Panthera the king-size bed, which left Xavier and him with the two remaining couches. However, Panthera refused and argued that because of Felis' size, he needed the bed more than she did. As she had previously stated at CiderLane, even a loveseat was a comfortable bed for a person of her stature.

Xavier scoped out one of the two chairs in the living area as a potential bed. He had learned during his brief cohabitation with Felis at CiderLane that Felis snored like a freight train, and there would be no getting sleep if he shared a room with him.

Xavier walked towards the sound of Felis and Panthera's voices; he guessed he was not the fastest dresser after all, he thought. The closer he got to the dining area, the better he could hear and understand what they were discussing. Once in the room, he realized the dining table was currently being used to study and mark known security measures and entrance and exit points on a blueprint of ISM. Panthera stood off the side of the table, looking at a tablet containing the security notes they had made during their leisurely tour of the facilities. A smartphone lay on the table off to the right of Felis, it appeared to Xavier as if they were conducting a three-way call with Castor, Sam, and Felis, but that changed when he heard Matt ask Panthera a technical question about the retinal scanner employed by the facility.

Panthera looked up from the notepad, placing her pencil in her hair as she addressed the room. "Xavier, welcome to the party," she said.

Castor's voice echoed through the phone, "Xavier, got some bad news for you. I need you to stay at the hotel while Panthera and Felis make the initial entry to bypass security."

Upon hearing Castor's statement, his first thought was to interrupt him and ask why he had been sent along if not to help breach the security and retrieve the device. However, the following statement stopped him in his tracks.

"Xavier, you have an uncanny ability to project a harmless carefree facade and persuade random strangers to open up and talk to you. I may have a lead on someone who knows something about my sister's abduction. All you need to do is show up at the rendezvous point and casually bump into the person and place a tracking device somewhere on their skin. It will have completely embedded itself into their skin within a few seconds. It is a new form of technology Sam and Matt have been tweaking in their spare time."

Felis' booming laugh echoed around the room, "If that is what the goobers do in their spare time, I would hate to see what they do on vacation," he said. The speakers crackled as both Matt and Sam protested being called a nut.

If Xavier did not know better, he would have thought that Sam and Matt were twins separated at birth and adopted by separate families.

"The meeting place will be at the old Kimpton Carlyle Hotel near Dupont Circle in the restaurant off the lobby area. The gentleman will be sitting at the bar awaiting the arrival of one of my associates. I suspect the guy knows what my go-to associates look like because he mentioned Felis and Panthera by name. So, you are an unknown element, and it might be easier for you to plant the device rather than by someone they already know and distrust," said Castor.

Xavier tried to remember what he had learned about the Carlyle Hotel; he vaguely recalled it was where former president John Fitzgerald Kennedy (JFK) slept with the blonde and busty Hollywood icon Marilyn Monroe. He also remembered that his mom had mentioned she had stayed there at one time when she attended a conference at the same time the presidential inauguration was taking place. She said the streets were packed with people. There was a party-like atmosphere, but she remembered the extreme cold and the snow that sparkled like diamonds against the backdrop of red, white, and blue hanging along railings, doors, and on every available open space.

"Well, I have never done something like this before, but I guess I can give it a go; time to put some of the specialized training you provided to good use," said Xavier.

"Good man," said Castor. "I hope this person is the real thing and not another con artist seeking a payday. Whenever someone contacts me, I am reminded of the story of the Dowager Empress Maria of Russia after the Bolsheviks murdered the Russian royal family. It must have been a nightmare for her to deal with all the con men and the actresses who pretended to be Anastasia Romanov, the Grand Duchess and last princess of the Russian empire. I know what it is like to get your hopes up and then be disappointed. However, unlike the Grand Duchess, I know man's manipulative and deceitful nature."

Everyone in the room remained silent; there was nothing to say.

At that moment, Xavier vowed that he would not mess up his first solo mission, mainly because this could be the way he started paying back Castor for his generous support and understanding in helping him with his struggle to find answers and return to his life. The rest of the meeting passed in a blur as each participant received their mission details and hashed out strategies to counter any potential complication that may arise. In the back of his mind, he wondered what he would do once everything was over, and he got his life back. The questions in his head started to pile up upon each other. They only served to increase his anxiety about the situation. Taking a nap would help him calm his nerves and make it so that he would be more refreshed and alert before he headed to the rendezvous site.

Xavier looked around the bar area of the Carlyle Hotel. He noticed it had a homey elegant feel to the bar area. Everything from floor to ceiling was adorned in Cherry wood tiles or panels. The brown leather booths blended with the wooden wall panels and floor tiles. Modern deco light fixtures in the shape of globes with blinding white shades and white padded chairs broke up the sea of brown. It reminded him of Castor's board room, except in this case, the bar was made of white marble with art deco stain glass windows located on the wall behind the bar allowing for additional light to filter into the room. Glass shelves were positioned in front of every other window to allow for storage of an eclectic mix of liquor. The light from the windows lit up the multi-sized bottles. It reminded him of a Tiffany lampshade and how it created a kaleidoscope of light and colors.

Some of the tables had circular brown ottomans for people to either sit on or use to prop up their feet after a long day at work; however, he doubted that the bar would be that empty to allow for unoccupied seats. The meeting was scheduled for 6 pm. One of Castor's security personnel sat at the bar waiting to contact the informant. Xavier located a bar stool close to the restroom; he figured it would make watching as people entered the lounge or headed toward the bathrooms easier.

His job was to blend in with the other patrons, and once the informant showed up it was up to Xavier to plant the tracking device on him. Pretending to be strangers, both Xavier and the security person ignored each other. They projected an air of preoccupation with their own issues and internal struggles with life.

The tracking device developed by Sam was nothing like anything he had ever seen. It was based on Nanotechnology and could only be detected with a microscope. The Nanite were waterproof and ran off the electrical impulses transmitted by the nervous system. While he had not seen the Nanites up close; he had to take Sam and Matt at their

word, that the vial contained the tracking device. It was
explained to him by Sam that as long as the Nanite was in a
glass vial or refrigerated, it would remain dormant, but
should it meet human or animal skin or be removed from
the glass vial, the increase in temperatures would re-
activate them.

The nanites had enough reserve energy to power
themselves until they could imbed themselves into the skin
and access the electrical impulses produced by the
biological systems of its host. Even if only one Nanite made
it on the host's skin, it would replicate until it was strong
enough and capable of transmitting a signal back to the
command center.

Xavier asked for a glass of water with ice and a Coke
without ice; he placed the Coke next to him and put his
jacket on the seat to make it look like he was with a friend
and to give the impression they had just gone to the
bathroom. He sipped the water and hoped that anyone
looking would assume it was vodka on the rocks. Looking at
the mirror hanging on the wall, he thought about how just
pulling his hair back and adding a tribal tattoo on his face
was enough to add five to ten years to his age, making him
look much older than his age, old enough that the bartender
did not feel the need to ask for his identification.

When the informant entered the lounge, he was quickly
picked out because of his rumpled and disheveled
appearance. Xavier could tell right away that the gentleman
was a novice at this type of thing, and he projected an
attitude of barely contained panic. He was about five feet
five, on the thin side except for the belly that could pass as a
baby bump on a female. His glasses' thick black frames and
lenses enlarged his owlish brown, gold eyes. He reminded

Xavier of a middle-aged balding Bob Crotchet from the book "A Christmas Carol," by Charles Dickens.

The gentleman stopped before the bar and asked for a Shirley Temple, which was nothing more than a little kid drink named after the famous Hollywood child actress Shirley Temple. The drink consisted of 7-up soda, maraschino cherries, ice, and grenadine syrup; just drinking that in front of Xavier or his friends made him want to laugh hysterically. The look on the bartender's face conveyed a sense of disgust, and any chance of the guy projecting an image of a successful businessman went down the drain.

Once the bartender placed the drink on the bar, the gentleman turned towards Castor's security guy. He said, "Hey Jake, is it true that JFK slept with Audrey Hepburn in this hotel?"

Castor's man responded disinterestedly, "No, Brian, that is Marilyn Monroe you are thinking of, " Hepburn starred in "Breakfast with Tiffany."

The informant looked at him and asked, "Are you sure it's not at instead of with," he asked. Completing the prearranged conversation signaled that they were speaking with the correct individual. The informant struggled to climb onto the barstool as his companion watched silently and offered no assistance.

He could not hear the rest of the conversation due to the sudden influx of individuals just getting off work as the start of happy hour heralded the end of the workday and the beginning of a long weekend.

Xavier waited until both the bartender and the informant were busy and not looking his way before removing the vial from the jacket pocket, he had laid across the adjourning bar stool. Looking around to ensure no one was looking, he poured the nanite vial into the remaining melted ice water.

He turned back towards the bar and waited for the informant to complete the transaction with Castor's man. Before the meeting, they agreed that the security officer would instruct the man to go to the restroom before leaving so that they did not leave together and rouse any suspicions in case someone watched the interaction between them.

He noticed the informant discreetly passing a yellow manila envelope to his neighbor, who provided him with a box shaped like a rectangle with assorted Lindt Milk chocolate truffles inside. The security guy instructed the informant to say hello to the wife and kids and give them his love and chocolates. Clapping a friendly hand on the informant's right shoulder, the security guy stood up, moved towards the front entrance, and exited the hotel, never looking back towards the bar.

Xavier wondered if he never looked back because he was confident that he would cover his six or if it was because another security person in the hotel lobby was assigned to watch how he handled his first solo mission. The informant got up with his box of chocolates and headed toward the bathroom. Just as he was ready to pass Xavier, he jumped up. He made sure to collide with him and splashed the remaining liquid in his glass onto the hand holding the raincoat and the chocolates.

Both men voices clashed as one said, "I am so sorry," and the other said, "Look what you have done."

Xavier attempted to dab the front of his shirt without touching the area where the liquid touched his skin.

The man angrily pushed away his hands and said, "I am fine; get away from me. I don't need your help."

In response, Xavier turned towards the door, and the informant continued to the restroom to dry his coat and clean up before heading home.

At the hotel room, Xavier got ready for bed. He looked forward to completing the rest of the mission and returning to Chicago and his friends. He had sent the folder back to Castor via a special courier. He hoped he had successfully planted the tracking device on the informant. He quickly made up two larger couches in the suite's living area. He doubted he could walk straight by the time he arrived in Chicago, what with sleeping on a sofa for three days and flying in a plane multiple time.

He knew that tomorrow night Panthera and Felis would make a foray into the International Spy Museum and photograph the portion of the disk so that Matt and Sam could copy it and replace the original with a look alike. Laying his head on the pillow he stole from king size bed, he listened to the sounds of Panthera and Felis playing spades in the next room; neither felt the need to go to bed before midnight, and it seemed to him that they functioned best when they only slept four or five hours a night. He knew his ability to function required eight hours of sleep or more.

The next day Xavier woke to the sun shining through the drapes and the sound of the door closing on the gentleman delivering breakfast to the three guests. The smell of bacon, sausage, pancakes, and eggs teased Xavier awake. At the same time, the sound of the adults helping themselves to coffee produced a Pavlov-type response in him.

He wanted to pull the covers up over his head and go back to sleep and pretend he was at home and that, at any moment, his mom would come through the door to wake him up. Releasing a long-suffering sigh, he kicked the blanket off and swung his feet off the couch.

Rubbing his hand over his face, he mumbled, "What is that awful smell," he asked. "It smells like my cocker spaniel did a number two in the house."

Panthera laughed and replied, "I will have you know the waiter told me it was high-quality coffee grown on the slope of an active volcano in Hawaii."

"Again, it smells like puppy poop," said Xavier as Felis grunted in agreement.

It was apparent to him and Panthera that Felis was not a morning person, at least not until he finished his coffee.

"What is the game plan for today? I know we have the mission tonight, but that is late tonight. So that means we have eighteen hours to burn until we head out." By this time, Felis seemed more awake and inclined to join the conversation, "I suggest we go look at some tourist sites, enjoy lunch, take a nap, and then get ready to have some fun."

Xavier waited until Panthera finished her last bite of toast before asking what monuments they planned to visit. He knew that he wanted to at least visit Lincoln's Memorial, the Holocaust Memorial, and the Smithsonian National Air and

Space Museum. The last time he took a trip with his family was for a college visit. Mom and Dad promised to go on a big family vacation as one last family trip after high school graduation. His parents had even told him he could pick the destination. He finally decided he wanted to go to Italy and see the Vatican, the Sistine Chapel, and the Frescoes painted by the Italian Renaissance artist Michelangelo.

But now that was just a pipe dream. After a moment he decided he would treat this trip like a mini vacation and make some memories that he could share with his family, future children, and grandchildren.

The sound of Panthera asking Felis if he had a preference pulled him from his melancholy thoughts. Felis then informed them that he had at one-time work on Embassy Row, so he really did not care where they went one way or the other.

However, as a man who did enjoy a good meal, he wanted to eat at a nice sit-down restaurant that makes a good steak. He suggested St. Anselm on 5th Street, near Union Market, around 1 pm. Afterward, they would return to the hotel, shower, and nap before preparing for the midnight reconnaissance trip to the ISM.

Xavier knew that there was no point in asking Felis what he did or where he worked on Embassy Row because those assigned to this part of D.C. often had to sign a non-disclosure agreement. The remainder of the day went just as Xavier and Felis planned, except when Felis picked up Panthera and threatened to dump her in the reflection pool near the WWII memorial. Overall, it was a good day.

Later that night, Xavier paced the suite, anxious and nervous about how long it took for Panthera and Felis to access the ISM building and photograph the disk. He knew that the disk would be easy to replicate once they sent the photographs to Matt and Sam and they would then receive the replica via special messenger. It was just a matter of patience; one of the things he discovered early on was that the waiting was more difficult than he could ever have imagined. The suite door opened, and Panthera and Felis walked in, laughing, and giggling like two teenagers. With his hands on his hips, Xavier assumed the role of the concerned parent and demanded to know what took them so long.

Felis laughed again and said, "Look, honey, our little cub is worried about us."

If Felis had been looking at Panthera's face when he called her honey and referred to Xavier as their little cub, he would have seen the longing in her eyes and the sadness on her face.

Xavier's heart went out to her, and his anger and impatience disappeared in response to Panthera's personal pain.

Panthera's good humor rapidly evaporated as she moved into the room, "we successfully found the object and took the required pictures without having to disturb or remove it from its resting spot. However, I suggest we all go to bed and get some rest because tomorrow we have a long day in front of us."

The door slammed shut; an audible engagement of the locking mechanism to the master bedroom signaled the end of all conversation.

Felis looked toward Xavier; his face showed puzzlement and confusion. "Did I do something wrong or say something wrong?"

Xavier wanted to help him, but he knew that when it came to matters of the heart, it was better if they figured it out between themselves. Shrugging his shoulders in response, Xavier turned towards his sleeping area.

"I guess I am sleeping on the couch tonight. I just wish I knew what I said or did." Felis said as he walked towards the area where Panthera had slept the night before.

The next day the group packed their bags and individually figured out ways to pass the time until they left on their mission. Felis watched forensic files on television, and Panthera read a historical romance book by an author named Barbara Cartland. While Xavier completed the New York Times crossword puzzle and then took a nap waiting for hours to pass by until they left to retrieve the item.

He knew the plan to recover and replace the item with the duplicate was low risk, but he could not help being nervous and anxious that something might go wrong. Some part of him wanted to confide in Panthera or Felis, but he did not want them to tell him he was a baby. He felt like he had started to earn their respect over the past month and did not want to do anything to jeopardize it. By the time 10 pm arrived, Xavier was so keyed up and anxious to get the mission over with and head back to Chicago.

The International Spy Museum and the area around it resembled a Western-style ghost town; the streets were devoid of life, lights on the poles flickered on and off, and the only sounds that punctuated the silence were the buzzing of insects as they made their final kamikaze flight into the heated streetlamps. If anyone had passed by or looked out an office window, all they would have seen were dark shadows moving low to the ground; in some cases, they might even mistake them for stray dogs searching for scraps of food, small rodents, or stray cats. If asked by law enforcement or interested parties, everything about that night was unremarkable.

Panthera took the lead, moving towards the electrical security control panel located on the side of the building; she quickly punched in an override code provided by Mathew and Sam. Once the panel was opened, she pulled out an electronic device she had received via a special courier earlier in the day. Xavier knew the device needed to be connected to the camera feed for at least three minutes. Once done, it would submit a program that would temporarily mimic the security system and loop the camera footage until it was removed.

In theory, this would make it appear to the remote-control team and the guard that the system was still functioning when every security system would be turned off in the facility, making it unnecessary to worry about passing the retina scan or the infer-red lasers. Xavier felt like Sam and Matt had given him the cheat code to defeat the system, like when Kirk from Star Trek, as a cadet, beat the no-win scenario, Kobayashi Maru. In theory, this would give the group the additional time needed to switch the disk piece and get in and out.

Once Panthera had connected everything, they waited for three minutes to pass before heading towards the back entrance of the facility. While three minutes does not sound like a lot of time, Xavier felt like time stood still, especially when you had to watch and time everything down to the last nanosecond. She motioned the two males to proceed her into the building using sign language like those used by airplane controllers on the tarmac. In response to her silent instructions, Felis moved toward the front position. Xavier assumed the middle, and Panthera pulled up the rear, guarding their sixes. The group moved from level to level in a silent and coordinated manner, each listening and watching for anything that might complicate the mission.

The gradual progression to the fifth floor was quiet and uneventful due to the late hour and the fact that the security guard had previously made his rounds and was supposed to be checking the video feeds and the security system in the control booth on the second floor.

Once the group had reached the fifth floor, they moved cautiously along the wall until they approached the Mata Hari exhibit. The silence in the room was only broken by the breathing of the three individuals; Panthera proceeded to the spot where the disk was hidden within a replica of the statue of Shiva Natara Ja; in Hindu religion, he was known as the creator, preserver, and destroyer of the universe.

The reproduction differed from the original one located in Birmingham Museum of Art Alabama because of the artist's usage of gold-plated materials for the coating of the statue and the incorporation of what appeared to be a portion of aluminum, gold, and silver or silver alloy in the shape of a circular piece precisely one-third of the size of a 360-degree circle located directly behind the head of the

Shiva Natara Ja. The metallic silver appearance of the wedge reflected light and made the statue appear alive.

Panthera held her hand out to Xavier, motioning for him to give her the fake disc as she removed the real one from the statue; suddenly, she stopped and gestured to Felis and Xavier to freeze; she tilted her head to listen.

Xavier also strained his ears to pick up any possible sound; at that moment, he wished he could lift his ears like a dog and magnify every sound. After a few minutes, he could hear the off-tune sound of someone whistling the theme song to the old television Andy Griffin show.

All three of them broke away from each other and crouched down low to the floor behind the other exhibit furniture and displays. The sound moved closer and closer and became more off-key as it became apparent that the whistler had forgotten some of the song and was recycling the parts he knew.

The whistling abruptly stopped, and a beam of light moved around the area, breaking up the shadows that pooled around each exhibit. Ironically, the security guard resembled the character of Barney Fife from the Andy Griffin show. Both the guard and the actor Don Knotts were about 5 feet 7 inches tall with a slender build and probably weighed only one hundred and thirty-eight pounds.

It was hard for Xavier to tell from his hiding place if the guard was as socially inept or high-strung as Barney. If he was, did that mean his revolver was empty or only had one bullet? He was in no rush to find out either way and just prayed that he would turn around and leave them in peace.

The few minutes it took for the security guard to scan the entire area was just long enough that Xavier felt his knees locking up and going numb with a loss of feeling in his lower extremities. The guard started to turn around when the sound of the air conditioning unit caused him to stop and jerk back around. Holding his breath Xavier froze and prayed that he would leave and go on his merry way. After a few moments, he did just that. He finally released his pent-up breath; he was ever so grateful for the breathing exercises his swim coach insisted he and the other swim team practice daily.

Felis stood halfway across the room, facing toward the entryway the security guard had left by; Panthera reached for the fragmented disk and replaced it with the replica. Turning towards Xavier and Felis, she made the prearranged sign signaling the wrapping up of the mission. An unknown sound alerted Xavier to the return of the security guard; When he looked towards the doorway, he realized that the guard had his gun raised and pointed towards him and Panthera. The weapon shook violently in direct proportion to the hand that held it. Xavier prayed that Felis would be able to reach the guard before anything wrong could happen; he feared that the guard might inadvertently pull the trigger.

Later when asked to detail what happened, Xavier told the others how everything seemed to move in slow motion. He remembered watching the security guard's trembling finger inadvertently apply too much pressure on the trigger, followed by a brief flash of light as the bullet left the gun's muzzle. He reacted instinctively and pushed Panthera to the side; throwing out his right arm, he yelled at the security guard to drop his gun and sit down. His thoughts were fragmented and confused as he tried not to cry out the entire time the bullet burned a path through his right shoulder. Panthera's concerned voice eventually broke through the fog that enveloped his mind, only to blackout from the pain as she pushed something into the hole in his shoulder to stop the bleeding.

When Xavier opened his eyes, he realized that his pain was real and not a figment of his imagination. The light streaming through the window temporarily blinded him and added to the pain he felt in his shoulder. Once his eyes had adjusted to the light, he looked down towards his feet and noticed Colleen sitting in a chair pulled close to the bed with her head resting next to his hand as she slept.

Packer's light snoring attracted his attention as he sat in a chair located near the windows. His sleeping body was contorted into what appeared to be an uncomfortable position. His legs hung over the arm of the chair as his chin rested on his collarbone. The position made Xavier uncomfortable just looking at him. While Matt sat in the other chair on the opposite side of the room working on his laptop.

Some unknown instinct made Matt lift his head to check on Xavier. Once he realized he was awake, he set aside the laptop and moved toward the bed.

Quietly he asked, "Dude, how do you feel?" Colleen opened her eyes and lifted her head in response to Matt's voice. Packer chose at that moment to swing his legs over the chair, approach the bed, grab Xavier's hand, and start pumping his hand up and down in his excitement.

Xavier groaned in pain, "Packer, please stop." The sound of Xavier's pain-filled command prompted Colleen to raise her hand toward the two males; "stop it, both of you. Give him a moment, and he will determine what questions to answer and how fast."

Walking towards the door, Mathew said, "Castor wanted me to let him know when you wake up so that we can answer your questions." In five minutes, the room became crowded as Castor, Pollux, Felis, and Panthera joined the teenagers in their desire to see Xavier and verify that he was on the road to recovery. Dr. Deralyn moved around the bed, checking his vitals, and monitoring the IV fluids being pumped into him.

Panthera was the first person to speak as she leaned over him and gave him a heartfelt hug. "Why did you do that, you crazy kid? I was in the process of taking the steps needed to avoid getting hurt," she said.

Xavier mumbled, "I didn't know that I just wanted to protect you the way you and Felis have protected me." Everyone in the room shook their heads in bemusement. "What happened after I was shot by the guard," he asked.

Felis stepped forward and stood beside Panthera as she held Xavier's hand. "Well, the strangest thing is I remember everything up to the point when the gun went off. I also vaguely remember you shouting to put the gun down and sit down," said Felis.

"I am a still little hazy about what happened until Panthera touched me on the shoulder. After she touched me on the shoulder, the fog in my mind lifted. That is when I helped her bandage your wound. The good thing is that

Panthera and I are trained as combat medics. However, you might not want to know what Panthera used to plug the hole and stop the bleeding," said Felis.

The occupants in the room started laughing, and Panthera, shockingly enough, started to blush a bright red. "Listen, it was the only thing I had, and I knew it would work," she said.

Xavier looked at Colleen and noticed her face was a bright red as well, and when he looked at Dr. Deralyn's face, he also saw it had a mild blush as well. The only female who was not blushing was Pollux and he wondered if that was because of her CIA training. With a puzzled look, he turned towards Felis.

His gleeful smile quickly alerted Xavier to the possibility that he might not want to know what she had used. "She used a tampon in her pocket, and it fits perfectly," he said.

The laughter from the males in the room only compounded the discomfort the young ladies felt.

"Oh, stuff it, you juvenile delinquents," said Dr. Deralyn. "I will have you know that a tampon is perfect for plugging bullet wounds, and the fact that Panthera is smart enough to carry one at all times is commendable."

The males in the room doubled over with laughter as the women just rolled their eyes and shook their heads at their antics. Even Xavier struggled to contain his mirth, but the pain in his shoulder motivated him not to give into hysterics.

Once everyone had control of their emotions, Panthera started from where Felis had left off. "Xavier, you ordered the guard to drop the gun and sit down; I am not sure why you told him to sit down but not only did the guard sit down, and so did Felis. It was weird watching two grown men sit down with legs crossed."

"That is weird," said Xavier. "When I told the guard to sit down, the nursery rhyme that my Kindergarten teacher used to say in class when she wanted us to settle down suddenly popped into my head. If I remember correctly, it went something like Criss cross applesauce, Knick knack paddy whack follow me and place your hands on your knees."

Now it was time for Felis to blush as Panthera confirmed that he had done just that, dropped his gun, and sat down as Xavier envisioned. She also mentioned that he stayed as still as a statue until she walked over to him and shook him repeatedly. Pulling at the collar of his shirt

Felis attempted to alleviate some of his discomfort before finishing the narration. "Right after Panthera told me you had been hit, we pulled down your shirt and discovered that your tattoo was lit up like a neon blue sign," said Felis. "We knew we needed to get you to the plane and back to Chicago as soon as possible without jeopardizing the mission. Thankfully, the plane is equipped with trauma care, medication, and intravenous fluids to stabilize patients before taking off."

Xavier interrupted Felis' narration; "What about the security guard, did he remember what we looked like? I am so sorry, I did not mean to jeopardize the mission," he said.

Castor stepped forward, placing a hand on his knee, reassuring him that he did not jeopardize the mission. "The security guard apparently doesn't remember anything that happened," he said.

Panthera confirmed his statement, "We took him to the control room and sat him down and left him there after administering a sedative known for eliminating short-term memories. By the time he woke, he had forgotten about us and thought he had fallen asleep on the job. Once the bleeding slowed, Felis carried you to the vehicle. I ensured all biological evidence was disposed of and turned the security system back on.

Dr. Deralyn spoke up and mentioned that it was time for Xavier to rest and sleep so his body could heal. He quickly objected and promised he would get some sleep, but he needed to know what happened. Castor agreed and instructed him that he could ask three more questions before they left for the remainder of the day so he could get some sleep.

He stopped and thought long and hard about what he wanted to ask first. Turning towards Felis, he asked, "Why did you drop your gun and sit down when I yelled at the guard?"

Felis shook his head and shrugged, "I am not sure why? One minute I was getting ready to tackle the guard. Still, before I could do anything, it seemed like I was hit by a shock wave, and then the image of little kids singing the nursery rhyme you mentioned popped into my head. I knew I needed to replicate the image, so I sat down criss-cross and placed my hands on my knees. It was like my ability to think and act independently was gone, and all I wanted to do was obey the command to drop my gun and sit down."

Deralyn reminded him he had two more questions to ask before he had to get some rest. "The second question I have is why were you immune to my command to sit down?" Xavier asked Panthera.

Her response was vague, but it was probably the best explanation he could get for now.

"I suspect that it might have something to do with the fact that you were touching me with your other hand when you yelled the command to drop the gun and sit down. The best explanation I could give would be that my proximity to you was close enough that I was within your personal space bubble, which protected me from your command's influence."

Xavier pondered her response for a moment before asking his final question. "How in the world did I do it?"

Castor looked towards Deralyn and asked, "Dr. do you want to explain this part to him, or should I?"

"You go ahead and explain," she said as she made a notation on Xavier's medical chart.

"We think that this ability may be the talent that Dr. Proctor kept referring to, and we think that the adrenaline surge resulting from the gunshot wound triggered the manifestation of your talent. We are unsure of your talent or how to use or control it. Another thing we noticed after we undressed you to attend to your wound, we also noticed that your tattoo has changed again, not as dramatically as it did with Colleen. The addition of a vine and a leaf branching out from the original tattoo extending across you back towards your right side," said Castor.

Ophiuchus: XIII

Xavier placed his arm over his eyes and exhaled deeply, taking this as a sign to leave. Everyone quietly said their goodbyes and promised to visit again as they slowly left the room. Rather than clear things up, Xavier felt more bewildered than ever and wondered where this new information fit in with what they already knew. Slowly, his eyes drifted close as the medication Deralyn had slyly administered via his IV began to take effect.

One week later, Xavier entered the conference room; his right arm was still in a sling to relieve the pressure on his shoulder wound. Thankfully, he could write and eat with his left hand. Sometimes being a Southpaw was alright after all.

Upon entering the conference room, Xavier's friends started clapping and congratulating him on his return to the land of the living. His face became uncomfortably warm as the blood pooled in his face and ears.

Castor called the meeting to order, "Ladies and Gentlemen, it is my pleasure to welcome back a valuable team member."

Ducking his head, Xavier tried to gain control of his emotions before telling everyone, "Thank you."

Laughing in good humor, Castor directed everyone's attention to the folder placed in front of every individual.

"I would like to direct your attention to the information in front of you and notice that we could decode a small portion of the information on the disk. The same encryption key that was used to decode Dr. Proctor's files. Thank goodness for unimaginative record keepers," said Castor.

"So far, we have determined that the next phase of the plan is to determine where the next part of the master disk is hidden and retrieve it. However, there is one thing we need to do before we attempt to figure out where the next portion of the disk is hidden," he said as he looked at Xavier.

With a puzzled look, Xavier asked if there was anything he could do to help.

Castor nodded his head affirmatively. "I would like for you to contact your parents, and with the proof, we have so far, we can use it to convince them to reveal what they may possibly know."

"Wait, My parents would never harm anyone, and they have nothing to do with Dr. Proctor and the Trundle family." Angrily Xavier pushed back his chair to face Castor. "I resent you implying that they are in cahoots with those evil people," He said. "I came to you for help; how dare you turn this around on my parents."

Raising his hand in a calming manner, Castor said, "I know you think that they have nothing to do with this mess, but even you have to admit that they know something and that whatever it is may end up helping us discover additional clues to what is going on. Remember, eleven other kids are out there just like you and possibly in just as great danger from those evil people as you were."

Xavier bent his head to acknowledge the underlying logic of what Castor had said.

Colleen reached across to take Xavier's hand, "I will go with you if you want? My entire week is free and clear."

Her comment pulled a chuckle out of Xavier, just like her, to make a joke and try to alleviate his anxiety.

Matt cleared his throat, "Xavier, I think it is a good idea; your mom is slowly wasting away. She took a leave of absence from work and never leaves the house. I talked to Will, and he said that all she ever does is hide in her room and cry. She stopped attending church, gave up her position on the parish council, and has lost fifty pounds since your death."

"I agree with that," said Packer. "Your mom is grieving herself to death, and if you see her and tell her what is going on, it may be just what she needs to save her and re-ignite that spark she once had."

Pollux picked up where Packer had left off, "Your mom has lost the will to live and no longer has hope for the future. She has given up on her faith, and her family and those who lack a belief in a higher power or lose hope are at a greater risk of committing suicide."

With a shake of his head, Xavier agreed that it was time to talk to his parents and get the secrets out into the open. He just wondered would the secrets bring his family closer together or if they would tear them apart forever?

Castor's voice filled the void of silence; "Who would like to volunteer to travel to see the beautiful and charming town of Huntington?"

Opening his eyes, Xavier was startled to see that every person in the room had raised their hand in response to Castor's question. He even laughed a little when he realized that Packer had raised both hands and his left leg while Matt had raised his hand and humorously crossed his eyes.

"Thank you, guys, I don't know what will happen nor what we will even find out, but I appreciate your support. You guys are the best friends a guy like me could ever have," said Xavier.

The car ride from the airport to Xavier's house was long and silent as everyone respected his wish to be left alone with his thoughts. Pulling up at the door, he knew his parents and Will would arrive within the next hour. Packer and Matt had headed back early to coordinate the visit and ensure that all the neighbors and family friends could handle what was guaranteed to be a messy and chaotic visit.

Xavier looked towards the house he had grown up in from the comfort of Castor's SUV, affectionately known as the Beauty and the Beast (B2). The lights were off, the seasonal decorations were absent, and the house gave off a Michael Meyers vibe from the horror movie "Halloween." He knew that once he stepped into that house and asked the questions that needed to be answered, there would be no turning back.

Taking a deep breath, he reached for the door handle and stepped out of the vehicle; it was time to face the demons of his past, demons he never knew existed. A hand on his shoulder alerted him to Castor's presence; it gave him the strength to take the few remaining steps needed to unlock the door and enter the dark foyer. If he thought the outside of the house gave off serial killer vibes, the inside was much worse. Xavier was shocked to see that the wall in the hallway looked like a puzzle with multiple missing pieces. It took him a little time to realize that every missing picture was the one with him in them.

The furniture in the foyer had multiple layers of dust, which his mother and her OCD would never have tolerated before his death. He could not move past the dining room because he feared that his heart would break even more than it already was as he saw the grief and misery that had replaced what was once a happy home.

Moving into the dining room, Xavier noticed pictures of himself and Will in a shoe box. Still, for his life, he could not remember taking these pictures. One shot showed him standing beside a miniature Statue of Liberty in New York City. The weird thing was the little boy next to him looked like Will but was too young to be his brother; maybe the boy was a cousin, especially since there was a strong family resemblance.

Moving aside from some photos, he noticed a piece of paper with what looked like a poem titled Alex's Room. The heartbreak in the poem was evident in every line; "footsteps echo down the hall, gentle sounds softened by walls, muffled snores travel through the door, your quirky laughter fills the air, six months later you are no longer there, quiet whispers and hush tones now dominate this once happy home."

It was agreed upon that Matt and Packer would eat with Will and Xavier's parents and then bring them back to the house. Matt would introduce Castor, and he would help soften the shock when Xavier revealed that he was still alive. He knew his parents would probably eat at Wise Guys downtown on Cherry Street. His mom would order a medium rare steak and loaded baked potato, and his dad and Will would follow suit. His family liked their red meat, especially if it was on the medium rare side. The key turning in the lock signaled an end to his introspection.

Closing his eyes, Xavier focused on his parents' voices. In his mind's eye, he could see them taking their coats off in the entryway and moving into the living area. The first thing his dad would do would be to start a fire and get his mother to sit down in her favorite spot on the couch. He would then cover her up, put logs on the fire, and stoke it until it roared and provided the room with abundant heat needed to ward off the cold.

Xavier stayed in the dining room, hidden behind the door waiting for Castor to finish talking to his parents. Matt started the conversation by introducing Castor to his parents and mentioning how he was the CEO of CaLa International, with offices in Chicago and Tokyo. Then, after introductions, he heard Matt deliver the prearranged phrase to signal that they were ready for Xavier to make his appearance. Walking across the foyer, standing in the doorway to the living area, he waited for his dad and Will to recognize him.

His mother sat in her favorite spot with her back to the portal. He knew when his dad and brother realized he was in the hallway. The glass of water his dad held in his hand dropped onto the hardwood floor, with a small amount soaking into the rug under the coffee table. Blaine's eyes widened, and his jaw dropped open as Will stood frozen, looking toward Xavier.

The words Xavier had meant to say dried up in his mouth; wiping his hand across his face, he tried to refocus on the words he had planned to say when he saw his family again. He was just as shocked by what he saw before him, Will and his dad seemed to have aged ten years overnight. Slowly Deanna turned towards the foyer in response to Blaine and Will's stunned reaction.

Xavier barely recognized his mother; her face was much thinner than it used to be and devoid of makeup; her hair was pulled back in a bun, and the dark circles under her eyes attested to many sleepless nights. Her blue eyes filled with tears and silently rolled down her face as she shoved her fist into her mouth to muffle her cries.

He could no longer remain still, he ran around the couch, hugged his mother around the waist, and cried into her lap. Matt, Packer, and Castor watched as Blaine and Will joined them in giving Xavier a collective hug.

Once everyone had dried their tears and found a spot to settle down, Castor stepped forward and played the host. "Packer, please make a pot of tea for everyone to sit and discuss everything."

Everyone sat quietly, contemplating their private thoughts until the arrival of the tea.

Packer entered the room with a tray of hot tea and teacups, "sorry, I was only able to find White Chocolate Peppermint tea; I hope you like it," he said.

The atmosphere in the room was tense and awkward, and for a moment, Xavier was grateful to have something hot for both his hands and to warm up his insides. He took a sip of the scolding liquid and knew he could not put it off much longer. Placing the saucer and the teacup on the coffee table, he looked towards his mother, "Mom, I need to ask you a few questions. I want you to know that I love you wholeheartedly and am not accusing you of anything. But I need to know your connection to Dr. Proctor beyond the fact he has been my physician for years," he said.

Blaine sitting next to Deanna, placed his right arm on her shoulders and said, "Xavier, you have to understand that everything your mother did, she did for you and Will. Please don't judge and think bad of her because of what she did."

Let me ask you this question, said Deanna. "What would you be willing to sacrifice to have a loved one back for a minute, an hour a day, or their entire life?"

She gave him a minute to think about his answer.

Then she responded "Throughout my life, all I wanted was to have a husband who loved me and children I could love and nurture in a way my mother never did. My first husband was not a kind person before he died, and he made my life miserable, but he gave me two wonderful little boys that I loved more than anything else."

Xavier held his hand, "wait, what do you mean by the first husband?

Deanna sighed, "I am sorry; we never planned on you finding out that Blaine is my second husband. While you do not share the same DNA, he has been more of a father to you and Will than your biological father could ever have been." Xavier took a deep breath, "Where is my biological dad," he asked.

"My first husband committed suicide when Will was two years old when he went by his given name of Hunter," she said. "Before you interrupt me, please let me finish my story, and then you can ask your questions. I will not be able to finish if I have to stop and start."

Everyone nodded in agreement and waited for her to start talking again. "I mentioned earlier that I had two beautiful boys, one was named Alexander Xavier and the other Hunter. We lived a wonderful life in Bowling Green, Kentucky, and had our share of difficulties. Still, for the most part, we loved each other and overcame the hardships if we stuck together.

Alex was the oldest and a mini-me in almost every way. Hunter, otherwise known as Will, was the youngest, with a four-year age gap between them. For fifteen years, I was a widow, and then one day, I met a wonderful man who made me happy, and we got closer and closer."

Deanna took a sip of tea and continued with her story. "Around my birthday, Alex took Blaine out on the back porch and asked him what his intentions were towards me and then gave him his condolences on the upcoming loss of his man card. I was so embarrassed but a few years later I would come to cherish the memory."

Xavier got impatient and interrupted his mother, only for Will to shake his head and caution him to listen to what she had to say.

She started talking as if she had never noticed the interruption, "On June 25th, Alex was coming home from work when he was killed by a drunk driver on my motorcycle. I knew when he died because I woke up from a

deep sleep and started having a panic attack. Alex and I
were extremely close. I would start a sentence, and he
would finish it. He loved to write fantasy fiction, and he
used to read my law books in the bathroom so he could
argue the finer points of the law. He was kindhearted and
loved to wear Hawaiian shirts. He hated bullies and would
stand up for the rights of others. He never cared about
being a follower. He just moved to the beat of his own
drum."

"When Alex died, I lost the desire to live, and for years
after, all I could think about was being with my son Alex. I
would drive across a bridge and think that with one wheel
jerk, I could end the pain. Then one day, Will got hurt,
waking me from my self-imposed trance. I realized that Will
deserved a good mother, and I promised to do everything I
could to be there for him."

In a subdued tone, Xavier asked, "Am I your third son,
and am I named after Alex? Is that why my name is Xavier
Alexander?"

Shaking her head, she leaned closer to Blaine, "I named
you Xavier Alexander because you were my second chance.
But I also didn't want to replace or erase Alex from
existence. You asked me how I met Dr. Proctor; this is where
he comes into the story. He approached me one day during
what I thought was a chance encounter, but I later found
out he had it all planned. He had seen me on television
during the murder trial that followed. I guess he picked up
on my desperation and despair. The first time we met, he
asked me the same question I used to ask you. What would
you sacrifice to have a loved one back for a minute, an hour
a day, or their entire life? I asked you that question because
of my innate sense of shame. I felt guilty because I knew

that I had chosen to sacrifice my faith in divinity and forced Will and Blaine to give up everything just to have a chance to be your mom again."

"When I met him again, I told him I would sacrifice anything and everything. He then told me about this government program known as ROME, Restoration of Minor Entities, and that they had the technology to restore a version of my son Alex; I thought they meant harvesting Alex DNA and providing me with a grandchild. They told me that the only individuals eligible for this offer were parents who had lost a minor child due to a tragic accident. Later I discovered that with the help of an eminent corporation they extracted DNA from Alex's teeth and made an exact clone of my child similar to what they did for the cloning of pets. I knew that it was illegal to clone humans, but I justified it by telling myself that I was not the one breaking the law."

Blaine said, "We went along with the idea because we saw that your mother was slowly wasting away. We did not think it was possible, but we felt it was the only option to prevent her from following Alex. The day your mother held you in her arms was the happiest I had seen her since before Alex's death."

Will nodded in agreement before adding to the statement, "You must understand we all loved Alex, and losing him and then Mom would have destroyed our family. I was willing to entertain the idea of another child in the house if it meant saving my mother. Gradually I grew to love you as much as I did Alex and then there came a time when I no longer viewed you as anything but the reincarnate of Alex."

"I did talk it over with Will and Blaine, and they agreed based on their desire to please me," said Deanna. "The only thing we had to do was enter a program called the Xerox program where we would receive new identities, new jobs, and move to another place. We also had to cut ties with every living family member or friend; I have parents and siblings still alive, and Blaine has a brother, a niece, and a nephew. But I would have done anything to have a second chance, and most days I don't regret my decision."

Packer chose that moment to raise his hand, "Momma D, why did you never tell Xavier about his being a clone?"

"Because," said Will. "Mom and Dad signed a non-disclosure agreement that stated if they told anyone about Xavier, including Xavier, the government and the company had the right to take possession of the said product and destroy it. Remember, clones and AI programs do not have any rights because they are technically not human or citizens of the United States."

Castor stood up and turned towards the mantel, "So what was your original name he asked Deanna?" She took a moment to respond, "My name is Elena Daniella, and I prefer my middle name over my first name. I was named after my grandmother on my father's side."

Xavier asked, "Does that mean that letter opener with the initials EDH are actually your real initials?" His mother nodded yes and sat with her head bowed in shame. "I never told you the truth about it because I was ashamed and afraid you would hate me if you ever found out. I was too weak to live without you, and I promise I love you just as much as I love Alex and Will."

Xavier looked at the woman who, for his entire life, was there for him in a way that no one else could have been. He now understood why he always seemed closer to Mom and Will and why they seemed so sad sometimes. It also made sense now why he did not look like Dad. Most people would start questioning a parent's love, especially when they discover that the person, they called mom or dad was not biologically related to them. Still, Xavier had no doubt that Blaine was his dad by choice, and even if they shared zero DNA, they were family by choice.

He knew that his parents made mistakes, and he knew he would eventually forgive them for keeping him in the dark about the circumstances surrounding his birth. Still, it was tricky when your world was turned upside down almost overnight. "Tell me, why do I have a tattoo on my left shoulder, and do you know anything about my talent?"

All three of the Hansen family looked at Xavier, confusion clouding their eyes and face. "What tattoo, and what do you mean talent?" Asked Will. "You have many talents," said his mom. "You were identified as gifted and talented in third grade."

Xavier shut his eyes, and he prayed for the strength to understand the choices his family had made on his behalf. "Never mind, I just want to know if there is anything else you know that might help me figure out why Dr. Proctor wanted to kill you, Mom, and why did you keep taking me to see him even after I told you I thought he was deliberately inflicting pain on me during my visits," he said.

Will and Blaine's exclamations following Xavier's statement briefly derailed the discussion as they threatened to take care of Proctor themselves. Deanna exhaled a shaky breath, "Proctor probably wants me out of the way because if you had simply disappeared, he knows that I would never have given up looking for you. Death for both of us would have been the only way to minimize exposure."

He stopped to think about what she said and had to admit she was correct in her assessment. If there were three things you could say about his mom, it would be she was intelligent, loved her family more than anything else, and was stubborn. Now he knew for sure that he got his stubbornness from her.

Blaine answered the second part of his question, "The reason we kept taking you to him was that it was part of the contract we signed, and the reason we didn't believe you when you told us about thinking he took pleasure in inflicting pain was that he told us that paranoia was one of the side effects of the medication you are on for your condition."

Looking at Will, Xavier directed his following statement specifically at him. "You must have resented the fact that you had to give up your birthplace as the youngest of the family.

Will's response surprised him, "Alex was my brother, best friend, and the only father figure I ever had. Then when you came along, we all fell in love with you, not with the clone but you. I still think it was the best decision we as a family made."

"What about my nightmares?" Asked Xavier.

Deanna responded, "We can't figure out why you have them. Since you don't remember anything except absolute blackness, we cannot explain it."

Silence settled among the room inhabitants as everyone held their breath, in anticipation of Xavier's next comment.

For the first time since the start of the family interrogation session, Xavier smiled and, with a catch in his voice, said, "Mom, Will, and Dad, I can't say I completely understand the choices you made, but I will tell you that you are the only family I have, and I love you guys."

The family stood up and hugged each other as tears streaked down their faces and mingled together.

Castor stood up, asked if anyone wanted a refill, and walked toward the kitchen, signaling the others to follow him. The interrogation of Xavier's family was officially over; meanwhile, the loving reunion that should have occurred immediately was finally underway in the living area.

Later Xavier stared at his reflection in the plane window as the group traveled back to Chicago. His parents initially objected to leaving, but they finally understood after Castor explained that he would be safer with him than in a small town. The trip back seemed twice as long as he wondered who he was and how he fit into society now? But the question that bothered him the most was the one he could not easily dismiss. ***"Was he just a mirror image of another?"***

Atlas Protocol:

- Procedure in which the subject is removed from his/her environment for confinement and observation in a controlled facility.
- Named after Atlas in Greek mythology sentenced by Zeus, to hold up the heavens as punishment, for attempting to overthrow the gods with the help of the Titans.

Aquarius: Feb. 16 to March 11

Aries: April 18 to May 13

Biophone:

- Subdermal implant
- Made of Silicone glass covered in glycine and alanine protein fibers.
- Used as a latest version cell phone/texting device.
- 1 tap = End call/text
- 2 taps = Call
- 3 taps = text

Blaine Lewis Hanson:

- Father of Will and Xavier
- Computer Genius

Brainbow:

- Technique that labels neurons in the brain and color codes various sections of the brain.

Brainbow KT:

- Next generation of mapping neurons
- Capable of transferring knowledge from individual to another.

Cancer: July 20 to Aug. 10

Capricorn: Jan. 20 to Feb. 16

Castro Oliver Lee

- Gemini birth sign
- Fraternal twin sister snatched and disappeared at the age of five.
- Founder of group Subreption
- Son of original member of "Anonymous"
- CEO of CaLa International

CITRUM Industry:

- Founder of the technology used to create the Xerox project.
- Collaboration between the families of two former presidential candidates.

Deanna Eva Hanson:

- College professor at St. Francis University
- Mother of Xavier and Will

Gemini:

- June 21 to July 20
- Sign of the twins
- Represented by Castor and fraternal twin sister.
- Gemini organization founded by Castor.
- Similar in nature to the Activist group "Anonymous," from 2004

- Goal includes social justice and equality for all.

Holocene:

- Futuristic technology in which TV shows and movies are played via holograms and the viewer can interact with the story line as one of the characters.

Kendra Parodine:

- Scientist in charge of the Xerox Project

Lauren Elizabeth Lee:

- Twin to Castor Oliver Lee
- Snatched as a young child.
- Leo: Aug. 10 to Sept. 16

Liam Mason Trudel:

- Grandson of former presidential Candidate Henry Simon Trundle
- Wife Rosalee Mason Todd
- Produced one child: Mason Todd Trundle
- Master's in mechanical and Chemical Engineering

Libra: Oct. 30 to Nov. 23

Ophiuchus: Nov. 29 to Dec. 17

Mason Rinehart Trundle

- CEO of CITRUM Industries
- Doctoral degree in Molecular Bio engineering and Genetics

NIMAGE:

- Company created by Michael Lee
- Father to Castro and Lauren Lee

Packer Warren

- Best friend to Xavier

Pisces:

- March 11 to April 18

Pollux:

- Lieutenant to Castor
- Former CIA Hacker, Behavioral coder/deprogrammer

Rosalee Mason Todd:

- Granddaughter of former presidential Candidate Dewitt Mason Cyder
- Married Grandson of Henry Simon Trundle
- Produced one child: Mason Todd Trundle
- Doctoral degree in Molecular Biology and Genetic Engineering from MIT.

ROME:

- Restoration of Minor Entities
- Government agency in charge of the Xerox project

Sagittarius: Dec. 17 to Jan. 20

Scorpio:

- Nov. 23 to Nov. 29
- Colleen Nadine O'Connor
- Require stability, routines, and value home life, passionate, loyal, and creative.

Taurus: May 13 to June 21

Virgo: Sept. 16 to Oct. 30

Harrison Will Hanson:

- Older brother to Xavier
- Restaurant Owner of Burger World

Xavier Axel Hanson:

- Zodiac sign Gemini
- Writer
- Artist
- Public Speaker

Xerox Project:

- Government project developed by CITRUM Industries

Zodiac Thirteen:

- Name given to the thirteen patients of Dr. Proctor